About the author

David's teachers often said he was someone who spent all his time daydreaming and living inside his own head. This apparently never changed and he still lives there. David spent much of his young adult life travelling around England for work and in his mid-twenties broke the borders and journeyed to China where he taught English to fund his travels across the land over the course of three years. Most people who receive writing from David these days tend to be in trouble with the law as he busies himself fighting for peace and justice in his home country. Of course, when you're this busy finding time to write is a challenge, and to this day, David will never understand how he managed to write this entire story using a smart phone.

Photograph by Lee Brazier.

MAGIKAL THINKING
VOLUME 2

... I MIGHT NOT BE
HERE WITHOUT YOU.

MUCH LOVE

David
X

DQZS ROBINSON

MAGIKAL THINKING
VOLUME 2

Vanguard Press

VANGUARD PAPERBACK

A CIP catalogue record for this title is
available from the British Library.

ISBN 978-1-80016-248-8

Vanguard Press is an imprint of
Pegasus Elliot MacKenzie Publishers Ltd.
www.pegasuspublishers.com

First Published in 2022

Vanguard Press
Sheraton House Castle Park
Cambridge England

Printed & Bound in Great Britain

Dedication

This is to everyone who wishes the world was a little bit more. To those who would prefer an imagined land to the one they stand on. To those who throw on a bed sheet, grab the fire poker and pretend to be a wizard when they have the house to themselves. I'll never grow up. I hope you don't either.

Chapter One
PTSD

The journey back inside the lift was a noisy one. Chloe had drenched both Amos and Alex with verbal diarrhoea the second she had stepped back inside the elevator and the doors had slid open to reveal the pair who looked surprised to see her back so quickly. In fact, Chloe prattled on without pause about Gowin and all the different warriors she had met in the armoury all the way back to the common room. It wasn't until she began talking about the sword she'd paired with and Yoshiro's name was mentioned that she was finally interrupted.

"Yoshiro?" asked Amos turning to look at Chloe, his voice and expression thick with curiosity. "Yoshiro Tokugawa?"

"That's right!" said Chloe cheerfully and she gripped the sword and held it up for Amos to see. The second her skin came into contact with Yoshiro he seized the opportunity to speak.

"About time!" he snapped which made Chloe jump, "Did I not make it painfully clear how urgent it was to speak with Amos?"

"Yes, but…" stammered Chloe to the confusion of Amos and Alex.

"Did I not explain that lives were in danger and that time was critical?"

Chloe said nothing this time, she simply stared at the floor with a guilty look on her face.

"Chloe?" asked Amos placing a steadying hand on her shoulder. "What's wrong? Are you talking to Yoshiro now?"

Keeping a grip on Yoshiro, so he could be heard if need be, Chloe broke into a hurried explanation of how she had ended up with Yoshiro. She explained how Yoshiro had recounted the time Amos had saved his life, that Yoshiro desperately needed to speak with him and explained her theory of how being paired with Chloe might still permit direct communication with Amos due to their unusual connection.

"Well," blustered Amos who was quite astonished by this strange turn of events. "it's a sound theory and it certainly can't hurt to try! Alex, would you excuse us, if this works I would like to speak with Yoshiro and Chloe alone."

Surprised but unoffended Alex gave a nod to Amos, a little wave to Chloe and headed off to sit next to Wade who was still at the same workstation he had been at earlier.

Chloe moved to sit at a desk in the common room and placed Yoshiro on the table in front of her. Amos sat opposite her and surveyed the weapon. Up here in the brightly lit space, Yoshiro's full magnificence could be seen. The ruby red scabbard bound and decorated with black rope and leather stood out starkly against the neutral colours of the common room and Amos couldn't suppress a low whistle. He was as impressed with it now as he had been all those years ago when Yoshiro had held it aloft and yelled at the enemy. Amos reached forward to grab the weapon but hesitated, it lasted for but a second, and with a sharp intake of breath, he gripped the handle firmly.

A voice sounded inside Amos' head, but it was very muffled, like listening to a conversation carried through the plumbing of an old house.

"Yoshiro, slow down I can barely hear you!" said Amos as he pointlessly leaned closer to the sword and strained his ears to hear better.

Yoshiro continued talking fervently but it was to no avail, the sound was too distorted. An idea suddenly struck Amos, and he quickly stood up, lifted his chair and carried it over to Chloe which he placed next to her and sat down again.

"The fact that I can hear anything at all proves your theory was right!" said Amos encouragingly. "But as we are still different people the connection is poor to the point of useless."

Chloe slumped disappointedly onto the desk and buried her head in her arms. Amos chuckled and gave Chloe a gentle nudge with his elbow. "Before we get too dismayed, I do have a suggestion!"

Chloe looked up and saw that Amos was holding the sword near her. "Do you know what an amplifier is?"

For a moment Chloe couldn't see what Amos was getting at, Yoshiro wasn't a guitar, but then it dawned on her.

"I am the amplifier?" she said uncertainly.

"Possibly!" said Amos. "It's certainly worth a try!"

Chloe turned to face Amos properly and took hold of the opposing end of the sword. It was as though someone had cranked up the volume on a stereo from one all the way to eleven. Yoshiro's voice boomed through both their heads, making them jump an inch or two off their seats.

"Little softer if you will," said Amos giving his head a cleansing shake. "I can hear you quite well now!"

"Amos, I am so pleased to hear your voice!" said Yoshiro with unmistakable relief in his tone. "I never imagined we would speak again… but then, I never imagined I would spend my afterlife housed in my ancestor's sword either!" Yoshiro gave a hollow laugh. "Price of being the best I guess!"

Amos gave a solemn nod and patted the handle kindly. "An honour I am told, though I am sure it does not always feel that way!"

"My opinion is still reserved on that!" said Yoshiro briskly. "But that doesn't matter now, listen, London is going to be attacked!"

This pronouncement was so outlandish it took a moment to properly travel from Amos' ears to his brain. Through a muddled feeling of shock and confusion Amos could barely form thoughts let alone words and he replied with a splutter of, "What…? But how…? I mean… Who…? and When?"

"I can tell you the 'hows' later!" said Yoshiro dismissively. "I'm still trying to understand that part properly myself! But who, or what… well that's a different matter!"

"Before you tell me," said Amos, regaining some composure, "you should know we are not permitted to engage in non-supernatural or mystical conflicts. Regardless of which country it is that England has offended this time, I'm afraid they are on their own!" he finished with a sad shrug.

"You don't understand Amos, it's not a country! And those things…" Yoshiro made a sound like a shudder and the metal in the concealed blade sang. "…whatever those things are they're not human!"

Chloe, who had been maintaining a contrite silence, stirred. "What things? What do they look like?" she whispered quietly.

"Well…" began Yoshiro but he hesitated, struggling for the words to explain. "To be clear they sometimes do look like humans… but they change!" he added quickly, desperate to be understood.

"Change into what?" asked Amos who was leaning closer to Yoshiro again.

"Into a demon!" replied Yoshiro darkly! "I heard others in the shadow realm call them Jinn! Part man, part beast and able to move on the wind!"

"Jinn!" repeated Amos, a crack of concern in his voice. "And you 'heard' this?" he added suspiciously.

"I know what you're thinking, Amos!" said Yoshiro defensively. "The insanity of an instance is all I will get from a shade, but they see too sometimes and rumour spreads amongst them! Besides, I have seen these Jinn gathering with my own eyes!"

"What is the shadow realm?" asked Chloe confused. Thanks to her borrowed knowledge from Amos, she thought she had an impressive understanding of other dimensions, but this was not a familiar term.

Amos couldn't suppress a smile. "I believe Yoshiro is talking about the astral plane, Chloe!"

Chloe's eyes screwed together and her nose crinkled. The only thought that came to mind was, "No he's not!"

"What's the point of knowing everything, if you can't put all that knowledge to any use?" said Amos kindly. "Sometimes you have to read between the lines and use your intellect to make a leap! We may have a word for everything but not everyone knows what they are. Please, do not get into the habit of relying on what I know and forget to use your own brain."

He gave her a reassuring pat on the back and returned his attention to Yoshiro. "Well, Yoshiro! We'll come to how you have achieved the incredible feat of projecting yourself into the astral plane later. Right now, we could use a little more information. For a start do you know when this attack is supposed to happen?"

"Yes! I heard their leader say it!" said Yoshiro.

"Their leader?" asked Amos giving his glasses a nudge up his nose.

"Some sort of child!" replied Yoshiro, unconcerned. "It's hooded and if you see its eyes it looks dead. Maybe it's some sort of shade, but the Jinn all seem to be taking orders from it."

"When?" demanded Amos who sounded urgent all of a sudden. "When is the attack?"

"I heard him say they attack on the 11th of November!" replied Yoshiro all too casually.

"BUT THAT'S TODAY!" bellowed Amos and he nearly released his grip on Yoshirou.

"TODAY?" repeated Yoshirou, alarmed! "But, but… that's too soon, there was time! There was more time!"

Amos stood up sharply, accidentally dragging Chloe up with him as both were still holding the sword, and straightened his clothes. "I guess the war starts now then!" he whispered angrily.

Giving his glasses another little nudge up his nose he rounded on Wade who had been chatting quietly with Alex.

"Contact Frank!" he said suddenly very business-like. "I want all senior staff ready for a brief in ten minutes, and transportation to London for…" he paused and rubbed his forehead. "Yoshiro, any idea how many enemies we are facing?"

"Not an exact count, but I have seen the force gathering and they are more than one hundred strong!"

"A hundred strong!" repeated Amos weakly and his knees buckled slightly. "Better tell Frank…" began Amos, turning back to Wade and massaging the bridge of his nose causing his glasses to slide forward again. "…we'll need to mobilise the entire Conclave!"

Wade gulped loudly, stood slowly and with a look of extreme dread at what he would say, made his way out of the room to go and find Frank.

"Miss Sterling, it may be best if you go with him. Frank will not react well to this and Wade may need some moral support."

Looking a little bit disappointed at being excused again, Alex got to her feet and stalked off after Wade with her giant battleaxe lolloping over her shoulder which made her look comically murderous.

Amos made his way to the elemortal living room at a run. For a man of his years, he was surprisingly athletic and as he and Chloe still held

Yoshiro, Chloe only needed to make the occasional hop as he dragged her through the air at an impressive speed. As he ran, Amos bashed emergency buttons that were stationed at several locations inside the Conclave. The voice of GOD chimed over those in nearby offices, classrooms and workspaces.

"Attention! All Conclave staff should return to their appointed stations and make themselves battle ready. Please report to senior staff for briefing!"

"Any ideas of what they hope to achieve with this surprise invasion?" asked Amos who was extremely mindful of how woefully unprepared they were if this was indeed true and it was being orchestrated by 'Him!'

"It just wants them to wreak havoc!" said Yoshiro. "They're targeting a big crowd, too! It will be chaos from the panic — they intend on killing!"

"A big crowd?" repeated Amos racking his brain. With a gasp of horror, he realised at once that the attack was going to be aimed at the Remembrance Day parade and he told Yoshiro and Chloe.

"*Kami wa jihibukai*!" muttered Yoshiro.

"Are they after anyone in particular?" asked Amos as he shoulder barged through a set of double doors and continued down a long corridor.

"I heard something about an actual target but I don't know who. For the most part I think it's just killing people at random!"

"A distraction?" yelled Chloe who was still bounding along in Amos' wake.

"Yes, I expect you're right!" agreed Amos. "That's using your brain!" he added looking back and giving her a genial smile. He failed to see the next set of doors however, and opened them his head. Wincing from the pain above his eye, he gave a little shake and blinked wildly. "Perhaps not the best use of mine though!"

Before long the pair had come bustling into the living room to find Shui, Aarde and Hoowo3oow already waiting at the large circular desk with their respective companions. Also present were professor of demonology, Steve Gathercole, resident veterinarian and tutor of cryptozoology, Piotr Gwozdek, physical defence instructor and tactical advisor, Theo Scales, coven mother, Elizabeth Westa, and public relations manager, Chris McNally.

Amos gave them each a wave in turn and sat down next to an empty chair which would have been Ignis' seat. Chloe made herself comfortable on the sofa holding Yoshiro on her lap and for a few moments the room sat in nervous silence. At once all eyes turned to the holographic display that had flickered into view in the centre of the table and showed a very stressed-out looking Frank with Barry, Wade and Miss Sterling standing behind him. Chloe gave Alex a very obvious and cheery wave and Barry, misreading the situation, waved enthusiastically back. Realising his error, he shot his hand back down and blushed which caused the group to laugh. A vein pulsed angrily on Frank's neck and he growled through a deep sigh causing the laughter to come to an abrupt halt.

For the next twenty minutes, the room was deathly silent, as Frank and Amos with the assistance of Yoshiro via Chloe, discussed the imminent attack which was being made possible due to a breach still open above Soho. All were in agreement that the Remembrance Day parade was the most likely target and with Frank's help, Theo plotted a defensive perimeter which allowed for ground troops to be supported by Conclave mages from several nearby rooftops. Gathercole and Gwozdek, suggested a few demons and creatures that may help with containment, concealment and forgetfulness while Mother Westa prepared a list of which spells would be best for her girls to cast to achieve similar results.

"The auxiliary ground units will need disguises," said Frank concentrating on a map of London. "British police issue will be best, that way they can operate without hindrance when the attack starts."

"We still have no idea who, if anyone, is the intended target!" sighed Amos grimly. "Each time the figure in black has attacked, assuming of course we have correctly interpreted Yoshiro's description and are right in thinking it's the killer we have been investigating, one person was made into some kind of example!"

"Yeah!" said Aarde. "He is obviously trying to make some kind of point. If it was just the 'Church of Dumbass' that was attacked I'd say he had a thing against stupid religions, but that doesn't seem to fit with the other killings!"

"We should not forget what the demons Bushyasta, Onoskelis and Rangda said!" snarled Hoowo3oow. "'A war is coming!', perhaps this

15

assault is part of that and the assassin is equally complicit and not acting separately as we had been thinking!"

"It's possible," said Aarde sceptically, "but they also went on about a paradox. Not exactly a staple of religious doctrine!"

"They said the Gods allow it!" snapped Hoowo3oow. "They said it was their idea!"

"There is a very obvious religious theme, Aarde," said Shui thinking aloud. "Look at the collection of all those theologically specific symbols and icons that keep popping up at each place! That's more than the quirky calling card of a serial killer. That's a message!"

"The ifs and buts of a primary target right now is irrelevant!" snapped Frank! "As is the motivation! The information we have lets us plan around a crowd assault. Wade will work with me here to see if we can determine any individuals who may be a candidate and we shall dynamically adjust our plan accordingly. Chris you should probably shadow the prime minister, I can't see how this is political in anyway but if anything happens to him there will be fallout and we will find ourselves in a world of shit!"

"I can control explanation and information output better from his vicinity too. The media will swarm him when things go down. I'll prepare some 'alternate facts' for press release."

"Should we try and engage them at the breach site?" asked Theo with a quick glance at Frank in between measuring distances on a paper map in front of her. "It would buy us time and reduce casualties if their numbers were thinned before they reached the crowd."

"That won't help!" sighed Frank. "Jinn can change their appearance at will and look completely human in the mortal plane. There will be no way to distinguish them from anyone else until they either attack or use their abilities."

"Which are?" asked Elsu with a greedy look at Gyasi.

Gathercole chuckled. "They don't grant wishes if that's what you're thinking!"

Both Gyasi and Elsu noticeably deflated in their seats and looked sulky.

"Conclave not paying you enough?" barked Frank annoyed. "Provide some useful input and then we'll talk about a raise!"

"Jinn…" began Gathercole heaving a giant leather-bound copy of *Things that go bump in the night!* onto the desk and opening it to a chapter marked 'Masters of Mental Mayhem'

have the ability to affect the minds of humans. They are able to cause hallucinations which can dominate every sense in the human body, creating illusions so realistic that they are indistinguishable from reality.

"Joy!" groaned Wun Chuan who had, up until now, been skulking in the corner of the room. "Half of London tripping their tits off, that's just what we need. The police will have no idea what's going on!"

"Much like us!" said Frank. "But we can't let a little thing like ignorance get in our way, not when we have…" Frank consulted his watch. "…thirty-four minutes before the parade starts! We go on what we've got! Everyone, you know what to do. I want confirmation from all units and commanders when in place. Shout up for anything suspicious and stay safe!"

He turned despairingly to look at Shui, Aarde and Hoowo3oow and closed his eyes as if praying for strength.

"Offer support to the auxiliaries if needed but your priority is that little shit in black! I want him bringing in, dead, alive, as paste in a jam jar, I don't care! This might be the only time we get the jump on him and I will… will… never speak to you again if he gets away!"

Even Hoowo3oow laughed at this and as he got to his feet, he caused an updraft of wind which blew everyone about. "I will have his skin for leather!"

"That's dark, man!" snorted Shui and they fist bumped as Frank dismissed the room.

Thirty minutes later the last few calls were being made to Frank to confirm positions in the throng of people who had gathered in Whitehall and around the Cenotaph. It was raining and very gloomy over the monument, but there was an atmosphere of good spirits among the chattering and smiling collection of locals and tourists alike. Shui, Aarde and Hoowo3oow had managed to push and shove their way to the front of the crowd to stand right next to the barriers which blocked pedestrians from

17

the parade route. Wun Chuan, Elsu and Gyasi received many admonitory looks from the parents of other children at the inconsiderate pushing in of the elemortals, assuming as intended, that they were the mother and fathers. But Gyasi by himself would be an imposing figure, the three of them together looked positively menacing in the rain and the other parents soon cowed their gazes and tried to avoid eye contact at all costs.

Scattered here and there within the uniformed officers in attendance, were Conclave wards, dressed in tunics and stood in formation. Unseen and unheard, friendly demons under Gathercole's control weaved through onlookers, visible only in the wet and puddled reflection of the tarmac beneath them. The rain that fell, glittered and sparkled as it gently tumbled from the sky and was surprisingly warm making everyone who touched it feel very good, very healthy. Frank, who was watching the BBCs coverage of the parade on TV, made use of the wet ground to keep tabs on everyone while Amos, the only active member of the Conclave to serve in both wars, was garbed in his military dress and actually marching in the parade.

As the chiefs and delegates, government officials and religious representatives made their way toward the cenotaph and gathered on each side, the Conclave members steeled themselves. It was an impossible situation, everyone looked like a threat. As the guard were brought to attention, Amos' eyes fell upon the queen as she approached, accompanied by her husband, the prince, and leading the rest of the uniformed royals. She had a front and centre position next to the monument and Amos suddenly felt his stomach clench. It was unlikely, but what if the queen was the primary target? They hadn't considered the Royal Family as a possibility, but why would they? If anyone had plenty of protection it was the queen and Amos couldn't think of a reason why the child in black would target her. But she looked so exposed standing there and Amos was the only fighter nearby, if the child in black did attack her, they wouldn't stand a chance. The last member of the royal entourage took up position on their allocated spot and a pre-emptive silence fell upon the crowd.

Over on the sidelines, Shui was fidgeting and causing a great deal of annoyance to everyone around her.

"Boooored!" groaned Shui loudly.

"Quiet!" hissed Wun Chuan reproachfully. "Do your job then you won't be bored!"

Shui shot her a dirty look then turned to face the cenotaph, muttering under her breath. To the mild amusement of Aarde but the absolute exasperation of Hoowo3oow, Shui occupied herself by aiming at the crowd with her hand shaped like a gun. If she deemed a person to be 'not a demon', she pretended to shoot them making little gunfire noises with her mouth. If Shui had been properly armed the assembled masses would have been thinned to a third of their number in a very short space of time as she rattled off pretend shots like a cowboy hammer-firing a revolver.

"If you are going to make the noises you could at least pretend to reload!" sniggered Aarde.

With a wry grin at Aarde, Shui mimed flipping open the cylinder of a gun and shook out the non-existent spent bullets. She then pretended to withdraw a bullet from an inside pocket and threw it into the air, catching it inside the gun chamber which wasn't really there. Snapping the chamber back into place, which Shui emphasised by making a 'click' sound, she raised her hand again and pointed her loaded finger back at the multitude of bodies on the other side of the road. With one eye closed, Shui began searching the faces for a target as Big Ben began to chime marking the hour of eleven o'clock.

The bells rang loudly over Whitehall as the clanging announced the approaching time and all around, heads bowed, eyes closed and expressions became sombre. All, Shui noticed, except a guy casually leaning against the opposing rail twelve metres down the road. For some reason he was grinning and this irked Shui. For all she knew this man's mind may have wandered off to something funny that happened earlier in the day, but Shui had decided he had a stupid face and was going to pretend die anyway! The chimes ended and with a sinister grin, Shui quietly whispered, "Head shot!"

In a single instant the clock struck the first of eleven chimes, Shui gestured shooting with her hand, a cannon fired and the man Shui had been aiming at seemed to pop like a balloon, leaving behind a wispy, electric blue cloud, that was dissipating amongst the stunned and confused people nearby. For a second Shui looked at the end of her finger in shock. But then reason caught up with her and getting to her feet she clambered up onto a disgruntled Gyasi's shoulders and surveyed the scene. In their obvious surprise, those stood near the cloud had taken a sharp gulp of breath, inhaling the sparkling vapour into their lungs. Some of them looked disgusted as if a grotesque flavour or smell had permeated their senses, many had collapsed or were doubled over in pain.

"What are you doing?" demanded Hoowo3oow. "You are drawing attention to us!"

Shui who was concentrating on several other pops in the crowd waved him into silence and, overlapping her fingers and thumbs, contacted Frank.

"Checks aren't for another ten minutes Shui, if you're that bored ask Wun Chuan for one of the fidget toys I gave her the other day!" said Frank distractedly as he gave Shui a half glance through the little window in her hands.

"Don't be a twat!" retorted Shui hotly and she flipped her hands over to show Frank what she could see. "Look!"

"What the...? gasped Frank.

Big Ben gonged one last time and a silence fell over Whitehall. For the first time in history, the silence was punctured by hissed calls of annoyance, whispered curses and inappropriately loud groans of misery which led to a general muttering of complaints, which spread out in all directions.

Frank, who was still viewing the events unfold on a TV as it was broadcast by the BBC, felt his blood run cold. With a sinking feeling in the pit of his stomach he sent word to every senior operative that all units should hold position. If they interrupted the two-minutes' silence they'd probably be charged with treason or something.

"When local forces involve themselves, that's when you move in!" whimpered Frank, helplessly watching as more Jinn revealed themselves by bursting and infecting the populace.

The man commentating on the broadcast hadn't seen the lightning edged clouds erupting here and there about the tumult of struggling bodies and spoke angrily about the disrespect of an entitled generation as the camera zoomed back and forth, focusing on various arguments that were breaking out everywhere.

The camera panned over to the queen, she did not look pleased. Despite her small frame, the queen seemed to grow as her anger mounted and Chloe, who was also watching everything on TV, was reminded of when her mother considered how best to tell her off. She inwardly thought to herself that a whole lot of big children were about to be in a whole lot of trouble.

At the end of the two minutes another boom of cannon fire echoed overhead and a chorus of trumpets began to play 'Last Post", but the queen gave them a sharp look and a gentle shake of her head, they stopped playing immediately. For a second or two the queen waited with her head bowed and Amos shuffled nervously in place.

Suddenly and without warning Her Royal Highness took a deep breath and at a volume you would not have imagined her capable, the queen roared into the masses. "WHAT THE BLOODY HELL DO YOU THINK YOU ARE DOING?"

Back in the Conclave living room, Chloe smiled.

"HOW DARE YOU CONDUCT YOURSELVES IN SUCH A MANNER, HAVE YOU NO RESPECT?" continued the Queen furiously.

Prince Philip moved forward and consolingly placed a hand on his wife's shoulder.

"Philip, no!" said the queen stubbornly. "Never, in the history of..." she gave a sort of restrained growl. "...not once!"

Stepping forward, the queen opened her lungs wide and began to berate the congregation once again, but as she did so, a wisp of the electric blue cloud rushed forward out of the throng and sped towards her.

Amos threw himself forward yelling, "Hoowo3oow, now!" and dashed toward the queen. This did not evoke a good reaction from the royal guard, and reacting on instinct they closed in on him.

Thankfully, Hoowo3oow had understood and breaking from the sidelines he summoned a gust of wind deflecting the wisp away from the queen who had spotted it just too late. The prince darted forward to get back to his wife who was hunching away from the wisp and drew his sword as the guard collided with Amos beside him. Calmly but swiftly, Amos dispatched the guard by throwing them to the side or tying up their limbs by interlocking them together. He then turned to face the prince who was pointing the tip of his of his blade at Amos' throat while sheltering the queen.

"My apologies," began Amos, flushing with embarrassment. "I am not an enemy. However, we are under attack and I really can't afford to be hindered, not even by the royal guard!"

The prince opened his mouth to question Amos but a fight broke out amongst several officers around the Cenotaph which spilled out into the space near the queen.

Yells of, "IT'S NOT MY FAULT!" or "GET AWAY FROM HER!" and "DON'T HURT HIM!" sounded from the brawl, punctuated by meaty punches.

Feeling a little panicked, Amos tried to lead the queen and her escort to safety but more fights erupted all around them blocking their escape. A large man was thrown out of the fray and Amos had to shunt the queen and the prince to the side as the man toppled over and cracked his mouth against the white Cenotaph steps. His face covered in blood and shaking, the man tried to push himself up but another man, followed by two more, launched forward and sank a large booted foot into the back of the man's head, smashing it further against the marble slabs.

Without pause the attacker continued to stamp on the limp and lifeless body, as did his companions and all were angrily yelling things like. "HOW COULD YOU?" and "WE WERE JUST KIDS!"

Amos stepped in, and subdued the attackers by forcefully hitting pressure points at various locations on their torsos. As they slumped to the floor unconscious Amos checked the injured man. He was dead.

"What the hell is going on?" snapped the queen, removing herself from the shelter of her husband and storming toward Amos.

"Er…" blustered Amos, but he was saved from having to invent an answer by more people falling from other fights and in their confusion, deciding to fight him and the queen instead.

Parrying the attacker nearest to him and throwing him hard against the floor Amos lurched in Her Majesty's direction. As the furious individual moved to punch Her Royal Highness in the head, Amos kicked him hard in the side. At the same time, the prince swept his legs out from under him with the blunt side of his sword and the man span fully upside down in the air, landing on his shoulders. Before either had moved to subdue him further, the queen swung her bag wide and brought it down with surprising force upon the back of the man's head as he tried to get to his feet, knocking him out cold.

"That's why I don't like carrying it for her!" said Prince Philip tonelessly as he looked down at the man crumpled up at the queen's feet. "Bloody thing is really heavy!"

Amos almost smiled, but there was no time for celebrations, the crowd was closing in and was so dense with swarming bodies it was impossible leave. Battles were being furiously fought in every direction and everyone was fighting, some for their lives as a terrifying number of people were outright killing others without concern for consequence.

The heaving wall of angry limbs suddenly shifted violently to the left and Amos, the queen and the prince were knocked over and against the cenotaph. A bulge appeared in the distance, like some giant bubble had formed under the crowd and was forcing the people into the air. It moved toward the cenotaph like a great wave in the sea, building in mass and Amos felt his jaw drop.

"Where the hell are the elemortals?" he whimpered.

Some thirty metres away on the opposite side of the cenotaph, Shui, Hoowo3oow and Aarde were having problems of their own. A large contingent of police officers had been forcefully subduing a group of war veterans and Shui and her brothers had intervened leaving the aggressors in a neat pile on the pavement. Almost at once, the veterans had turned on the elemortals. White haired, wild and brandishing walking sticks the elderly men marched purposefully in their direction. Even those previously bound to wheelchairs had miraculously gotten to their feet and were advancing on the trio. They looked at each other for suggestions, but they could only shrug. From the anxious looks they wore it was obvious each were scared to hit the old men in case they killed one. Shui's face lit up with an idea, but Aarde seemed to have had an epiphany too and he stood up straight, held up a hand to Shui and placing the other on his chest, nodded solemnly as if to say, 'I got this!'

He dashed forward and brought himself to within striking distance of the closest veteran. He raised his hand up to the old man's forehead and braced his middle finger against his thumb. Wincing and hardly daring to look, he the flicked the soldier right between the eyes causing his head to snap backwards like he'd been shot. Before the old man fell, Aarde caught him, and gently lowering him to the floor, he checked his pulse.

"He's alive, but maybe do it a little gentler than I did!" said Aarde who sounded relieved.

"He killed the captain!" came a voice from the huddle as a glass bottle came hurtling out of nowhere which Aarde managed to smash with his elbow just before it hit him, inches from his face.

"NAZI SCUM!" shouted another man and a brick came flying at Aarde this time.

Aarde reduced the brick to dust with a glance and red powder scattered over his face and clothes. "Where'd they get a brick from?" muttered Aarde as he stood up and over the man he knocked out and braced himself against the aged unit that had broken into a run.

Hoowo3oow and Shui joined Aarde and descended upon the veterans who were charging to the call of, "DIE, YOU JERRY BASTARDS!"

"Just want to say…" grinned Shui pulling up in front of the man who had thrown the brick and flooring him with a blow from her finger, "…not a Nazi!"

"They must be having flashbacks to the war!" yelled Hoowo3oow over the din of battle cries and the clash of walking sticks as he deftly dispatched two more.

"Them and everyone else by the looks it!" replied Aarde, striking three more men down before kicking a younger man back into the crowd who had broken free from a different fight and had attempted to grab him.

Suddenly the frantic voice of the tactical advisor, Theo Scale, crackled into life inside Shui, Aarde and Hoowo3oow's heads.

"Guys, you have incoming, ten o'clock!"

As the elemortals turned to look in that direction, the maelstrom of rioting bodies shifted violently as one before collapsing onto the veterans, crushing them beneath a pile of heaving limbs that continued to fight and thrash around. Aarde reached out to try and help the buried men but several blood-curdling, terrified screams tore through the air and like birds disturbed from a tree, people fled and scattered in every direction, buffeting him left and right as legs and knees bashed his head. As the crowd thinned, Hoowo3oow caught sight of what had caused the panic.

"DEMONS!" he roared, pointing to a large group of men and women who were barging, smashing and ripping their way through the scared civilians towards the elemortals as blood rained over them from open wounds or severed joints.

They were grinning maliciously and from their smiles, black slime oozed out over their chins and dropped to the floor burning anything and anyone it touched.

One of the demons possessing a woman grabbed a man as he attempted to run past them to safety. Another demon possessing a tall, bulky man grabbed his feet and as the victim was hoisted into the air the two demons who had seized him began to pull him like they were trying to open a giant Christmas cracker. The poor man screamed, cried and begged through the pain as he felt his muscles rip and his bones dislocate. With one massive heave, the victim was torn in half and while his legs were thrown to the side, his torso was thrown at Hoowo3oow.

"Make a wish!" cackled the female demon to her companion's delight who were laughing like barking dogs, spraying more black slime onto people running by.

Hoowo3oow stared at the bisected remains of the man who was wailing in pain and choking on his own blood with a mixed expression of sorrow and revulsion. The man was reaching for Hoowo3oow with a pleading, desperate look on his features, but there was only one way to help this man now.

Crouching low beside the man's bloody head, Hoowo3oow cradled his neck and closing his eyes whispered, "Forgive me!" before snapping his spine.

A chill wind swept through the scene, swirling the rain in the air and kicking up litter and leaves which drifted haphazardly above the crowds. Hoowo3oow rose to his feet again, his long hair wet from the rain hung in front of his face and he was shaking.

"Aww, did the mean ol' demon upset you little boy?" crooned a smaller, plump demon to Aarde's right. "Are you scared? You gonna cry?"

Hoowo3oow lifted his head and the demons flinched under his gaze. His face was contorted into a look of outright fury, his fists were clenched so tightly he drew his own blood with his nails and he was grinding his teeth. Hoowo3oow took a step towards their attackers, who backed away a few steps, but they did not lose their sneering smiles.

"I have eyes behind them!" said Theo who was using the mirrors in the Conclave control room to get a first-person view of the action as she flicked between tendril-like orbs on the display at Frank's terminal, switching from eyewitness to eyewitness.

"There are another nine demons flanking the ones you can see and twelve more closing in on your six."

Aarde and Shui exchanged significant looks. Casualties were already high, as were deaths and many more would follow if this wasn't ended quickly. Unfortunately, 'ending things quickly' did not involve subjugation.

"Frank, I know the hosts aren't dead yet but…" Shui shrugged feebly before adding, "…this is a utilitarian situation right here!" in a hollow tone.

"Yes Shui!" sighed Frank grimly, understanding her meaning straight away as he had been thinking the same thing. "The greater good!" he said through a heavy breath. "We have no choice! Use of lethal force is authorised!"

At once Hoowo3oow burst into action. Vanishing on the wind he reappeared behind the demon in the female's body and grabbed her around the waist. He then wrapped his legs tightly around hers and pulled. The demon began to scream with fright and shock as she realised what was happening.

"I wish…" began Hoowo3oow through gritted teeth as he felt the thoracic vertebrae separate against his cheek, "…you knew how that man felt!"

With an angry roar Hoowo3oow heaved and tore the demon in two smashing it's head into the ground as he doubled over backwards from the force of pulling. Kicking the legs at her companions in magnificent foreshadowing, he stomped over to the remains of the dazed and whimpering demon who was trying to hurriedly mutter an incantation in an effort to eject from the now useless and agonising remains of her host. Hoowo3oow stood above her and looked down at the bloodied face with raw contempt, and without a word or further pause, he smashed his heel

26

through the forehead of the demon and buried his foot several inches into the tarmac.

So alarmed was another demon at the brutal end of his companion, he too began muttering the same incantation clearly feeling this was not going to end well, but Shui, spotting this, gathered all of the surrounding raindrops and used them to encase the demon in a giant bubble of water which he could not shake off. The demon glubbed as he tried to keep speaking, but a garbled gloop of noise came out instead.

"When trying use the mystical forces," began Shui in mock imitation of a teacher delivering a lesson, "one should keep in mind that while all words have power..." she strolled up to where the demon was drowning, looked into his wild eyes and grinned, "...it only works if you enunciate!"

The last word had barely left her mouth when Shui launched herself upwards, upper cutting the demon into the air and smashing the giant globule of water apart. As the demon fell through the air his mouth flopped open because his jaw was broken and useless. It was as Shui had intended, as before he hit the ground, Shui redirected the water that was splashing away in every direction back through the air and into the demon's unprotected throat. The torrent slammed him hard into the concrete but the demon could not make any sounds of pain and he thrashed around as he struggled for breath.

"AARDE, STATE CHANGE!" bellowed Shui as she took hold of the demon's ankle and threw him in Aarde's direction.

In the brief moment Shui had been holding the demon before she threw him, she had slowed down the water molecules sloshing around inside him. When the demon slammed into Aarde's waiting and immovable palm, the molecules stopped entirely as the body froze solid.

A second later Shui crashed into the demon's back with her foot, exploding the body apart and sending bits of icy limbs and viscera in every direction.

As the chunks twirled grotesquely through the air, Aarde span off one foot a full 720° and kicked the bigger pieces at several of the charging demons, sniping them in the head, killing them outright.

Unexpectedly and to Aarde's immediate chargrin, Gyasi, Elsu and Wun Chuan burst out of the wall of writhing bodies to his left and began subduing a few stragglers that were attempting to rush him.

"What the hell are you doing?" roared Aarde, rounding on the trio.

"Kicking all kinds of ass and being generally awesome! Thought that was obvious!" said Elsu as he bobbed to avoid an errant punch and knocked the attacker out with a swift blow to the neck.

"Here!" bellowed Aarde. "What are you doing here?"

"We are guarding your backs!" said Gyasi, a little hurt at Aarde's tone.

"Does it look like our backs need guarding?" growled Hoowo3oow as he appeared out of thin air behind two large red-eyed men and drove his elbows into their spines. The crack of bone resonated through the crowd and made Elsu shudder.

"Amos is alone guarding the royals and Frank said he had heavy incoming!" shouted Shui who was re-purposing raindrops as bullets, spraying them into the oncoming hordes like machine gun fire.

"Are you kidding me?" spat Wun Chuan. "It will take forever to reach him through this mess!"

"She's right!" said Hoowo3oow surveying the distance from atop a dazed, pensioner's shoulders.

"Not a problem!" said Shui with a half a grin. "We'll just have to throw you!"

"Sod that!" protested Elsu at once.

"Yeah, that's not happening!" agreed Gyasi waving a hand and backing away from the group and toward the crowd.

"Well, they're not throwing me!" snarled Wun Chuan marching over to stand behind Gyasi with her arms folded.

"Oh for…" muttered Shui, rolling her eyes and whirling around to face Aarde. "Going up!"

Aarde nodded and knelt on one knee. Hoowo3oow also turned to face Aarde and kicked up a strong gust of wind which whirled like a tornado around him.

Shui sped forward and within five strides had reached the spot where Aarde was kneeling. She leapt onto his lowered shoulder and Aarde straightened up fast as Shui jumped hard. The force launched Shui high up into the air who, at the apex of her jump, spread her arms and legs wide and exploded into droplets of sparkling water. The tornado that had been gaining speed as it twirled violently around Hoowo3oow shot in Shui's direction and caught the globules of water that was Shui in a fierce gale. The glistening drops shot toward Amos like a thousand sparkling beams of light, and as she approached, Shui could see Amos and the prince exchanging blows with various deranged strangers, some of which seemed to be royal guards, then she saw what had made Amos send an SOS to Frank. A giant wave of people moving like a lumpy tsunami toward Amos and the queen. A wave that was seconds away from breaking over them.

Amos had seen it loom over them too and he dived into the prince and onto the queen, knocking them behind what little protection the Cenotaph might offer and rose to face the crest of falling bodies towering above him and blotting out the sky. But as he braced himself to deliver his best attack, the wave split and a mass of flesh and clothing rushed past him on both sides, blocking off any escape for both Amos and the royals.

Amos glared into the maw of oncoming bodies. Like a kaleidoscope of humans, it swirled and tricked the eyes, unbalancing the senses. With a start Amos spotted a small dark figure that had appeared in the centre of the vortex. A stoic figure that seemed entirely unaffected by the mass of humans it was walking through, its black cloak flapping against the tumbling limbs. With a thrill of horror, Amos realised who it was. He had arrived at last!

No sooner had Amos drawn this conclusion when the figure in black darted toward him. Sheer fright made Amos react on instinct and he bent over backward to avoid being hit as the dark assassin sailed above him. For a fraction of a second Amos caught a glimpse of his eyes, they were the same white eyes he once found comfort in when he looked at Ignis or the others, but these filled him with fear. In that instant Amos registered the murderous intent gleaming behind the white irises, had seen where it was looking and knew with a sinking feeling that he wasn't the boy's intended victim. A blade was drawn and a flash of steel highlighted a path toward Prince Phillip's exposed neck.

'No!' Thought Amos realising at last who the target had been. But it was too late. He had lost his footing, the blade was out of reach and he didn't have the skill even if he could have got his fingers to it.

'I've failed!' he thought to himself bitterly.

Out of nowhere Shui reformed just next to the queen and kicked the assassin away from the prince with the force of a train. He clattered through the throng and smashed bodily into the doors of The Red Lion pub causing brick and wood to shower those nearby.

Shui helped Amos to his feet and turned to face the wreckage she had just caused, looking for the sign of a body moving in the rubble. When nothing happened, she shepherded Amos, the queen and the prince directly behind her

"When I say so take these two and run!" ordered Shui jerking her thumb over her shoulder at the queen and her husband.

Amos murmured his understanding and clutched an arm of each royal, who did not protest. Everyone stared at the dust settling in the distance, waiting, ready.

"You're not an elemortal if you are going to go down like a bitch after just one hit!" yelled Shui who was growing impatient.

"Shui, I really don't think…" began Amos imploringly but Shui ignored him.

"Really?" mocked Shui with a dry laugh. "You're seriously trying to tell me that you just got knocked the f…"

Shui's sentence was interrupted by a fist that came at her so quickly it caught her cheek as she deflected it a fraction too late. She stumbled a step back but recovered just in time to trap a second lightning-fast blow to her throat. Holding the hand tight she gazed into the shadowed face and drunk in the glare of the white eyes that were staring back. Cold fury had wrought them into a manic expression, and as they narrowed, Shui broke her hold, barely blocking two swift kicks which caused her to slide into Amos.

Capitalising on Shui's poor footing the assassin dashed forward and shot a foot at Shui's abdomen, but with unerring speed and precision, Shui gave the slightest side step and smashed her elbow and knee together, sandwiching the assassin's shin between them. Before he could react to the pain, she kicked the knee of his other leg unsteadying him and, hopping a little, kicked him firmly in the chest sending him several feet away from Amos and the royals. Unlike the assassin, Shui wasted no time and sped straight after him as he soared into a thick wall of bodies. She buried her foot into his gut the second he hit the cluster of people, causing them to collapse and creating a path to safety.

"Amos, run, now!" roared Shui, as she drove a fist into the assassin's upside-down face. Before she could strike again, the assassin span around, sweeping her legs and with tremendous force, punched her into the cenotaph which cracked and leaned precariously toward nearby rioters. He leapt to his feet and moved between Amos and the collapsed wall as they bolted for the clearing, blocking their escape. Amos took up a fighting stance and prepared himself for what would surely be death against this abomination. But the creature shook his head, waved him aside and pointed to the prince.

Whatever it had been trying to imply was lost on Amos, who took nothing but offence to this gesture.

"I AM NO COWARD BOY! FIGHT WITH ME AND SEE WHAT POWER REALLY IS!" growled Amos in a transport of rage.

His body seemed to swell as his clothes tightened against his muscles and the air seemed to ripple and flow over him like a heatwave.

The assassin's eyes widened somewhat with surprise but he was undeterred. He moved toward Amos with one huge leap. For a moment it looked like he was literally flying as he sped across the ground, his fist raised for a decisive blow. Before it struck, Shui's own fist had collided with the assassin's forehead and with a thunderous crack had blown him over the collapsed wall of bodies and out of the crowd.

He landed next to a woman with long brown hair and dressed in a smart black dress suit. She screamed in fright as he collapsed in a heap to her left, and looking where he came from, spotted the prince and squealed. "Your Highness, help!"

Prince Philip looked for the voice calling his title and spotting the woman tried to beckon her over.

"Miss Gibson, this way quick, get away from him now!"

The assassin rose to his feet once again, but as he did so his movements were thick with frustration. For a moment he looked back toward his quarry.

31

He had to do it now, before it was too late. He had just dug his feet into the ground and tensed his legs about to jump, when Miss Gibson clumsily ran into his peripheral vision. For a fleeting moment time seemed to stop as the assassin's brain caught up with the impossibility of what he was seeing. Realisation dawned on him and all thoughts of the prince were driven completely from his mind. He thrust out a hand and grabbed Miss Gibson by the neck and with a jerk, forced her painfully to her knees so he could hold her at eye level. Shocked, Amos and Shui made to lurch forward but the assassin withdrew another blade and held it to her neck.

They backed off instantly and satisfied that they would not attack him just yet, the assassin grabbed Miss Gibson by her cheeks and turned her face to his so he could look into her eyes. She whimpered at the sight of his cold, dead looking glare, but the assassin became increasingly excited at the sight of hers. He held her at arms' length and looked at her stomach. After a cursory glance he leaned in and sniffed her belly. His eyes widened so much they almost boggled. A moment later the eyes narrowed instead. It was clear he was smiling.

"I thought it would take longer to find you!" the assassin crooned menacingly into Miss Gibson's ear. "I thought I would have to send Abyzou after you, perhaps even that we would find you too late, yet here you are, gift wrapped so to speak."

The boy clenched Miss Gibson's neck tighter and she winced with pain and let out a barely audible cry.

"I think I should open my present right here and show everyone what I received!" the boy breathed through deep excited gasps of air.

Miss Gibson's expression stretched wide with fright as the boy wrenched her head backward as Shui and Amos looked on helplessly.

Without warning he raised the knife high and made to bring it down to stab her torso before Shui could even think to stop him.

Back at the Conclave, Chloe, who was still sitting with Yoshiro and had seen her mother taken hostage via the BBC coverage of the parade, snapped. It happened without thought, without decision and it was entirely unexpected for both Chloe and Yoshiro, though Chloe would have no memory of it later. As Chloe watched the assassin raise the knife on the television, she burst off the sofa and ran at the screen, screaming wildly.

She grabbed Yoshiro by the handle and in one smooth motion withdrew the blade and swung it at the scene. As she did so, the screen seemed to bleed into reality, or reality bled into the screen, whichever it was, Chloe suddenly found herself in Whitehall in the middle of the riot she had been watching and bracing the blade of Yoshiro against the knife the assassin had been about to kill her mother with, the tip of which quivered an inch above Miss Gibson's navel. Their attacks had collided mid-swing and in the confusion of her appearance everyone seemed momentarily frozen.

Amos blinked a little stupidly then rubbed his eyes. "Chloe?" he said in a small voice.

Cassandra looked down at the little girl straining to hold the sword against the assassin's knife and gasped with surprise.

"CHLOE?" she wailed, shuddering with fright.

This last shock was one too many for Cassandra and she fainted against the assassin nudging him away from Chloe. Cassandra collapsed in a heap on the floor but Chloe paid her no attention. She hopped across her mother's crumpled frame, and thrust Yoshiro at the assassin's chest. It was blocked easily but another attack came swiftly after and soon the assassin found himself trapped beneath an onslaught of steel. Chloe seemed to be in some sort of trance and her body was acting on its own. Her mind had left, the red mist had descended and all that remained was impulse as muscles and senses took control. Smashing the knife away with the length of the sword Chloe stepped in close, and slapping away the assassin's protesting hand, spun the sword around and used the butt of the grip to strike the assassin hard in the face. It was a surprisingly powerful strike and blood burst from his nose and mouth as the boy toppled to the ground.

Shui rushed to Chloe's side and prepared to continue the fight but as the assassin stood up and, spitting a puddle of blood at their feet, readied himself to attack, they were joined by Aarde and Hoowo3oow, the latter of which still clutched the dismembered leg of his last enemy and looked as though he intended to use it as a weapon.

For the briefest of moments, it appeared that the assassin was about to launch himself at them, but whether unwilling or unable to confront this many aggressors, the assassin turned and fled into the crowd, and down the street.

Chapter Two
Their Darkest Hour

Shui was first to break and give chase, but moments later Aarde and Hoowo3oow had followed after. The three of them ducked and weaved between stumbling legs and falling bodies, barging people out of the way and smashing through barriers where necessary as they desperately tried to keep the assassin in sight.

Shui could just see the black cloak swishing and floating behind their quarry as he wound through the crowd ahead but her attempts to gain ground were impeded by the swelling masses. As they neared the statue of Winston Churchill and the street opened up into a park, she saw the assassin break left and head toward Westminster Palace. As she, Aarde and Hoowo3oow broke free from the rioters they spotted him running across the Old Palace Yard, he was limping and this was hindering his escape. A thirst for blood erupted deep in the pit of Shui's stomach and baring her clenched teeth she bolted after him like a hyena closing in on a wounded gazelle. Aarde and Hoowo3oow shadowed her flank and they scorched a path toward the Victoria Tower Gardens as the assassin and his cloak disappeared along the side of the House of Lords and toward the River Thames. They reached the corner and saw once again the cloak flapping out of sight down a path at the rear of the building.

Hungry for the kill they sprinted after him, determined to exterminate this bastardised imitation of their own existence. Just as they turned the corner, a figure that had been sprinting in the other direction collided into all three of them, and together they tumbled over the river railing and plunged into the cold murky waters of the Thames.

A few seconds later the water began to churn and boil and steam exploded from giant bubbles as four small bodies floated to the surface, spluttering through wet faces.

Shui was thrashing around trying to get her bearings. Her expression was livid and spotting the fool who had crashed into her used the river's mass to push herself above the waterline and leer down on him.

"You, massive twat!" roared Shui with unsuppressed anger. "Do you have any idea what..." began Shui but she broke off mid-sentence as the little body she had been yelling at rolled over in the water and the face of Ignis looked back her as he spat a little spout of water from his mouth which instantly turned to steam.

"Hi Shui, I missed you too!" he said with a weak smile.

Far from being happy to see him, Shui launched from her watery perch and hit Ignis with such force the water exploded as though a bomb had just been detonated. Ignis shot beneath the surface and slammed into the river bed causing a tremor to surge through the Thames upheaving the waterline which spilled waves out onto the adjacent streets.

"Shui, we don't have time for this!" bellowed Aarde. "We must regroup, that assassin could be heading back to the cenotaph to finish the job."

As Aarde spoke, as if his words had been a cue for terror, a loud blood-curdling scream echoed over the palace and within seconds they had set off back toward the parade route and the source of the newly erupted chaos, with a winded Ignis in tow. As they drew close the sound of more screaming grew loud in their ears. The crowd was still scattering in several directions but the throng had at least thinned and it required little effort to navigate back to where they had left Amos and the others.

When they at last reached the cenotaph they were greeted with a heart-stopping, defeated scene of despair.

The rioting had all but subsided with only a handful of people still scuffling somewhere off in the distance. But any sound they made was obscured by the wailing of pain coming from Elsu. He lay on the ground before them clutching at a bloodied stump below his knee which was being treated with gauze and bandages by Gyasi who was heavily bruised and covered in deep cuts. Behind them stood Chloe in the centre of what appeared to be a mass of slaughtered bodies, each with obvious blade marks upon them. Chloe herself was caked in blood and her face was still vacant, almost serene. Yoshiro hung loosely in her hand, the tip of his blade rested against the tarmac and a steady trickle of blood streamed along the metal as it drained off Chloe's clothing. Every now and then she gave a twitch but otherwise was as still as a statue. Despite this terrible vision the true horror of the scene lay further still behind Chloe where Amos could be seen pressing down on a body that was slumped against the Queen. For several long moments they refused to believe what they were seeing and each stood rooted to the spot with ill-disguised revulsion on their faces.

His Royal Highness Prince Philip lay upon the floor weak and limp. His head was being cradled by the Queen and his chest was drenched in blood which had evidently come from the wound that Amos was trying to treat. Amos wore an expression of stout determination and worked frantically to pack the wound as he bellowed instructions to anyone with enough sense to listen. Upon the ground beside him was Cassandra Gibson. She had fallen and landed at an oblique angle and was clearly in discomfort and distress, but she was unable to better position herself on account of the fact that she was trapped beneath the lifeless body of Wun Chuan.

Wun Chuan's body lay bent backwards and broken across Cassandra's torso. Her lifeless eyes were fixed open and she stared unseeing into the endless grey expanse of cloud above them.

As Aarde and Hoowo3oow moved to assist Amos and Gyasi, Shui shot to Wun Chuan's side, and through muttered sobs of "No, no, please, please, no", lifted her gently off Cassandra who clambered away, desperate to escape her morbid circumstance.

Shui placed Wun Chuan in a space of her own and hurriedly began checking her body for a fatal wound. Eventually she found the culprit, a patch of skull at the back of her head which was soft to the touch and kneeling at her side Shui began to perform CPR.

"We can fix this!" said Shui, her voice cracking as her eyes pooled. "We can get you back, fix you with the Conduit. You'll be fine...! AARDE! MEND HER SKULL!"

She gave two breaths into Wun Chuan's mouth whose chest rose and then fell, defiantly lifeless. She resumed chest compressions and with each press tears tumbled from her cheeks and splashed Wun Chuan's face. "Just got to keep you from rotting!" rambled Shui with half a laugh. "Keep the blood pumping, that's all you gotta do! AARDE!"

Aarde glared wide-eyed at Shui as he handed Amos a fresh batch of dressings. He had realised what Shui had not, or perhaps had ignored and right now the prince was the priority. Hating himself, he turned back to face the prince but his assistance was lacklustre and he kept stealing guilty glances at Shui over his shoulder.

As Shui stared at Wun Chuan's empty eyes, a panic inspired fervour seemed to overcome her and she began to press harder.

"Come on!" growled Shui through gritted teeth and gave Wun Chuan another two breaths.

"COME ON YOU, BITCH!" She pressed harder still.

"Shui!" said a soft voice from behind her, but Shui ignored it.

"Breathe!"

"Shui!" said the voice again but a little firmer this time. "We are outside… there is nothing to hold her sou…"

"NO!" roared Shui. "BREATHE, YOU COW, OR SO HELP ME I WILL…" CRACK.

The sound of Wun Chuan's ribcage collapsing made Shui recoil with fright and anguish at what she had done. Her hands dithered in front of her as she held them up to her face and stared at them with disgust.

She shook her arms as if trying to rattle the hands away from her wrists and when Ignis walked over and wrapped his arms around her, holding her tight, she broke into a fit of crying. Her sobs and wails were like that of someone being tortured. All around, people stopped in their tracks and fell silent under the weight of Shui's pain. She fought against Ignis' grip but he held her tight and she eventually convulsed herself into a ball on the floor, whimpering as she rocked back and forth.

Aarde who had completely stopped helping Amos, just stood and stared at Ignis who had sat down beside Shui and was positioned with her head in his lap so he could shield her from view of the onlooking crowd.

His face must have been showing something other than sympathy, as a moment later Aarde received a blow to his arm which snapped him out of his torpor.

"If you want to punch him for being a friend, punch him later!" snapped Hoowo3oow impatiently as he joined him next to Amos. "Right now, your energy would be better used to heal the prince, his condition appears to be worsening!"

"Hm? What? Shit you're right!" spluttered Aarde, clearly wrong footed by this remark. "How's Elsu?" he asked, hastening to stretch out his hands and sense the prince's physical form with his energy and feel the vibrations of his structure.

"He'll live!" replied Hoowo3oow coolly. "With your help we should be able to grow him a new leg back at the Conclave."

Aarde felt right down to the strands of DNA, then to the molecules and finally the atoms where upon he began to realign them, encourage growth and reform bonds. A moment later he heard Amos tell the Queen the prince was stabilising and Aarde relaxed, allowing his thoughts to return to Shui.

"I don't want to punch him!" said Aarde after a minute or two of keeping the prince healing.

"Didn't look like it!" said Hoowo3oow sarcastically.

"Since when were you sarcastic?" retorted Aarde.

"Since when were you a liar?" sneered Hoowo3oow.

Aarde seemed lost for a response so Hoowo3oow pressed on. "You guys have always clashed and I have always known that it is in the main, at least for your part, because of Shui and her relationship with him... but I never thought you hated him!"

Aarde sank at the shoulders at these words and looked disappointed. "I don't hate him!" he sighed, then added after a disbelieving look from Hoowo3oow. "I don't... Honestly I don't! He's a dick but he's also a friend! I just... hate that it's not me!"

"Our situation never excluded us from feelings of love, Aarde," said Hoowo3oow consolingly. "Whether it's equal I couldn't say, but you do know she loves you too... and so does Ignis!"

Aarde didn't respond. He instead concentrated harder on the task of healing the prince.

"Just tell her!" pressed Hoowo3oow.

"Shh, a second!" commanded Aarde. He sounded suddenly stressed.

"Don't you shush me!" grumbled Hoowo3oow menacingly. "It may not be what you want to hear Aarde but..."

"Quiet!" demanded Aarde again. "Something's wrong!"

"What is it?" asked Hoowo3oow after a pause.

"He isn't healing!" replied Aarde who sounded very concerned.

"What do you mean it's not working!" snapped Hoowo3oow. "He's alive, isn't he? Half the work is done for you! Just push the molecules back together!"

Hurried voices erupted around the prince as he suddenly slumped further to the ground. Amos yelled for a first aid kit and a defibrillator and began clearing people away from the space around him as he prepared for the worst.

"What do you think I've been trying to do?" replied Aarde who was panicking now. "For some reason the molecules won't bond... they won't even meet... it's as if some force is pushing the wound further apart!"

At Aarde's words Hoowo3oow marched forward and with impatient roughness, shoved Amos out of the way and, disregarding the protests of the Queen, tore away the prince's shirt and removed the bloodied dressing.

Amos held a guard the Queen had summoned at bay and tried to placate Her Highness while Hoowo3oow scooped up a handful of bandages and wiped the wound clean of blood.

With the flesh exposed, Hoowo3oow could distinguish the shape of the wound that was refusing to heal.

"The spider web!" whispered Hoowo3oow so only Amos could hear as he examined each icon, symbol, and sygil upon the prince's breast, directly over his heart.

"The wound is like the others from previous assassinations?" asked Amos with surprise.

"It must carry some sort of curse..." said Hoowo3oow pensively. "If that is the case, it's unlike anything I have ever heard of... I... I don't think there is anything we can do!"

The sound of sirens echoed between the tall buildings, the police and ambulance were on their way.

"What are you doing to my husband?" demanded the Queen over Amos' shoulder.

Hoowo3oow ignored her. He turned instead to where Shui was still curled in a ball sobbing. "Ignis is there anything you can do?"

At once Amos started. "Ignis?" he blurted, wheeling around to look for his charge. "But he isn't... he's still..." stammered Amos confused. But then his eyes found him, cradling Shui.

"IGNIS!" yelled Amos jubilantly, forgetting the prince and the queen. "My dear boy I was starting to worry. Thought we'd lost you to the tides of time!"

He strode over to Ignis, dropped to his knees and hugged him enthusiastically.

"I just got back ten minutes ago!" said Ignis in a squashy voice, his face was half buried in the crook of Amos' elbow. "I ran into these guys while I was chasing that dude." Ignis paused a moment then added in an apologetic tone. "I'm afraid we lost him!"

"We can catch up later!" growled Hoowo3oow impatiently. "Ignis, can you help or not?"

"What do you expect me to do?" said Ignis indignantly. "My powers are plasma based. If you need him burning or electrocuting then I'm your guy, but healing? Not my area of expertise!"

Amos got to his feet, his face alight with an idea. "That's it!" he said excitedly, Burn him!"

"Wait, what?" said Ignis and Hoowo3oow together.

"You can cauterise the wounds!" replied Amos confidently. "Burn the edges together, it probably won't be a permanent solution but it may keep him alive long enough to have the coven break whatever curse is stopping us from healing him properly."

Ignis looked at the prince who had turned very white, he had lost a tremendous amount of blood and was fading fast.

"Are you sure about this?" asked Ignis to Amos. "My techniques are not really suitable for small and accurate procedures. There's a good chance I'll burn more than just the wound!"

"If we do nothing and the prince dies then we have no way of making this disaster disappear!" said Amos gravely. "We can make them all forget this travesty of a celebration easily enough, but not if the pain of loss is heavy in the queen's heart. That pain will force the memory to surface eventually and when it does, we will all be exposed for what we are. What follows… ." Amos drew a deep breath and sighed. "…I don't want to imagine!"

Ignis felt Shui stir in his lap and he looked down to see her face still wet with tears gazing up at him.

"Do it!" she said. "End this shit storm so we can go home!"

Nodding, Ignis raised Shui to a sitting position and got to his feet. He strode with purpose toward the prince and began rubbing his hands together. Within seconds black smoke was rising in plumes from his palms.

The queen, spotting him approaching, tried to shield her husband from him.

"What are you doing, no, get away from him!" she roared.

More guards hurried towards Ignis, this time armed with rifles but at a glance from Ignis they stopped in their tracks as though they had run into an invisible wall. Ignis, now only a foot away from the prince and the queen, crouched down to be at eye level with them both and fixed Her Majesty with a kind but sombre stare.

"Your Highness," he began with a small bow of his head. "I understand your trepidation, this day has been traumatic for everyone and I know that our appearance and methods are unsettling to the uninitiated."

Ignis spoke so softly that it was almost a whisper and the look of fury the queen had been wearing slowly melted away at the sound of his voice.

"We are too complicated to explain right now, but please understand if you want your husband to live you must let us help, in any way we can, and right now that means moving out of my way! So move!"

A queen does not take orders, she gives them. She is a woman who expects and demands obedience from her subjects and is not accustomed to being told what to do. Never the less at his last words, the queen slowly pulled away from the prince and got to her feet, helped by the one of the guards.

"This will hurt!" said Ignis coldly to the prince and his eyes burst into flames that lapped his forehead and fringe. "Everyone, stay back!"

Ignis upturned his palms which were glowing like hot iron and without preamble thrust them against the prince's chest. At once the prince began to convulse and howl in pain as the flesh beneath Ignis' hands began to sear and melt. The queen made to move toward her husband but a sudden blast of heat from Ignis' body made her stop and recoil and she buried her face into one of the guard's chest, sobbing profusely.

"Aarde," said Ignis without looking, "can you tell if it's working?"

Aarde stretched out his hands again and felt the subatomic vibrations within the prince's writhing body. It made him sweat at once. For a few moments Aarde said nothing. He was concentrating hard as though he were trying to locate an object in a dark room.

"Crap, that's hot!" said Aarde a few minutes later.

"Not what I asked dude!" Ignis shot back. "Have the cuts fused or not?"

"It's hard to tell!" replied Aarde wiping sweat off his brow with his forearm. "The molecules are too excited by the heat to see properly!"

"Well look harder!" demanded Ignis. "If I keep this up much longer, he's going to catch fire!"

Aarde screwed his eyes tight and focused hard on the task. "Just a sec, I'm almost there!"

The prince wailed harder as Ignis continued to press his hands against his chest and he made attempts to wrestle Ignis' limbs away from him. The skin was turning black under the heat and the flesh up his neck and abdomen was blistering and peeling away but Ignis continued to hold him down. A moment later the prince lost consciousness, and slumped dead-looking to the ground.

"Aarde!" roared Ignis impatiently.

"I know, I know!" said Aarde in a panic. Sweat was pouring into his eyes now and his hands were looking red and raw.

Several tense seconds passed in silence as everyone looked on bewildered and scared. Without warning Aarde dropped to his knees, growling with pain and clutching his own hands to his chest. "It's not working!" he whimpered. "The curse is too strong!"

As Ignis relinquished his hold on the prince, Amos stood up and kicked the cenotaph step in anger. A chunk of marble broke free and Ignis shot him a worried look.

"That's it!" he moaned weakly. "We are well and truly fucked!" and he picked up the piece of marble he had knocked off and threw it in disgust. It would have sailed into the crowd of onlookers, likely killing someone had it hit them but Hoowo3oow caught it with an outstretched hand and crushed it to powder. Amos, realising his error, sank to the floor and sat with his arms resting on his bent knees and drooped his head to stare blankly at the ground.

The uncharacteristic loss of cool from Amos stirred Shui from her grief and her watery eyes fell on Ignis who had turned to face Amos. Her vision blurred with tears, she could just make out the expression of sadness Ignis wore for his broken friend. Was it the salt stinging her eyes, maybe the light, but for the briefest of moments she thought she saw something else in his face, but it was gone so quickly, she didn't register it properly.

With a growl of fury, Ignis wheeled round and threw himself upon the prince. It was so abrupt it made Aarde and Hoowo3oow jump. The prince began to scream in earnest once more as Ignis' hands slammed against his chest.

"Ignis, leave it!" roared Aarde. "It's not helping, it's just torture!" and he and Hoowo3oow ran forward to pull Ignis away. But they hit a wall of freezing air that was so cold they fell to their knees gasping.

"Ignis? What… what's happening?" yelled Aarde under his arms.

Shui got to her feet to see what was happening to Aarde and Hoowo3oow. She stumbled slowly toward Ignis and felt the air with her fingers which appeared to be sparkling like scattered diamonds. Small ice crystals gathered on her outstretched hand as she waved it in front of her and she noticed frost forming on her hair. A shimmer of green light caught her eye from up above and she saw, along with countless other bewildered Britons, the aurora borealis illuminating the sky over London. Understanding hit her like a brick.

"You could never do it before!" she said in a voice so quiet it was barely audible over the cries from His Highness.

"Do what?" asked Amos with a shiver. Despite his distance from Ignis he too was beginning to feel a wave of cold creeping over him.

"Freezer burn," said Shui with a half a laugh.

"Freeze… are you fucking kidding me?" barked Aarde who had backed away enough to breathe effectively. "When were you planning on telling us that?"

Ignis said nothing. He was still intently concentrating on the task and it appeared to be requiring a great deal of effort. Ignis' face was contorted and he was shaking, not it seemed out of cold, but pain. The prince was becoming quiet and his chest was turning a purplish blue. He outwardly appeared to be rapidly succumbing to hypothermia. The centre of Prince Phillips chest was ice white now. It appeared to have frozen solid and he was now silent and still.

"Shit, Ignis!" whispered Aarde. "Is… is he dead?"

Ignis released his touch and got to his feet. "Not yet," he replied flatly. "I'm going to crack him open, when I do be quick about building him some fresh meat, you won't have long."

"Right," said Aarde, then thinking about what Ignis had said, panicked. "Wait, what?"

But too late. Ignis was already winding up a punch. Flustered but quick to react, Aarde assumed the position and braced himself for some fast work.

Helpless and entranced Shui looked on as Ignis brought down his fist with well-judged force. In the split second before it hit, she noticed something that caused her thrill of unease. 'Did he just say…' thought Shui, but SMASH! The top layer of the chest cavity shattered revealing splintered ribs and an un-beating, frozen heart.

"Aarde, I'm going to thaw him out. As I do, you'll need to chase the edge!" commanded Ignis, getting to his feet and rolling his shoulders.

"Do it!" replied Aarde with grim determination and together, under the renewed warmth that spread to everyone as Ignis reverted to his usual skill set, they created a new, albeit heavily scarred, chest. As the Prince inhaled his first life affirming lung full of air, Aarde and Ignis shared a fist bump and collapsed with relief.

Half an hour later, the crowds had been dispersed through carefully controlled security points that were being orchestrated by the Conclave. Calming drinks were being handed out for shock, and as each person drank, a soothing forgetfulness overcame them and a medic carefully escorted them to a recovery tent to sleep it off and eventually wake to their new memory.

"Thankfully most of the camera footage showing the cenotaph was corrupted due to high levels of microwave radiation in the area," said Frank to Amos as they debriefed through Amos' outstretched hands. "There was live coverage of the riot so there is no hiding that, but the cause is being attributed to an unexpected clash between opposing political activists that spread out to the rest of the civilians."

"How is our Majesty and her husband?" enquired Amos as he surveyed the flock of professionals swarming the palace. "I expect there will be some backlash for this."

"I don't even want to think about it," groaned Frank. "I don't think this can be buried. It was too traumatic, especially for the prince who will flashback to what happened every time he sees his scar, but that's a later on problem. Right now, I just want to get everybody back here, we need to talk!"

"Sounds ominous!" replied Amos suspiciously. "Don't tell me there's another attack!"

"No, no… well not that we know of at least." reassured Frank. "It's Wade, he says he's cracked it!"

"Cracked what?" asked Amos.

"No idea!" said Frank. "He called me up, demanded I set up an urgent meeting, fumbled and dropped the phone, then said he'd cracked it and hung up! He was very excited!" concluded Frank with an exasperated nod.

"Well, we're nearly finished here," sighed Amos observing several units reporting to their commanding officers and readying to leave. "Aarde and Hoowo3oow have already left with Gyasi and Elsu, the latter needing limb rejuvenation so they will have teleported straight to the medical suite."

"And Shui?" asked Frank tentatively.

Amos came to an abrupt halt, hung his head and massaged the bridge of his nose. He stole a glance at the tent still erect near the cenotaph that housed Wun Chuan's body and shook his head slowly. "Shui will be travelling with… with…" Amos' voice cracked.

"Are they travelling with Nephthys?" interjected Frank sparing Amos the need to say the name. Amos nodded.

"I'll get everything prepared and meet Shui in the lounge, have Nephthys take her directly there."

Amos, showed his understanding and bid Frank farewell before wiping his eyes on the handkerchief he had in his pocket. Giving himself a final dust off he peered around looking for Ignis and spotted him a few yards from the tent. Ignis was sat on the ground leaning back on his hands with his head lolling behind him. Amos came and sat beside him and gave him a gentle nudge.

"Quite the welcome home party, eh?" said Amos bitterly.

Ignis gave a half-committed laugh, and turned his head to look at his friend.

"You all right?" he said nudging Amos back.

"Better now you're here," replied Amos as a small tear fell from his cheek.

Ignis chuckled weakly. "That's only because you didn't see what was 'here', 250,000 years ago!"

He swung his arms forward and got to his feet before pulling Amos to his and together they went to the tent to wait for Nephthys to bring them home.

Chapter Three
The Second Law of Thermodynamics

A grim mood had gripped the Conclave by the time everyone had finished piling back to their stations and quarters. Throughout the building, staff carried out their business in near total silence, the only voices being heard were of those asking for some paper or to bring up a file. The day's events were still replaying on various feeds throughout the Conclave and even those who didn't need to view them couldn't help glancing at the carnage every now and again.

Down in the lounge the usual faces had gathered to pay their respects to Wun Chuan. Shui had placed her upon a cushioned and quilted ottoman positioned just outside her bedroom door which was becoming harder to see behind the ever-growing collection of flowers sent from friends and department heads. Shui had cleaned and redressed Wun Chuan's body as soon as they had arrived. She had worked without speaking for over an hour, refusing offers of help and slamming tools and cupboard doors with unnecessary force. She had clothed Wun Chuan in the only dress she owned, a blue silk embroidered frock and her hair had been tied up in a plaited bun. Once Shui had laid Wun Chuan's body down for her wake, she had taken a blue leather book from a long-legged stand upon which a photo of Wun Chuan had been placed, had locked herself in her room and had not come out since.

Ignis was sat next to Amos with his arms folded and his head bowed. He was bouncing his right knee on the ball of his foot and Amos could be seen visibly wobbling from the vibration. Aarde, Hoowo3oow and Gyasi were clearly visible on a giant display projected into the room from the centre console. They were sat around a bed where Elsu was sleeping, his leg bandaged but regrown and whole again.

Frank could be heard in the background from a second display. He was arguing with someone from MI6 regarding the continued security of Prince

Philip and the poor provision of information the Conclave was providing the government. The words 'need to know' were said multiple times.

Chloe was still not fully with it. She was swaddled in a blanket and was huddled between her mother, Cassandra, and Alex at the back of the room where it was quiet. Cassandra was weeping silently and rubbing Chloe with an arm wrapped around her as though trying to keep her warm, she clearly had no idea where she was or who these people were, nor did she seem to care. Alex darted her a snide look every now and again as though waiting for an opportunity to argue with her and shuffled bitterly away a little when Cassandra's arm grazed hers.

Wade, was the only one who seemed truly restless. He was pacing back and forth, a roll of paper held in his right hand was being tapped frantically against his leg and he rubbed his neck relentlessly.

Eventually Frank's conversation concluded with a loud pissing contest during which Frank pulled rank with a security clearance level the agent had never even heard of. After agreeing to smuggle a contingent of conclave auxiliaries to stand inside the palace, the agent hung up with the sincere wish they wouldn't speak again until Barry was in charge.

"Arsehole!" barked Frank as he slammed down a phone handset. Several faces shot up to look at him and he gave an embarrassed apology with a solemn glance at Wun Chuan.

Amos got to his feet and interrupted Wade in his pacing.

"At a risk of sounding indelicate," he began with a cautious look around the room, "I understand you have something very important to relay to us, Wade."

"Yes!" blurted Wade. "I do, but I wasn't sure if…" he broke off staring at Shui's door.

Amos patted him gently on the shoulder. "I think it's best to let her grieve. We are having a service later, she should rest until then."

He turned to address the rest of the room. "In the meantime, I think we should press on. We survived today by sheer luck." His tone was serious now. "Without the miraculous intervention of Yoshiro, what happened at Whitehall would have done so without our interference and undoubtedly would have ended even more catastrophically, than it did."

"I shudder to think!" murmured Frank who seemed temporarily lost in thought. "The loss of life would have been immense and there is no doubt the attempt on the prince's life would have been successful."

"He nearly died even with our help!" growled Hoowo3oow over the speakers. "That attack, those symbols. We were powerless against it. There was a deeper magic at work. Whatever force that freak is using, it is old and we have no defence!"

"Not no defence!" said Amos slyly with a knowing look at Ignis. "Freezer burn, eh? That's a new one!"

Ignis seemed to struggle for words. He looked uncomfortable and apprehensive. Finally, he said, "It's painful!" He looked at Amos who was gazing back sympathetically. "I've never been able to push past the pain enough to do it properly."

"When did you realise you could do this?" asked Amos kindly. "I never suspected there was a different dimension to your abilities, it's remarkable to say the least."

"It happened once, a long time ago," said Ignis as if it wasn't important.

"How long is long?" enquired Aarde ill-disguised annoyance.

"I don't know, a hundred years or so!" replied Ignis who sounded equally nettled.

"A hundred years? What the hell Ignis!" snapped Aarde. "You didn't think that was something we ought to know about?"

"And why would it be any concern of yours?" retorted Ignis coldly. "When it happened, it did so on its own. I had no control over it." Ignis got to his feet and walked to the sink to get a drink. After a few gulps of water, most of which had turned to steam in his mouth, he added, "And it hurt, real bad. Like my body was collapsing in on itself. I wasn't in a rush to make it happen again so I put it from my mind."

"Put it from your mind? Ignis you are evolving. You have developed a skill that is separate to the powers you were given!" Aarde took a calming breath before he continued. "For better or worse you've managed to transition and if it happened to you it could happen to us."

"No, it couldn't!" barked Ignis, but then as he stared at Aarde and saw the disappointed frustration hanging on his face he deflated. "I'm not evolving, it's still plasma, still matter, I'm just using it in a different way!"

"By freezing things…" said Hoowo3oow with obvious disbelief.

"Obviously!" sneered Ignis who was becoming more restless.

Aarde was no longer sitting next to Elsu's bed, he was stood up and was too close to whichever mirror was casting his location so that all that could be seen was one enlarged eye and ear.

"A hundred years or so…" mused Amos. "…that's about the same time the human race invented freezing technology if I'm not mistaken."

"Aye!" interrupted Frank. "The first mass production unit was still in our cafeteria when I started working here. A far cry from the Smeg we have upstairs!"

Amos chuckled immoderately and punched Ignis jovially on the arm. "That's it isn't it! Let me guess, solar winds to push down CFCs from the atmosphere? That would of course account for the Northern Lights being seen over the palace for the first time in living memory."

Ignis rubbed his arm unnecessarily and with a coy, sideways look at Amos cracked a wide smile.

Aarde looked close to tears, his watery, blurry eye wobbling with reflected light. "You told Shui, but you didn't tell us?"

Ignis knew what Aarde was getting at straight away, he didn't need the knowing look given to him by Hoowo3oow. "It's not like that!"

"Really, then what is it like?" snapped Aarde. "No, Hoowo3oow!" he continued when Hoowo3oow pulled him back toward his seat. "Thousands of years… of being brothers and you hide something like this from us!"

"Don't give me that!" growled Ignis. "This isn't about how I use my abilities! You think I didn't notice you gorming at me when I was comforting Shui? You've had a bug up your arse about her for over a millennium and you like nothing more than to blame me, like it's my fault you're too much of a pussy to be honest with her and tell her how you feel!"

Ignis had become increasingly louder the more he ranted and he positively bellowed the last five words.

Aarde stood with his head lowered. His shoulders were rising and falling as he took deep steadying breaths. When he spoke, his voice was quiet but there was a cold fury laced in the words.

"Fuck you, Ignis!" he said simply before raising a fist and punching the mirror, terminating the feed.

Ignis kicked over a stool in temper which buckled the metal leg and he sat himself down, his right leg shaking restlessly.

Amos was the first to speak following the intense and awkward silence that followed this debacle.

"Can we just be thankful that Ignis was able to pull something like that out of the bag and afford him the dignity of telling us the hows and whys in his own time?"

"Agreed!" sighed Frank. His nerves were fraying again from the continued stress this day had presented. "Wade! I think now would be a good time for you to weigh in and tell us what you found."

"Finally!" said Wade impatiently and marching imperiously forward.

He tapped a few details into the centre console and a third display appeared showing notes, photos and video snippets of the murders the assassin had committed in date order. There was a collective grimace from everyone present, they were no less hard to look at the second time around.

Wade enlarged a still image of Alfred Braskin, one of two of the first victims that they knew of that had the iconic calling card of this mysterious counterpart. Beside his picture was a résumé of sorts. It listed the man's career history, his education, previous addresses, known affiliations and memberships along with a list of close friends, relatives and associates. Once again, the photo of Alfred standing with Pacal Chan and the elusive Bernard Godfrey came into view.

"Have you found him?" asked Ignis eagerly, the argument of a few minutes before forgotten in an instant. "The other man in the photo, is he here?"

"No, his location is still to be determined, but it is paramount we locate him before the assassin does!" said Wade sternly. "On the back of my conclusions I am certain Mr Godfrey is a target!"

"What makes you so sure?" asked Frank between sips of coffee. "We don't have motive for the other killings yet, we can't poss…"

"But we do!" interrupted Wade.

Frank spluttered into his mug and choked. "I beg… *cough*… your pardon!" he said between gasps.

"Because Mr Godfrey shares one thing in common with Alfred, the high priest of cosmic rebirth and Prince Philip!" said Wade matter of factly.

"And that is…?" pressed Frank.

"That they are, or at least were in the case of the first two, mortal but unmistakably…" Wade took a deep breath. "…Gods!" he finished dramatically.

A few seconds of ringing silence followed this pronouncement which was quickly broken by the hysterical and unabashed laughter of Frank who was beside himself with mirth. "Say that again, but to my good ear!" he chortled.

"It's true!" said Wade sulkily.

"This lot, Gods!" Frank continued through thick, unsuppressed giggles. "You can't be serious, I mean no offence to the prince but he doesn't strike me as the Herculean type and the others, bugger me mate, I know I told you to bring me a theory but far-fetched doesn't cover it! I mean you do remember that we have an entire dungeon filled with Gods, right? You know the ones, they're big and really broody…!"

"Alfred Braskin, a white alien man, appears in the midst of people who have been excluded from the technological age," spat Wade crossly. "Clarke's first law states any technology sufficiently advanced is indistinguishable from magic."

Frank stopped laughing but sat with his head cocked to the side, his expression still dubious.

"When people can't explain what they see, how do they reconcile it in their minds?" yelled Wade in frustration. "What has the human race been doing for thousands of years and what has happened as a result? This entire institute manipulates the fabric of that principle on a daily basis for our own convenience and we do it with absurd ease. How did we make the Conduit? How did we make him?" At his last words Wade had pointed at Ignis who gave him a very stern look.

Waving his hands apologetically Wade pressed on. "C'mon, you know I'm right! Alfred was seen as a God! That tribe believed it so deeply he became one in a limited way." Wade changed the file being displayed on the projection to the high priest. "And so did this guy. His followers believed his claim so much that not only did he become a God in title, but he died the way he told them. We all saw it!"

53

Frank was taking Wade more seriously now. He was leaning forward in his chair and was looking at the files on his end too.

"What about Prince Philip?" asked Amos. "How could he possibly be included in this. The British public have no delusions about his mortality!"

"They don't…" said Wade smugly. "…but members of the Prince Philip Movement are very confused about that!"

"I'm sorry, the who?" asked Frank.

"A tribe in the southern island of Tanna in Vanuatu," explained Wade. "The Kastom people had a legend that the son of a mountain spirit would one day take the form of a light-skinned man, voyage across the sea, marry the most powerful woman alive and return to his island with his wife. They think Prince Philip is that man!"

Amos and Frank looked dumbfounded. Ignis remained sat shaking his head.

"You're shitting me, right?" said Frank unable to suppress a smile.

"Not at all," continued Wade. "The royal family visited Vanuatu during a commonwealth tour in 1974. At that time the Queen was… and arguably still is… the most powerful woman in the world. She was shown due respect wherever she went and the villagers of Yaohnanen saw this. A few questions to the right officials would have told them everything they needed to know to learn their identities and someone applied it to their lore. It fitted, so the rest followed suit!"

"Boom! God! Just like that!" said Frank with a snap of his fingers.

"Why though?" asked Amos more to himself than anyone else. "Why now, or even at all? Gods by title they may be, but they have no divine power, no supernatural prowess. They were no threat to anyone!"

"The paradox!" said Wade grimly. "Bushyasta said that the hole was already there. It was probably caused by whatever paradox they were talking about. That means it caused the breach and bled reality. Considering everything else that has been manifesting around the planet, maybe the breach has changed for them what being a God means."

Frank looked hopefully at Amos who raised a quizzical eyebrow.

"I still don't get the point!" he said puzzled. "Even if that were true, it still doesn't make sense to kill them. The effort and risk alone, outweighs

54

the end result. There was no gain! No claiming of followers, no transfer of power. Nothing!"

Amos pondered this for a moment while he gave a characteristic clean of his glasses. "Well then," he said at last, "if there was nothing to gain, maybe we should consider what there was to lose."

"Again, nothing!" argued Frank. "Those men couldn't have challenged a demon let alone another God! A real one!"

"Frank's right!" agreed Shui from across the room. Her sudden appearance startled Amos who had been facing the wrong way. "But then maybe the loss wasn't theirs to lose." She walked slowly along the length of Wun Chuan's outstretched body stopping at her head to gently reposition a strand of hair. "Maybe it was ours!" she said sadly.

Amos hurried to her side and hugged her tightly.

"How are you dear? he asked softly.

Shui simply shook her head softly. Feelings were difficult for Shui, expressing them even more so.

"Miss Sterling, would you be so kind as to put the kettle on?" asked Amos as he slowly escorted Shui to the sofa.

Alex looked alarmed at being addressed, but she understood and made her way to the sink while casting frequent dark looks at Cassandra. As she walked past Amos she whispered with a hiss. "Why is she even here?"

"She is Chloe's mother!" said Amos firmly. "Right now, Chloe needs her!" He gazed sadly at them for a moment then added. "And she needs Chloe!"

"You're not threatening her with lasers though, are you?" spat Alex as Amos walked away.

"Maybe the demons think they would be valuable to us in this war the demons mentioned," suggested Wade. "If they are somehow going to be able to break into this realm in their own forms then who knows what a mortal god would actually be capable of?"

"What a time to be alive, eh!" groaned Amos sardonically.

"I've just tripled the guard on Prince Philip!" said Frank absently as he worked away in the background. "The assassination may have failed, but if Wade is right, he should also be considered a viable target!"

He continued typing for a few minutes while Amos got Shui settled and Alex made tea. After a couple of minutes, he added, "Five units en route to Vanuatu as well. Considering what happened to Pacal Chan it may be better to play it safe."

"Excellent, Frank! Be sure to relay this to Hoowo3oow and Aarde immediately," ordered Amos politely.

"Already done. They are on their way down here now, with a dossier I just compiled," replied Frank smugly.

"Shui, do try to drink," whispered Amos softly. "Would you like something to eat maybe? A biscuit perhaps or a…"

Shui looked mournfully up at Amos and he fell quiet. He was holding a very forced smile. She knew he was just trying to be helpful so Shui, just to make him stop asking, agreed to have an apple.

"Wade…" Amos continued absently as he rummaged through the cupboards. "The other man…" he closed and opened a few drawers, "…the author. What's his name?"

"DQ… something… Robinson?" offered Frank.

"That's the one," said Amos a little grumpily, banging a few doors shut and trying another set of cupboards. "Is there no fruit in this damn kitchen?"

"What about him?" asked Wade who brought up his file. The grotesque, posed figure came into view.

"Do we really need to see that. Y'know… never mind," said Amos averting his eyes and continuing his search. "How does he tie into all this? You spoke to his wife, she said he was an atheist, right? I can't see how that would warrant him a death sentence. Ah, here we are… oh!"

He had withdrawn an apple from the cupboard, but it was beginning to rot. He looked at the others, they had also started to putrefy in varying amounts.

"You really must stay on top of the cleaning you guys!" he moaned dropping the rotten fruit into the bin. "How about a sandwich instead, Shui?"

Shui was busy looking at her feet, her head propped in her left hand. She raised her right arm into the air to show her agreement then let it flop down again to droop over the edge of the sofa.

"Maybe it was a copy cat!" suggested Alex who was hovering somewhere between Shui and Chloe.

"It's not impossible," mused Frank bobbing his head from side to side. "Thanks to that utter tosspot plumbthumb6759, the formation of symbology was highlighted on Youtube for all to see..." Frank massaged his temples as though the thought was painful, "...but it's such an accurate representation etched in his brain I have to believe it's still our guy!"

"He must have really pissed him off!" said Alex staring at the victim's photo with her nose screwed up.

"Maybe it was something he wrote!" offered Wade. "His book apparently had religious themes, maybe something in it touched a nerve."

"What are you trying to convince me of, Wade?" asked Frank smirking. "That this guy attends a book club with his demon mates and that was on their weekly reading list!"

Wade did not look amused.

"Where is the respect?" he muttered throwing his paperwork over his shoulder.

"Fine," snorted Frank with a laugh. "Make obtaining a copy of that book a top priority. I suppose there might be something in it that sheds a light on why he was butchered. It had better be good though! I'm not reading it if it's crap!"

"We should probably put considerable effort into working out whether anyone else could qualify as a God. If they can, it stands to reason our assassin will make them target," added Amos as he pulled a loaf of bread out the bread bin.

"That's probably something I should get started on," said Wade wide-eyed and he gathered his notes and strode out of the door with a warm wave to Amos.

Amos took out a slice but then threw it down in disgust. "Are you kidding me!" Amos emptied out the contents of the bread bag onto the counter. Every slice had turned blue and was growing mould. "When was the last time you went shopping!" he demanded of Ignis throwing him a rare reproachful look.

"A couple of hours ago!" said Ignis defensively as he got to his feet to have a better look.

Amos opened the fridge and gagged. A pungent smell quickly filled the living space as Amos pulled out several bloated and discoloured items of food from the shelves that were dripping a cheese-like liquid on the floor. He quickly checked the milk Alex had left out on the counter by giving it a reluctant sniff before pouring it down the sink.

"Good lord, Miss Sterling!" Amos said aghast and retching slightly. "You made us drinks with this?"

Alex stood, looking mortified. "No, I mean yes… but it was fine a minute ago!" She looked down at her cup of tea, it had congealed. "No, that's not possible!"

A sense of urgency stole over the room. Something strange was going on. Shui looked over at the flowers that had been placed around Wun Chuan. They had all wilted and turned brown. Even Cassandra had noticed something odd was going on as she had calmed down enough to help herself to a Jaffa cake she'd been carrying in her pocket, only to discover it was hard as a rock and was now busy tapping it on a table.

"Something is here!" hissed Ignis angrily as he turned slowly and surveyed the room. Shui suddenly got to her feet too and placed herself back-to-back with Ignis, ready for a fight!

A voice. A horribly familiar voice called out to them from across the room. A voice Shui thought she would never hear again. In an accent no one could place, it said quite calmly. "Now, there will be no need for violence!"

Everyone in the room slowly turned their head in the direction of Shui's room. Cassandra screamed, stumbled over and promptly fainted at the sight that greeted them. Wun Chuan was busy getting herself off the ottoman and examining her surroundings with polite interest.

Shui let out an angry snarl and lurched at her but Ignis held her back.

"Whoa, calm down love!" said Wun Chuan sounding highly amused. "You don't want to go starting something you don't know how to finish."

Shui was bucking and wrestling with Ignis' arms in an attempt to break free but he held her fast. Shui cast him a disgusted look but she was too distracted by the reanimated corpse in front of her to throw him off properly. As she thrashed around, desperately trying to reach Wun Chuan, she sobbed angrily, shaking her head and silently mouthing the word 'no' over and over again.

"I'd watch that tone, if I were you!" warned Ignis as Shui's body gave a particularly forceful jolt. "You don't want to go pissing off something you don't know how to stop."

Wun Chuan gave an indulgent smile. "If you like."

She strolled across the living room like she didn't have a care in the world. It was a slow, almost lazy walk that allowed her take in her surroundings and there was something odd too. A shadow maybe, something dark for definite, tall too. It followed behind her like a thick plume of smoke and then it was gone. It was as if it only existed when you weren't really looking. Whatever it was it had the shape of human and it towered over Wun Chuan. Eventually she reached an armchair which she flopped into, the shadow falling after her, and made herself comfortable, delighting in the bouncy nature of the cushions.

"It's a brave soul," began Amos, sliding in front of Shui and cautiously moving toward Wun Chuan, "coming here, to this place of all places," he added as he gestured to the building at large.

Wun Chuan gave a sideways nod of the head, her mouth down turned with derision as if to intimate, 'If you say so'.

"It was reckless to possess that body," he gestured to Wun Chuan. "in front of us, her friends!" Amos had moved quite close now and Wun Chuan was looking up at him from a reclined position. She was very relaxed.

"But it was really fucking stupid, to do in front of her!" he finished pointing an outstretched hand at Shui.

A heartbeat's worth of time passed during which Wun Chuan blinked. Amos dived at her with his fists raised. Ignis, alarmed at his attack, released Shui who immediately shot forward. Wun Chuan just appeared, standing, and in front of Amos before his fist were even fully back. His expression had not had time to even register his surprise yet but she was upon him, her left hand holding his arm in place and her right hand pressing on his chest. Amos immediately turned a pale grey and began panting for breath, his knees buckling beneath him. Shui was already across the room, and she leaped over Amos, her foot aimed at Wun Chuan's face. The leg didn't connect though. Instead Shui's entire body collapsed into water upon contact with part of Wun Chuan and she landed as a puddle behind her with a splash that hit the wall.

Ignis had been hot on Shui's heels, ready to back her attack but when he saw what happened to her, he came to a halt.

"Smart move kid!" sneered Wun Chuan. "I did warn you."

"I'm not a kid!" growled Ignis as he sized up his opponent, looking for a weakness. "You all think that, like you've been around forever. I'm almost certainly older than you."

Amos let out a wheeze, and a sound that was like dying followed.

"Let him go!" demanded Ignis desperately, his hands raised in surrender, all bravado drained away. "Please, don't kill him, not him, please, PLEASE!" Ignis bellowed the last word as he dropped to his knees.

Alex could be heard crying in the background, she was covering Chloe from the fight and was obviously frightened. Wun Chuan noticed and released her grip. Amos dropped to the floor with a single thud — he wasn't moving. Ignis glanced from Amos to Wun Chuan, he was scared and confused in equal measure and he dithered on the ground, torn between wanting to go to Amos and uncertainty over what would happen if he moved.

"He will live!" said Wun Chuan coolly. "And you can stand!" she added as she sat back down in her seat and made herself comfy again.

Ignis stood very slowly. He dried his eyes and then for need of something to do with his hands brushed himself off. He shot covetous glances at Amos and each time he did the shadow appeared behind Wun Chuan for a fleeting moment.

After a long pause he finally asked. "What are you?"

"Clever boy!" replied Wun Chuan, smiling. "Don't bother!" she added in a bored tone to Shui who had reformed behind her and was sneaking toward her.

Shui froze on the spot, her expression torn between frustration and apprehension.

"Yes indeed!" continued Wun Chuan with a nod. "Not who, but what?"

Shui came around to stand beside Ignis and as she did, she noticed the black figure each time her eyes moved away from their guest.

"You say you are older than me?" chortled Wun Chuan. "I think not."

"That's what everyone says!" muttered Shui, rolling her eyes.

"Well," began Wun Chuan with a casual flick of her hair. "in my case it happens to be true. I have always been and always will be. I will concede that having thoughts, feelings and a shining personality is rather new... relatively speaking you understand," she added almost as an afterthought.

"Are you a God?" croaked Amos unexpectedly. He was slowly clambering back to his feet, massaging his chest and flexing his left arm which was evidently aching. "No demon could do that to Shui!"

"Heavens above, no!" chuckled Wun Chuan immoderately. It took a few minutes for her to stop laughing, so Ignis helped Amos to a seat and checked him over.

"I'm good, my friend," said Amos, pulling Ignis in for a hug. "I think she was giving me a heart attack, but I don't think there is any lasting harm."

"Spill!" roared Shui impatiently. "You... you..." she stuttered, struggling to find the right words to describe the indecency of the situation. "Fuck, just tell me, what are you?"

Before Wun Chuan could reply, the elevator doors hissed open and in walked Hoowo3oow and Gyasi. They were deep in conversation discussing the contents of Frank's dossier and made their way across the room, oblivious to the oddness of the scene. Hoowo3oow sat next to Wun Chuan at the edge of the sofa, Gyasi sitting next to him and he turned a few pages with keen interest. A moment later he and Gyasi were in a state of utter confusion as the pages began to crumble like frail ash at his touch.

Hoowo3oow leaned over to Wun Chuan with the file held out in front of him. "Have you seen this?" he said absently before he looked up and saw who he was talking to.

He let out a rare yell of fright, and pulled away from Wun Chuan so fast he fell over Gyasi. Gyasi noticing the cause of his alarm also jumped back and landed on Hoowo3oow, pinning him to the floor.

"Oh, for the love of..." groaned Shui as she grabbed Gyasi with one hand and lifted him off Hoowo3oow, placing him back on the sofa at the opposite end.

"Thank you," said Hoowo3oow with an abrupt return to his usual strict tone as he rose to his feet. "Anyone care to explain?"

"She was just about to when you guys walked in, weren't you!" replied Ignis with an expectant look at Wun Chuan.

"And I thought you guys were supposed to be smart!" whispered Wun Chuan disappointedly and she leaned forward and stood sharply.

This time Hoowo3oow and Gyasi saw it too. The dark shadow that accented her movements. The tall black figure that shared her space.

"What the…" said a puzzled Hoowo3oow taking a few steps back.

"You're Death, aren't you!" came a small, partially muffled voice from behind Wun Chuan who turned with interest to see who spoke, her expression incredulous but amused. Everyone else leaned to see around Wun Chuan with equal surprise.

It was Chloe. She was peeking out from under Alex's arm and attempting to push her off! "That's right, isn't it?"

The black shadow billowed out momentarily as though it had caught a breeze and then was gone.

"Give that child a gold star!" said Death happily. "What gave it away, the decaying food? My effect on the girl? The near fatal heart attack he nearly had?" Death finished pointing at Amos.

"Um… no!" said Chloe almost apologetically. "Y… Yoshiro told me. He… he said you've met before."

"Ah!" said Death softly. "My work precedes me! Not often I meet one twice, where is he?"

Alex let Chloe move free and she approached Death with Yoshiro held in front of her. "He's in here!" she said weakly.

"He's… really?" said Death, snatching the sword out of Chloe's hand and giving it a rattle. "You don't say." Death turned the blade over a few times and then tossed it back to Chloe. "What on earth did he do to deserve that?"

Chloe looked hurt and upset. "Nothing. He's my friend," she said holding Yoshiro tight.

"That's how you treat your friends?" asked Death in astonishment. "Maybe I've misunderstood the term, is friend perhaps synonymous with enemy?"

"Excuse me, but we are getting sidetracked," said Amos and he ushered Chloe back to Alex. "To my knowledge you have never presented yourself to the Conclave before," he continued cautiously. "I do not wish to offend, but I must ask why you have chosen now of all times to meet with us and… forgive me… in such poor taste."

"This is poor taste?" asked Death. "What is wrong with it? Am I rotting already?"

"No, no, you misunderstand." interrupted Amos with a scared look at Shui. "The body you have borrowed belonged to a friend of ours, she died in battle earlier today, we are mourning, especially Shui!"

"Oooh, that's why…" said Death through an understanding breath. "…the whole trying to kick me and tempers flaring all over the place!"

"Quite!" said Amos lamely. "So… why are you here?" he asked coaxingly.

"Hmm? Ah, yes!" said Death distractedly, then in a very matter-of-fact tone added. "I'm here to help you stop the end of the world!"

"Come again?" asked Frank who seemed to have found his voice again. "What possible incentive could you have for getting involved?" he continued bemused. "I mean you're Death! Surely you can't die!"

Death gave Frank a penetrating stare and he was grateful to be on the other side of a holographic display.

"You are correct in essence," began Death sharply. "But not in the finer distinctions!"

"How so?" enquired Amos interestedly.

Death let out a deflating sigh and gave a scratch on Wun Chuan's chin while considering how to explain.

"I am a fundamental part of the universe…" said Death a moment later. "…I'm not a thing of whimsy, I wasn't invented, I was always here and I will be all that's left when all else has perished."

"Of course!" said Ignis as comprehension dawned. "You are entropy! An actual system within the laws of the physical universe." He smiled for a moment, pleased to be on the same page at last, but then faltered. "Hang on…" he said waving his hands doubtfully. "…physics isn't sentient. Physics just is! Since when did you have a personality?" he asked, dubiously.

"Since you lot came along…" Death cast a lazy hand towards everyone in the room. "…and started making things up to explain what you were too stupid to understand."

"Whoa, hang on," growled Hoowo3oow. "We may be old but we didn't…"

"Ugh, not you specifically!" interrupted Death before adding impatiently. "Your breed, or species! Humans in the general sense. They gave me life because for them, dying is scary!" Death gave a shrug. "You fear the unknown like no other life I have ever encountered… and the cosmos is huuuuge!"

"So you are Azra'il, then?" asked Amos sceptically.

"To some," replied Death. "To others I am King Yama, or Thanatos or the Shinigami, or Ankou, or El or whatever other nonsense persona I have been forced into over the aeons!"

"Forced into?" asked Frank who was sat bolt upright and was taking notes with the enthusiasm of a journalist interviewing their favourite celebrity.

"It means that for every soul I meet I am forced to don the appearance they expect." A sudden look of indignation came over Death who folded Wun Chuan's arms defensively. "And act how they expected at one time too!"

"Your character changed dependent on the cultural beliefs of the soul you collected?" pressed Frank.

"Exactly! In fact, the whole collecting souls thing too, what is that about? Do I look like a UPS driver?"

"You mean you don't collect souls?" said Frank puzzled.

"Well, I obviously do now! From time to time anyway," guffawed Death who seemed amused by the fact. "But I'm not supposed to. Those things should float off on their own as part of the cycle. They shouldn't be part of this universe any more!"

Frank sucked the end of his pen a moment as he processed this. "Then what are you supposed to do?" he asked eventually.

"I am supposed to bring order to chaos!" said Death loftily, raising a hand in exultant praise. "Y'know… entropy… the eventual death of the universe." Death added at the puzzled look on Frank's face. "I do therefore I am!"

"But that won't change. You won't be affected by casualties of a war!" argued Frank. "We humans are not your only concern!"

There was a murmur of agreement at this.

"Maybe not…" crooned Death. "…but you are my biggest concern."

Death began pacing a little, a look of worry drawn upon Wun Chuan's face. Its shadow paced along behind as usual but it looked more hunched than before, like it too felt weight on its shoulders.

"How?" blurted Frank in disbelief. "We take up like what, two per cent of time in the existence of the universe and even less space inside it. What could possibly be so damn important about us!"

"Because without humans…" began Death, taking a deep dramatic breath. "…I am just something that happens." There was a sadness to Death's voice and a distant look in the borrowed dead eyes.

"I have thoughts and feelings… wants even! I have more than an existence, I have experiences," there was more than sadness behind the words now, there was pleading. "You know how it works. You've seen enough of them die by now."

"When no one else knows!" said Amos softly.

"We vanish!" agreed Death dismally. "I love having a mind. To be able to understand and appreciate what I get to experience, you have no idea, it's incredible."

Death looked wistfully into space for a moment then continued with a sudden abruptness.

"I mean yes, the chess games do get tedious, none of you are any good, although I did always wonder what would happen if someone won," added Death with a chuckle. "But that's not the point, I can't afford the world to be filled with demons and the realms to merge, the concept of death would be meaningless and I would disappear."

"So what you're saying is you need us!" sneered Shui, testily.

"We need each other!" snapped Death. "Without me you're all dead!"

"That is a matter of opinion," replied Amos coolly.

"No, it's a fact!" said Death. "Does anyone else know how you get a living human into the other realms? Hmm? No, I didn't think so!"

"And why on earth would we want to do that?" growled Hoowo3oow. "Here is where our abilities are the strongest. If we stand our ground and work together, we can fend off anything that comes through."

Death laughed raucously and without restraint.

"You must be joking!" said Death with a gasp. "Do you realise how stupid that is?"

Hooowo3oow screwed his eyebrows together angrily, but this made Death laugh even harder.

"Young man, at most you have four able fighters whom could prove effective in the fights to come! Four!" Death held up four fingers. "Your opponent comprises of the majority of the population of every single other realm. I don't even know what you'd call that number? You and the planet will be overwhelmed in less than a minute and you are a fool if you think otherwise."

"How then," began Shui with a touch of impatience, "will entering the other realms be of any benefit? We will still be outnumbered but we won't have the support of the Conclave."

"It's a trap!" spat Hoowo3oow. "Ambush us when we're out of contact then attack the Conclave?"

Ignis fired up at once, his whole body, bursting into flames. "Who wants to see what Death warmed up actually looks like!"

Shui and Hoowo3oow came to his side at once and readied to fight but Death just sat down looking exasperated.

"Calm the fuck down, ginger!" said Death waving at them with a quelling gesture. "And we already know, how this ends!" Death added pointing at Shui. "Such tempers. How you have not murdered more people is simply astonishing."

All three dropped their arms and shuffled awkwardly on the spot, looking comically like the children they outwardly appeared to be. They opened and closed their mouths stupidly for a few moments, searching for a retort but they were completely lost for words, all except for Ignis who ran a hand through his hair and managed to mutter. "It's not ginger, it's red!"

"The benefit, my dear," said Death with a derisive glance at Shui. "…is closing off the breaches and stopping the realms collapsing — period! I honestly thought you people were smart!"

"What do you mean, 'you people?'" demanded Shui indignantly, and Ignis sniggered under his breath.

"Don't be crass!" said Death firmly. "I'm not in the mood!"

Frank was still visible on the projected display and was flipping through a humongous tome just off screen.

"Is that actually possible?" he enquired as he peered more closely on a particular page. "Closing the breaches in realms beyond just ours I mean?"

"Of course it is!" said Death brusquely. "You just need to collapse the energy holding the hole open."

"Oh! Is that all?" said Ignis, mockingly. "Fuck me, Frank. We should have just done that in the first place."

He stormed around to the other side of the centre console and examined the panels with exaggerated interest.

"Here, let me just press the close breach button!" he said slamming his hand down on a button that wasn't there. "Sorted! I guess we can all relax now!"

"Don't be absurd, idiot child!" barked Death aggressively. "How can anyone be so infuriatingly impatient? I swear if I didn't need you, I'd leave you all to your doom!"

Amos gave Ignis a consoling pat on the back and strolled over to sit beside Death. He saw the shadow out of the corner of his eye loom over him as he lowered himself onto the sofa and a chill ran up his spine. He managed to force a smile onto his features, and when he spoke it was in as polite and gentle a manner as he could muster.

"Please accept our apologies," he began with a warning look at Ignis, "it has been a very trying week and I'm afraid our nerves have worn as thin as our patience."

Death's expression softened to a more sympathetic one.

"And I have made things more tense by showing up in this meat suit! I keep forgetting I'm wearing your friend, please, it is I who should apologise!" A few seconds of silence passed before Death noticed Amos looking expectant and added. "I'm not going to though, it's goes against

67

my character, but believe me when I say I feel it, you know…" Death bumped a closed fist against Wun Chuan's chest, "…in here!"

Amos allowed his face to drop into his palm for a moment but recovered his poise quickly. "Then how about we get straight to tactics?" he said clapping his hands together and rubbing them vigorously. "Should I presume that you know some sort of spell that would cause the energy to collapse?"

Death leaned close to Amos and gave him a pitying smile. "A spell wouldn't do anything… but a weapon would!"

Amos blanched. "What kind of weapon?" he asked quizzically. "Like a bomb?"

Death chuckled immoderately. "Humans and their bombs!"

For the next ten minutes, Death explained to an enthralled audience about a very special sword, a sword that had been thought into existence by man thousands of years ago. This legendary blade had been attributed to a variety of characters over the many millennia it had existed for, but always it was recognisable by one very obvious detail. The sword was ablaze with a divine fire. A fire that burned so hot and bright, that if anyone tried to wield it who wasn't divine in nature, they would be immolated in an instant, erased from existence, body and soul together. The most important detail of this incredible blade was that the divine fire was infinite. An energy source that is inexhaustible, perpetual, a violation of nature.

"The only way to collapse the energy inside the barrier is to increase its entropy," said Death who was speaking animatedly now, the black shadow trailing behind with equal vigour. "The sword like all manifestations of the mind given form are infinite low entropy objects. They remain in existence ad infinitum, because that's the kind of crap you humans make up and wholeheartedly believe." Death patted Amos on the knee. "Bless them, it's like they can't seem to evolve past childhood…"

"Was the sword once yours?" asked Chloe who had been lurking behind the sofa. "When you were the angel of death?"

"I really like this kid!" said Death grinning broadly. "Yes indeed, mine for a long time." Death looked reminiscent and appeared to have stopped paying attention.

Amos coughed loudly, drawing Death's attention back to the conversation.

"How precisely would we use this sword to close the breach?" he asked reasonably. "It's not like there will be something to hit. It is just a hole!"

"Tut, tut!" said Death slyly, wagging a knowing finger. "Just because you can't see it, doesn't mean it's not there."

"Sounds ominous!" said Shui.

"Oh, it is!" said Death. "Here, pass me that paper and I need a pen!"

Alex came bustling over and handed Death a black sharpie while Hoowo3oow slid a sheet of paper across the console toward Amos who hurriedly handed it over. Death flattened the page out on Wun Chuan's lap and pulled the cap off the sharpie with her teeth. With clean broad strokes, Death began to etch out a shape that was spiral in appearance. Long lines intersected the design, and in the spaces made by the intersections, Death had drawn a number of symbols and icons which were terribly familiar.

"What are you doing?" demanded Amos suddenly and he backed away from Death and placed a hand inside his jacket to hold something metal, a sliver of which glinted in the light. "Why are you drawing that?" he added more loudly.

"Now what?" said Death indignantly, slapping the marker down on the paper. "What possible problem could you have now? Are you afraid of spiders or something?"

"Spiders?" said Hoowo3oow, marching forward and snatching the paper out of Death's lap. "This is the mark of the assassin! What do spiders have to do with it?"

"This…" began Death, taking the page back from Hoowo3oow and holding it up for all to see, "…is what is holding that breach open. This is a web created by Anansi, although as far as he is concerned each one is a chapter."

This pronouncement was not greeted with the gasps of amazement Death had been expecting, but with glares of indifference instead. "So you're not scared of spiders then?"

"The boy!" snarled Amos, determined to have an answer. "Who is he?"

"The boy?" repeated Death. "What boy?

69

"The boy, the boy!" raged Amos. "The boy that's been running around murdering plastic Gods with impunity!"

Death suddenly looked concerned. "What do you mean plastic Gods?"

"I mean Gods who aren't really Gods," growled Amos who was still visibly angry. "They're just humans, but some well-meaning, but misguided people, thought they were and somehow it counts!"

Death's face turned stony.

"Clever… they've thought it through! But this is bad! This is really bad!"

"Yeah, we know that!" said Shui scornfully. "Try to keep up!"

"Then why on earth are you not more alarmed?" yelled Death standing abruptly and marching over to Shui to stand nose to nose. "Mortals made God are rarer than astatine and they live about as long too. You do realise if you have no Gods left then the plan is rather scuppered, don't you?"

"No, it's not!" said Shui just to disagree, then thinking about it added, "Maybe… Ugh! Why? Why is it scuppered?"

"Because, you massive twat," sneered Death an inch from Shui's face, "you need a God to wield the sword!"

"No, we don't!" said Ignis noticing Shui shift her weight to her back leg and swiftly pushing her away from Death before fists started flying again.

"Fire is quite literally my name. Flaming sword kinda sounds like m'jam!" he finished pointing both his thumbs at himself.

"Divine fire, my dear. You need to be divine to hold it!" said Death, looking Ignis up and down. "And I'm afraid to say there is nothing divine about you!"

Ignis raised his eyebrows and opened his mouth but said nothing. Instead, he turned away from Death looking crestfallen.

"There it is!" said Frank mournfully and unexpectedly. "That's the motive. He's making sure we can't draft any of these Gods into our ranks, taking away our only means of closing the breaches. Death is right, that is clever!"

"I'm afraid you still don't appreciate how bad it is," said Death irritably. "You need a God to do more than use the weapon."

A few seconds of dejected silence followed this pronouncement during which a vein throbbed in Frank's temple and Amos massaged the bridge of his nose. Hoowo3oow ground his teeth and Shui rolled her eyes.

"Of course we do!" she muttered quietly.

"You need a God to get to the other realms," said Death with a touch of derision as if this ought to be obvious. "They are the only ones who can open the gates that take you beyond. The only ones who can unlock them."

Nobody reacted to this, so Death spoke loudly as though addressing someone very dense. "You also need them to see what will be guarding the web at each breach."

"Let me guess, big ass spider, right?" said Ignis, lolling his head back and sounding disappointed. "We can handle spiders!" he said confidently. "Just more legs to break!"

Hoowo3oow growled his approval but Shui looked troubled.

"Why Anansi?" she asked. "He may be addicted to mischief and causing shit but he's all right mostly," she added fairly. "And while he may be a clever bastard, he wouldn't stand a chance against us in a fight. What's in it for him, beside my size three shoe up his arse?"

Death gave a great sigh and then said cautiously. "This is about more than power, it's about stories. That's what this mess means," Death added waving the paper straight and giving it a sharp tap.

"The Gods are bringing their stories together but they can't do it on their own. They need a great storyteller and Anansi is nothing if not a lover and great teller of stories."

Death traced a finger around the spiral.

"Anansi is using his silk to reach out and weave one tale into another. As a result, each web is a nexus for an ungodly amount of power and the creatures spinning them are benefitting from all that power. I repeat, infinite low entropy."

Death took a deep breath and exhaled very slowly.

"Anansi is smart, he is a God of knowledge after all and he will be using signal threads to get information from each web and to him it's all plot fodder. Even the spiders here on earth allow him to spy on us. It is only because of the protection and filtration systems in this building that we can talk about this at all."

71

Tired of waiting for a break in the conversation Frank banged a fist on his desk a couple of times to bring everyone to attention.

"Just how many Gods are in on this?" he asked incredulously. "And just what has pissed them off so badly?"

"Yeah!" agreed Shui. "What's their problem? They must know this will seriously affect their fan base, right?"

"Surely you recognise these symbols!" interrupted Death condescendingly. "They are marks of commitment from each God you are up against and it isn't exhaustive, more will join and this diagram will get bigger," said Death with sombre finality.

Another deep sigh cut the tension and Death's frustration ebbed away.

"As for why?" Death shrugged looking apologetic. "I have no idea. It's utter madness! There is no telling what will happen if the realms collapse. The demons talk of ruling the mortal world, but I don't think they understand the gravity of the situation. There will be no mortals left to rule, they'll all be dead. They were probably just told this to get them on board, get them geared up for a fight."

"Then a fight is what they will get!" said Frank defiantly. "The Gods seek to unbalance the realms? They have forgotten their place, it's time we remind them."

"What's this 'we' shit, Frank?" said Shui curtly. "You coming too?"

"Ooh, I would," replied Frank, "but y'know, I don't want to."

He turned to address everyone. "Look, this has been a lot to take in! It's worse than we thought, but we need to stay focussed. I have faith that Wade will find us another God if one exists. Any ideas to speed up the search, I'm all ears!"

"What about Prince Philip?" suggested Alex. "We know he definitely counts as…" she sniggered. "…a God. And thanks to you he's still alive."

"Alex, was I mistaken in thinking you were smart," scoffed Frank with rude impatience. "Aside from the fact that he is still recovering from extensive burns that will have him bedridden for a few more months and apart from the fact that the amount of work that went into reworking his memory of today was so extensive putting it right will be almost impossible…" Frank paused for thought before ploughing on. "Oh! And let's not forget that his absence will most certainly be noticed, His Royal

Highness is nearly 100 years old. We can't be drafting him into a war, he wouldn't last five minutes."

Alex muttered something like. "Amos could do it." before falling silent and folding her arms defensively.

"Amos..." began Frank scathingly. "...is not only expertly trained in these matters, but he has also received a boost from our resident deity too, just like Gyasi, Elsu and..." he broke off, unable to say Wun Chuan's name aloud.

"There is just no comparison," he continued abruptly. "The prince is not an option!"

A minute of confused silence hovered about the room like an unwelcome guest before Gyasi, clearing his throat and then clearing it several times more, tentatively raised his hand.

"Can't we just make one?" he asked hopefully. "We made the Conduit, what's to stop us creating one ourselves?"

"Not possible mate," said Frank sadly. "There is not enough time. Creating fresh theology takes years. No, we need one ready-made. We need this, Bernard Godfrey."

Someone stirred with a confused groan at the back of the room and the sound of heavy limbs flopping onto a sofa accompanied a weak whimper that repeated. "B-Bernard Godfrey?"

"Mum?" whispered Chloe gently. "Mum, are you OK?"

Everyone had turned to stare in bewilderment at Chloe and the woman she was helping to a seat. Cassandra was still reeling from fainting but her colour was returning to her cheeks and her eyes were starting to focus. She had been roused by the sound of the name but it seemed to be adding to her confusion.

"Did you say Bernard Godfrey?" she asked, rubbing her forehead.

"I did," said Frank suspiciously. "Do you... do you know someone with that name, madam?" he asked politely.

"I do some translation work for a university professor named Bernard Godfrey. I doubt it's the same man you are after though."

A thrill of anticipation ran through the room like a crackle of electricity.

"We shall see," said Amos, intrigued. "Tell me has he ever mentioned a man called Alfred Braskin?"

"Actually, he has," said Cassandra. "His best friend is called that. They used to…"

"Work together?" supplied Frank who was rummaging through his notes.

"Exactly!" said Cassandra with surprise.

A few seconds passed in silence until Frank held up a photo so it could be seen clearly on the display. "Is this them?"

Cassandra seemed lost for words and she simply nodded. Amos bore down upon her with a hungry look in his eyes. "Have you a phone, madam?" he asked holding out his hand expectantly.

Unnerved and trembling, Cassandra reached inside her jacket and pulled out a smart phone. A fingerprint scan and a few swipes later and Amos was staring at the photo and contact information for Bernard Godfrey. Amos' eyes momentarily boggled and he let out a short laugh like a bark which he quickly stifled.

"Apologies, madam," he whispered delicately "I was not expecting… well… can I just check…" Amos turned the screen so Cassandra could see too. "Professor Sex, is the same man we are looking for?" Amos scratched his chin to disguise his obvious amusement and added, "The picture of an Aztec phallus didn't really clarify."

Cassandra turned a deep shade of beetroot red. In her confused state the details of the contact information had escaped her attention.

Clapping a hand over her mouth she yelled. "Oh my God!" before stifling herself.

"Our secret," said Amos, giving his nose a couple of taps. He quickly scrolled to the bottom, pressed call and held the handset up to his ear. A moment later his hand dropped with frustration, the call had gone straight to answer phone. He brought it back to his ear and waited for the beep.

"Good evening Mr Godrey. My name is Amos Cromwell and I am here with Cassandra Gibson," began Amos in his best telephone manner. "I'm afraid she has had a rather traumatic day and has asked for you as someone to come and collect her. I would like to add that she is fine, no injuries, but she is a bit shaken and is feeling a little fragile. It would be best if you could return this call as our address isn't listed and we are a little hard to find, I dare say you will need directions. Thank you and goodbye."

With that Amos hit the 'end call' button and handed the phone back to Cassandra.

"Like I said, astatine!" crooned Death who was sauntering across the room to stand next to Amos. "Best keep looking, just in case he is in a meeting with your… acquaintance!"

This apparently had been Frank's first thought, too.

"Damn right!" he said. "It always pays to be paranoid, we keep searching till the Prof is under this roof. Gyasi, please escort Cassandra to Rich's office. Tell him to spam that number until he answers. Alex, take Chloe down to Mother Westa. She can have the coven soften the impact of today. Last thing she needs is PTSD kicking in at two a.m. tonight."

Gyasi and Alex sprung to their feet and made their way over to the elevator with their charges in tow. Cassandra looked worried at the idea of parting company with Chloe but was being consoled by Gyasi's deep soothing voice. It was almost hypnotic. Chloe chuckled and took hold of Alex's hand.

"Death…" began Frank. "…er, quick question!" Death smiled gently and gestured for him to continue. "This sword you were on about."

"Yes?" replied Death.

"Where is it?" asked Frank, bringing up a map in front of him. "Once I have the lay of the land, I can plan an op for these guys."

"Probably in the artefacts section," said Death casually. "You won't need to steal it," said Death dismissively. "Divinity in any form is permitted to just take it. It'll come back when its quest is over."

"Not what I meant… although that is good to know," said Frank, making a note. "No, what I meant was which country? And if you know it, which city?"

Death screamed and rocked with laughter, the shadow laughed even harder.

"Oh, you do make me laugh!" intoned Death slapping the air in Frank's direction. "Which city, he says? Ooh, that's good!"

Death dabbed at a tear with a handkerchief stolen from Amos' pocket and eventually the giggling subsided. Spotting the look on Frank's face,

Death gave a placating look and passed the handkerchief back to Amos who noticed a spot of blood on the corner.

"I'm sorry... really," said Death sincerely. "I just wasn't expecting... never mind, the sword is currently on display in the artefacts section inside the Akashic Hall of Records, second floor, just after the golden fleece exhibit."

"The Akashic Hall of Records?" asked Frank. "Akashic as in the Akashic realm?"

"That's the one!" said Death happily. "Have you been there?"

"No," said Frank dejectedly. "But it's on my bucket list," he added weakly.

"We have to go all the way to the Akashic realm to get it?" asked an appalled Ignis. "What about the gates in between? How are we supposed to murder Incy Wincy?"

Death hadn't considered this but rallied quickly. "You'll have to sneak past," said Death offhandedly.

"Sneak?" repeated Ignis. "Past a giant spider?"

"Yes!" replied Death who didn't seem at all concerned.

"With a human who is our only means of knowing where it is and will probably shit himself when he sees it?" added Shui, testily.

"Yeah!" said Death with a grimace. "They probably will, won't they?"

"Great!" said Shui turning her back on everyone and punching a nearby pillar which cracked and crumbled.

Amos gave Death a nervous tap on the shoulder.

"Um, madam... er... Death?" he said hesitantly and then showing her the blood stain on his handkerchief added. "I think it may be time for you to leave."

"Oh no!" whined Death, snatching the handkerchief and dabbing at her eyes to see more fresh drops of blood. "That is disappointing."

"You're rotting?" asked Shui in a panic. "You're making her rot?"

Shui dashed over to Death and looked at the face closely.

"You are, you fucking are, she's decomposing," Shui yelled angrily as she began to pace on the spot. "Get the fuck out of her body, now!"

"Ugh! Fine!" snapped Death, tossing the page at Shui. "I'll go and you're fucking welcome by the way!"

Without warning, Wun Chuan's body collapsed. Shui darted forward, catching her an inch from the ground and as such was the only one who didn't see the shadow of Death, stood in place for a fraction of a second before it was gone. A cold silence sat over the room like frost as Shui picked up Wun Chuan's body and gently placed her back upon the ottoman. She leaned forward and kissed her softly on the forehead. A single tear fell from Shui's cheek which she wiped away with stoic force. Without speaking she walked toward her own room and opened the door but before she walked inside, she cast Ignis a lingering dark look. Ignis caught her staring and stared perplexedly back. Before he could ask her what she wanted, Shui had gone inside and closed the door, locking it behind her.

Amos gathered up some flowers that had been knocked to the floor when Death had first arrived and placed them back on the ottoman.

He patted Wun Chuan's hand and whispered under his breath. "I hope you end up in the right place!"

"Aww, me too," Wun Chuan replied as her eyes snapped open. "Fingers crossed."

Amos let out a loud yell of surprise, stumbled backwards with fright and tripped over the raised flooring.

"What in the world was that?" he demanded as he clambered back to his feet.

Wun Chuan was sitting upright and staring at him by the time he was upright.

"Didn't mean to frighten you. Something I forgot," chortled Death unabashed.

"And that would be?" asked Amos through gritted teeth.

"You will also need a nephilim!" said Death in what was assumed to be a helpful tone.

"Nephilim?" asked Amos with forced calm. "I've never heard the term, what is it?"

"I think you mean, 'what are they?'" said Hoowo3oow gravely. "Abominations, is what they are!"

Amos cast a hopeful look at Ignis. "Would you care to elaborate?" he asked placing a delicate emphasis on the word 'you'.

Ignis gave a resigned smile.

"I always knew we'd have to have this talk one day," he said nodding his head slowly. "You see Amos, when a human and a demon love each other very much, one of them puts their…"

"Surely not!" interrupted Amos aghast. "You can't mean offspring from their copulation!"

"Yes, I do and most of them are right mutant messes!" said Ignis dispassionately. "Cannibalistic lunatics too!"

"Now, that's not fair!" said Death reproachfully. "Not all of them are… 'messes'… and not all of them are from demons!"

"True," said Hoowo3oow flatly. "Angels in one guise or another have been known to…" he cast around for a suitable word, "…stray."

Ignis snorted derisively. "Stray? That's the word you're going with? Thousands of years old and you still can't say the word sex?"

Hoowo3oow growled menacingly at Ignis, but Ignis ignored him. "Yes, angels do it too, but their spawn are a lot rarer and tend to die early in life."

"Can't they survive in our realm?" asked Amos, intrigued.

"No, it's not that!" said Ignis. "They are usually murdered as infants. Humans tend to be affected a lot more by the angel half than a demon half. I'm not sure why but mortals tend to go insane when they are in their presence."

"Because they carry within them the voice of a God, dear boy," supplied Death. "Any sound they make is not only incomprehensible, but it's downright intolerable. Imagine if you will, a baby, crying and screaming in tongues and making a noise that is so piercing and loud that your brain literally starts to turn to mush. A human would be driven to kill it to end their own suffering."

"That will certainly shorten the odds on us finding one of them," said Amos sadly. "What do we need one for? If it's something we can do quickly we can perhaps make do with… one of the other ones."

"Hmm, possibly!" said Death hesitantly. "But it would probably be better to bring them along for the ride."

"Uuugh, this isn't a babysitting service, mate," said Ignis frustratedly. "It's already turning into a suicide squad. What use are they gonna be, really?"

A long pause of consideration followed this question, as if the response was being crafted.

"Well, you see, nephilim are born with a song inside them," Death said at last in a surprisingly fond tone that bordered on wonderment. "A composition of such complexity and wonder no mortal could ever recite it and no angel or demon could ever imagine it. It's a song they probably don't even know they have. However, stand them on the site of a God gate and this magical melody will overcome them and they will play a tune that will shake the very fabric of space. The vibrations will rearrange reality in an overture of seismic proportions and in the grace of the coda will the gate be revealed. This of course will work in every realm, so should you find sneaking through a breach impossible, they could summon another gate and progress can continue."

"You know…" said Ignis thoughtfully, as he strode in a circle around Death appraisingly, "…that would have been a beautiful sentiment were it not for the fact that you turned a weird bluish, yellow colour halfway through."

He stared at Death a little more intently.

"In fact, dude…" he poked gingerly at Wun Chuan's cheek. "I think you're starting to bloat."

Death reached up to touch Wun Chuan's cheeks. Sure enough, they felt swollen and distended while the skin felt loose and fragile. "Shit! I'd better go before I pop like a beached whale."

"Wait!" hollered Amos urgently. "We don't know how to find a nephilim? What are we even looking for?"

"It would be useful to know where this gate is too while you're at it!" grumbled Frank who was resting his head on his hand, while gripping a clump of his own hair.

"Oh, that last one's easy!" said Death. "You just have to go to the God's birthplace… by that I mean the place they became a God."

"Oooh!" said Amos with happy comprehension. "That I would very much like to see… and, er… the nephilim?" he asked hopefully.

"No idea!" said Death carelessly before adding "I can smell myself. I need to leave before chuckles comes back in and sees the mess I'm making of her friend."

Indeed, the skin on Wun Chuan's exposed flesh was starting to split and peel and the colour was now turning a greenish black.

"All I can say is…" began Death in a hurry as the left side of Wun Chuan's face drooped, "…they always have a deformity, regardless of parentage that is exactly the same. An additional digit on each limb… although you may be looking for scars if they've had it amputated… you humans are a bit vain when it comes to that sort of thing."

Understanding bloomed between Amos and Ignis and they gawped at each other in amazement.

The busker!" they both said in unison.

"Well, you seem to have all you need," said Death lying back down on the ottoman and getting comfy. "I will bid you farewell and…" Death gave them all a tragic look, "…good luck. You'll need it!" and closing Wun Chuan's eyes was gone once more.

Ignis crept forward and gave a tentative prod in Wun Chuan's ribs. The body shook lifelessly and Ignis sighed, as did Amos.

"So, can I assume you guys know where we can get hold of one of these nephilim?" asked Frank a little feebly. It had been a very long day.

"We know where one was," corrected Amos but he sounded pleased. "We met him, a pleasant lad and very musically talented."

"Yeah!" agreed Ignis. "He spoke with song lyrics because his vocal cords had been…" Ignis' eyes widened with excitement. "…cut. Shit, he really is one!"

"He shouldn't be hard to find," declared Amos confidently. "Buskers don't try to hide, they want to be seen and he will have caught a lot of attention."

"Perfect!" said Frank bracingly. He clapped his hands together and gave them a rub. "I'll leave that little mission in your capable hands then," he added with a roguish grin.

Behind Frank on the display Barry entered the room carrying two mugs. "Coffee, Frank?" he asked rhetorically, handing one of the mugs to Frank before blowing into his own.

"Look at that!" said Frank, taking a soothing sip and sighing gratefully. "It's all coming together."

Chapter Four
Divide and Conquer

Although Amos had been confident that finding the nephilim shouldn't be too hard, the busker was proving to be very elusive. Weeks had elapsed since their meeting with Death, and to everyone's disappointment, the Conclave had accomplished nothing. They had not located the nephilim, there had been no word from Professor Godfrey and they had no other leads on where to find another to fill his place. Morale was definitely low. To make matters worse, Shui had not come out of her room since the wake. Food was being sent in, in Tupperware boxes and left outside her door by catering staff, they had to make sure she was still eating. Thankfully the boxes were being taken and empty ones left in their place, but only when no one was looking.

Much of the institute had become festooned with Christmas decorations as the season of goodwill had descended upon them with brute force. No one actually felt like doing much celebrating, the prospect of Armageddon had that effect, but it was the done thing, and appearances were important.

Elsu was back on his feet and busy helping Hoowo3oow and Gyasi in one of the rarely used spare control rooms. Together they were trawling through the populous using the mirrors to see what each individual was looking at before switching to another. Wade had realised that they couldn't see anything but static when they looked through Bernard's eyes because his status as a God must be causing some kind of interference. As such, others like him must show the same static if you hack their vision too. The real work was building up profiles of likely candidates to narrow the search. Searching through all eight billion people on the planet just wasn't practical. Wade had made some good strides. He had developed a set of criteria that would illustrate what events or aspects of a person would allow for the technicality of becoming a God and it had proved effective at finding some good candidates. Despite his best efforts, however, they had all so far turned out to be regular old, boring and completely useless, normal people.

As an unexpected guest, Cassandra had been given a room at the institute where, on her part, she could remain close to Chloe while she settled in and on the Conclave's part, they could keep her nearby until Bernard was found, alive or dead. Her husband had been called by Richard, who had been supervising Cassandra's time during her stay, and notified him of the situation. An argument had erupted when he had been met with a complete lack of interest in Cassandra's well-being and an almost equal indifference to Chloe's health too. A family man through and through, Richard had yelled himself hoarse about the duties of a father and general human decency. Cassandra's husband had eventually hung up on him and they had not bothered him since. The search for Bernard Godfrey, had by now, become worryingly fruitless. While the Conclave panicked over what was probably their only hope lying dead in a ditch somewhere, Cassandra fretted ceaselessly over her missing friend whom she also assumed was probably dead somewhere in a shallow grave.

Richard did his best to keep up her spirits, consoling her as best he could while maintaining the adage, 'No news, is good news!' Secretly, Richard had been practising how to deliver bad news in the mirror, just in case. To keep her busy, Cassandra had been subcontracted by the institute as a research assistant where she translated ancient texts in their archives and deciphered dead languages. To Richard's, and indeed Chloe's delight, she had thrown herself into the role enthusiastically.

In the control room, Frank and Barry were slowly being buried under a torrent of cases as the weakened barriers allowed more and more figments to materialise in the real world. Overactive imaginations across the globe were summoning all manner of strange and bizarre monsters that were wreaking havoc and stretching the resources of the Conclave to the limit. The impending war, once thought of so lightly not too long ago, now seemed like an insurmountable wall of doom which would collapse and crush them all any day now. The stress had been so much for Frank that he had started smoking again. This was much to the annoyance of Barry who worked in the same room as him and was not tolerant of Frank's flagrant disregard for office policy as he chain-smoked one cigarette after the other right at his desk.

"Twenty years you told me!" preached Barry during one particularly busy morning after he had walked into the control room carrying two cups of coffee as usual and collided with a thick cloud of acrid tobacco smoke.

"Twenty years without a single one and now you can't seem to exist without one in your mouth."

"Well," said Frank without looking at him, "twenty years, is a long time. I've missed out on a lot of cigarettes, I'm simply catching up." And he placed his current lit roll-up in his mouth and held it there while he worked, occasionally taking a drag without pausing from the keyboard which was causing a pile of ash to build up on the space bar.

"Seriously mate, you'll end up in an early grave," warned Barry.

"Probably gonna die soon anyway," said Frank apathetically. "Might as well make the most of it." Frank paused in his typing looking thoughtful for a moment then added. "Wonder if I could get hold of some heroin?"

Barry spurted his mouthful of coffee all over his trousers. "Frank, what the hell man! Are you serious?"

Frank laughed through a plume of smoke but promptly stopped due to a coughing fit.

"You... *cough*... are a... *cough, cough*... bit thick sometimes," he said banging his fist on his chest to shake loose the phlegm. "Of course I'm not serious. I don't need to get hold of some heroin... I've already got some."

Barry eyed him suspiciously for a moment then said, "Oh, ha, ha! Very funny!"

Frank gave him a wink, then spotting something over his shoulder, pointed at Barry's screen saying. "You've got incoming, by the way."

Barry spun in his chair and pulled himself close to the active displays. It took him a few seconds of squinting and tilting his head side to side before he understood what he was looking at. With a gasp of amazement, he began tapping enthusiastically on the mirror.

"Wow, Frank. Get a load of this!" he said happily.

Frank shuttled his chair next to Barry's and peered at the display which was live streaming the sight of a farm boy in Norwich. The young boy was staring intently at a small animal, like a baby goat, but it was suspended off the ground by a long thick plant stem that was rooted in the earth. At the end that touched the goat, Frank could see the stem blending smoothly from flora green to a patchy white and flesh colour as it joined seamlessly to the goat's stomach. The goat's legs and head, hung limply as though it couldn't be bothered to move them. Occasionally, the stem bent and flexed in an unheard wind at which point the goat would snap aggressively at anything close enough to reach. Plants, objects and people all seemed to be viable food for this bizarre creature.

To make matters worse, there was a crowd of at least twenty people gathered around the strange hybrid creature and they were taking photos of it and posing next to it for 'selfies'.

"Shitting, shit!" barked Frank irritably. "Goddamn smart phones!"

He scanned through a list of available units who were not on deployment. The list was a short one and the only names on there were for auxiliaries who had been in post for three days. Fearing a media stampede if someone uploaded a picture or video to the Internet and it attracted the attention of a local news channel, Frank considered alerting Shui. He couldn't decide if he was brave enough to bother her at the moment. As no one had been able to speak to her he wasn't sure how she would react to being disturbed. He decided he didn't want to be the one to find out.

"Find Aarde!" he said in a resigned tone. "He's sulked enough, it's time he made himself useful."

"What about Ignis?" suggested Barry helpfully.

"Nah!" groaned Frank. "He's still out with Amos looking for that busker. I need them to stay on it. I need something to go right for once."

Frank gave his temples a firm circular rub and sighed deeply.

"Just get Aarde. Have Nephthys send him to the farm. Get those people gone." After a moment of contemplation, he added, "Better give him a tactical EMP grenade, he will need to 'brick' those smart phones... and when he's gone, get on social media and nip this shit in the bud."

Barry put down his mug and got sulkily to his feet. "He's probably going to shout at me," he muttered quietly.

"Not as much as I will if you don't get a move on," snapped Frank.

Barry scurried from the room looking a little dejected and Frank turned back to his own displays and checked the list of outstanding events. It was getting bigger. He checked the map. Across the oily surface, lights blinked in and out of existence as monsters appeared and were eliminated. The trouble was, for every light that went out, three more appeared somewhere else. Frank checked the south-east coast of England. A massive surge of energy had just appeared there causing a very bright light to illuminate fifty square miles of land mass.

"Aarde has landed!" he mumbled before making a soft explosion noise with his mouth.

Looking further north he watched another bright light source somewhere up in Nottinghamshire. The light was much more muted than Aarde's, but Frank knew it was Ignis and that it was less bright simply because he was obviously in a better mood. This made Frank raise his eyebrows expectantly. The good mood had better be for good news.

Amos and Ignis had nestled themselves into a thicket of people at a local Christmas market in the centre of Nottingham City. Amos was busy trying to fit his mouth around a very large turkey and stuffing pasty while enjoying music being played by a brass band that were stationed near a large fountain at the end of the market square. Ignis, on the other hand, was busy eating a bag full of churros while showing off on an outdoor ice-skating rink that had been erected for the festive period. Ignis was quite literally cutting a swathe through the other skaters who were keeping themselves to the fence edge to avoid being sliced as Ignis leaped and twirled and span through the air with speed. When Amos eventually called him off the ice, he left to the sound of applause and appreciation.

"Frank is trying to get hold of us," whispered Amos as he pretended to help Ignis remove his ice skates. "I can't answer him here though, it's too loud and there's too many people. Someone will notice."

Ignis nodded his understanding and kicked off his boots. He marched over to the rental desk and swung them onto the counter. One of the blades embedded into the wood surface.

"Sorry," he said, fishing out a piece of paper from his pocket and slapping it down next to the boot. "...my bad man! Locker thirty-one, please."

The clerk jerked the boot out of the desk and slid the ticket toward him. He held it aloft, gave Ignis a haughty sneer, then turned about to look for his trainers. Once found, the clerk slammed them onto the counter and gingerly discarded the ticket into a bin as if was something dirty.

"All right, minimum wage," said Ignis in a sarcastic tone. "Calm down or I'll have to call your mother."

The clerk leaned over the counter to leer at Ignis.

"Listen here you little shit…" he began but he was interrupted as Ignis grabbed his shirt and pulled him over the desk.

"What part of calm down didn't you understand?" he whispered menacingly.

The clerk looked very alarmed as he dangled half upside down and struggled uselessly, against this small boy's surprising strength. Unable to articulate a response to Ignis' question he simply shook his head stupidly.

"Behave, there's a good lad," said Ignis and he gave the clerk a couple of slaps on his cheek before releasing him, at which point he collapsed in a heap on the wrong side of his counter.

As Ignis and Amos walked away leaving the dishevelled clerk behind, Amos gave Ignis a stern, enquiring look.

"Everything all right?" he asked delicately.

"Yeah, course!" said Ignis a little unconvincingly, then noticing Amos' continued mute staring added. "Really, I'm fine… I'm just sick of being treated like a child. It really pisses me off!"

"You're always sick of that," replied Amos dismissively. "You've been complaining about that for quite literally my entire life!"

"It's all right for you," began Ignis waspishly, "people treat you with respect automatically because you look old. What do I get? Condescending looks and arrogance." Ignis shoved his hands aggressively into his pockets and picked up his pace to walk slightly ahead of Amos.

Amos looked sadly at his companion and sighed deeply. "I can only imagine your frustration," he said softly. "It is an unimaginable burden, but, forgive me, you are deflecting."

Ignis spun around and cast Amos a filthy look.

"Don't look at me like that," said Amos firmly. "You are not normally this irritable and you have been like it all week. What's actually bugging you and please don't pretend it's this!" Amos waved a hand in gesture to the crowd around them.

Ignis looked defiant but as he raised his head to speak his eyes met Amos' who was still eyeing him expectantly. His anger abated instantly. He could never be angry with Amos.

"I guess I'm still a bit irritated with Aarde," he said at last. "Storming about the place like I owe him money… it's starting to wear thin."

Amos gave him a consoling pat on the back. "I thought that might be it. He'll calm down," he said softly. "Jealousy is a difficult guest and getting it to leave takes time. He'll come around."

"Hmmm!" replied Ignis through tight lips. As far as he was concerned, Aarde could behave however he wanted, just as long as it wasn't around him.

A moment later, Ignis and Amos had found themselves a quiet spot across the road near Nottingham Castle. After a cursory look around to check they were not being watched, Amos formed a window with his hands and sung the reflection whistle quietly.

"About friggin' time!" barked Frank the second he appeared in view. "What took you so long?"

"Hello to you too," said Amos coolly. "You may remember that we are in a city, specifically the centre! It's quite busy and difficult to find somewhere private."

"Plus, Amos was taking a shit!" bellowed Ignis loud enough for Frank to hear.

Frank snorted with laughter and went into another coughing fit while Ignis chuckled at the mortified look on Amos' face.

Amos blushed and cuffed Ignis on the back of his head with his elbow. "I was not… er… having a constitutional!" affirmed Amos awkwardly. "Anyway, what was so urgent?"

"I need a progress report!" said Frank through an exhalation of smoke. "Please tell me you are close to finding this guy!"

"In regards to our busker, the local paper shop informed me that the young man we described plays outside his door every Thursday at seven p.m. We should know if it's the same person in…" Amos checked his watch. "…about twenty minutes!" he said confidently.

"I'll contain my excitement for now then," said Frank sceptically as he stubbed out his cigarette with unnecessary force.

Ignis poked his head up in between Amos' arms so Frank could see him properly.

"Cheer up mucker! It's not like it's the end of the world!" he said giggling.

"Don't Ignis!" pleaded Frank in a tired tone. "My brain can't handle sarcasm today."

"It'll be OK!" assured Amos kindly. "We've always prevailed in the past!"

"There's never been a mutiny among the God-tier beings before," replied Frank as he lit another cigarette. "This is completely unprecedented. It doesn't even follow their lore. Rapture, fine. Ragnarok, whatever… but this? This? Why does it have to be happening on my watch!" At this Frank actually banged his fist on the desk which startled Amos.

"Easy mate!" said Ignis sympathetically. "Every watcher says the same thing when things start going south. All of them. It always seems bleak, but we elemortals always win! If we have to kill a God to do it then that's what we'll do."

"Wouldn't be the first time!" said Amos supportively over Ignis' shoulder.

"Yeah, well. There's not exactly a feeling of unity among you guys at the moment," replied Frank darkly.

"That's not true!" said Ignis lightly. "I really like Hoowo3oow!"

Amos couldn't help but laugh, and despite himself, neither could Frank.

Once they'd composed themselves again, Amos pulled the window closer to himself again.

"How is Shui anyway?" he asked sadly. "Has anyone seen her yet?"

"No!" groaned Frank with an abrupt return to his stressful demeanour. "Heard her banging about, and probably breaking things…" said Frank before taking a deep gulp of coffee. "But no, no actual sightings!"

"I'll try and speak with her when I get back," said Amos helpfully. "This much time alone can't be good for her."

"Yeah!" said Ignis. "She's becoming a right recluse!"

"Not to mention her help with the ever-growing list of problems would be greatly appreciated," groaned Frank miserably.

"Do you need us to weigh in on anything, mate?" said Ignis brightly.

"No, you concentrate on bagging this nephilim," replied Frank determined. "Let's tick that box, yeah?"

"Understood," said Amos respectfully. "We'll be in contact once we've confirmed one way or another if this is our boy."

"Good luck!" wished Frank, holding his hands together as though in prayer.

"Hypocrite!" chuckled Ignis a second before Amos broke his hands apart and the connection was lost.

"You are a bugger!" grinned Amos. He shivered and gave his arms a brisk rub. "I'm cold," he said through a bloom of icy breath. "Let's go get a cup of tea while we wait."

Back in the spare control room, Elsu and Gyasi were still scanning through the seemingly endless collection of possible contenders for the vacancy of mortal God. Hoowo3oow had grown impatient with 'All this sitting around!' and was sparring with what appeared to be a copy of himself made with smoke from Elsu's pipe. Gyasi winced every time a kick came too close to the back of his chair, while Elsu seemed to be quite used to this behaviour and remained slumped against the desk with a bored look on his face.

"Do you have to do that in here?" bellowed Gyasi unexpectedly, after he felt the wind from another kick, tickle his neck.

Hoowo3oow came to an abrupt stop mid punch and turned to look at Gyasi with a scandalised expression creasing his features. "What?" he asked sharply.

"All this flailing about you're doing?" grumbled Gyasi, waving his arms about in demonstration. "Do you have to do it so close to me?"

"Yes," replied Hoowo3oow flatly. "This room is exactly three metres in length and three metres wide. It is not possible to do this without coming close."

"Then do it somewhere else, man!" whined Gyasi, turning his back on Hoowo3oow and making a big deal of scanning the next subject.

Hoowo3oow dropped into a chair next to Elsu and folded his arms crossly. "I can't do it somewhere else!" he said bitterly. "I have to stay with you two in case you get lucky!"

"Then why don't you help instead?" suggested Elsu tonelessly.

He appeared to be struggling to stay awake and pushed his keyboard toward Hoowo3oow and made himself comfortable on the desk.

Hoowo3oow snarled as he dragged the keyboard in front of him and he shoved Elsu further across the desk to give himself more room to work.

As an unperturbed Elsu slipped into a light sleep, Gyasi and Hoowo3oow worked without speaking, as if it were a contest to see who could ignore the other the longest. After nearly twenty minutes of mute defiance, Hooowo3oow broke the silence.

"Doesn't Aarde ever train next to you," he asked in a tone of forced politeness.

"He does," said Gyasi with equal politeness. "Only he is kind enough to do it away from my face."

After a pause, Hoowo3oow said. "I apologise for making you nervous..." and Gyasi looked hopeful, but his face dropped when Hoowo3oow added, "I know you are sensitive and not very brave, I should have known better."

"Bra..." began Gyasi in retort but he held his tongue. "You know what, doesn't matter. At least I know why 'he' is stoned all the time now."

By 'he', Gyasi had meant Elsu. Hoowo3oow span in his chair looking affronted. "And what is that supposed to mean?" he spat through clenched teeth.

"You are a stressful person to be around," said Gyasi calmly, clearly pleased to have gotten a rise out of him. "I am just thankful that Aarde is the one with the level head."

"You take me to be emotional?" roared Hoowo3oow, jumping to his feet which, considering his child body, made no difference to his height.

Gyasi gave him a sneer and snorted derisively.

"Oh no!" he said, his deep voice oozing with sarcasm. "You're totally in control. Like a Vulcan you are!"

Hoowo3oow opened his mouth angrily, a venomous response was sat on the tip of his tongue, but as Elsu stirred, he seemed to become aware of himself and realising that Gyasi had a point, sat back down again.

"You may be right," he said at last. "I know I have been provocative lately. I think things have just been so tense recently that it's become hard to have a positive attitude."

Gyasi inwardly thought to himself that he couldn't remember a single day when Hoowo3oow had ever displayed anything like a positive attitude but refrained from sharing this, he wasn't sure how far he could push Hoowo3oow before he punched him, and much as he would never admit it, Hoowo3oow was right, he was sensitive.

"Everyone has been on edge lately," said Gyasi empathetically. "We lost one of our own and we are on the brink of a war that we are not prepared for. I mean look at this…"

Gyasi had pointed to the map of the world in the room which worked just like the one in Frank's station. This one was starting to look like a map of electrical power usage, so many were the beacons of light bursting in random locations across the planet.

"Have you ever seen this many incursions?" he asked weakly. "It's insane."

"Yes," growled Hoowo3oow in an undertone. "And I'm stuck in here when I should be out there making those lights go out!"

"You know why you're here," said Gyasi in an effort to maintain calm. "If one shows up you need to get straight on it in case that other kid shows up."

"Chance would be a fine thing!" snarled Howoo3oow, checking his current candidate with very hard presses on the keyboard.

Gyasi looked nervous. "You really want to fight him?" he asked tremulously.

"Damn right!" said Hoowo3oow confidently. "End this shit right here and now! I'm sick of all this waiting."

Hoowo3oow took a look at his display, the vision was clear and the person whose eyes they were viewing from was busy watching pornography. Hoowo3oow growled in disgust and banged his fist on the enter key, switching subjects and Gyasi glared at him.

Hoowo3oow rubbed his eyes lazily with one hand and without bothering to look raised his hand to mash the keyboard again.

"Wait!" yelled Gyasi, sliding over to him and knocking Hoowo3oow's hand away. "Look!"

Hoowo3oow followed Gyasi's outstretched finger and his gaze fell upon the display. It was full of static. They both stared at the crackling display and froze with shock, neither seemed to know what to do. Gyasi gave Elsu nudge which roused him from his sleep.

"Seriously Hoowo3oow, it's not hard," he said groggily. "Just press this and it switches to the next person."

And before Hoowo3oow or Gyasi could stop him, Elsu pressed the enter key which loaded the next subject and settled his head back down on the desk with his eyes shut.

"NOOO!" yelled Gyasi and Hoowo3oow together.

Elsu jumped with a start and slid off the desk.

"What happened?" he asked, suddenly upright and wide-eyed.

"You, absolute arse!" raged Hoowo3oow and he grabbed Elsu by the back of the jacket and threw him out his chair and against the door.

Hoowo3oow kicked Elsu's chair out of his way and began hammering the keyboard in an effort to retrieve the previous candidate, it took him only a handful of seconds, to realise he had no idea how to do that.

"Get it back! Get it back!" he demanded with a sharp sideways glance at Gyasi.

"I don't know either," said Gyasi helplessly. "Wade wrote this search algorithm and it doesn't look like he included a back button!"

"FUUUCK!" roared Hoowo3oow furiously and he rounded on Elsu and bore down upon him. "You, incompetent idiot," he snarled, staring into Elsu's confused and cowering eyes with impatient contempt.

"What did I do?" whined Elsu holding his shaking arms defensively in front of his face.

"You just lost a viable candidate!" said Hoowo3oow with calm fury. "And you can be the one to go and tell Frank!"

Elsu couldn't bring himself to speak. He simply nodded nervously and scrambled to get to his feet so he was no longer face to face with Hoowo3oow. He bounced anxiously on the spot for a second before giving Hoowo3oow a scared look as he too was standing, but in the way of the door. Hoowo3oow stepped to the side allowing Elsu to leave without speaking.

As Elsu tore off down the corridor he heard the control room door slam shut with such force it broke the latch and swung outward. He had never been so relieved to be going to give Frank bad news. In less than a minute he was at the door to Frank's room and he raised a hand to knock, paused to take a deep breath, then knocked half-heartedly, as if he hoped it wouldn't be heard.

"Come in," came Frank's voice from the other side.

Elsu opened the door with a shaky hand and peeked inside. Frank had his back to him and was busy coordinating Conclave units across the globe. After ten seconds had passed without Elsu speaking, Frank turned around to see who had entered and found Elsu frozen mid-step in the middle of the room like a deer caught in head lights.

"Why do you look guilty?" asked Frank suspiciously.

Elsu quickly explained what had happened in the other control room, and as expected, Frank exploded with manic fury. After yelling at Elsu for a full five minutes, during which he smoked two full cigarettes and had a coughing fit, he grabbed a headset from a drawer and tore off to the other control room. He called Wade as he ran, praying he would be able to fix it and within moments he had burst into the room and was at the desk with Wade in his ear.

"All right mate, what's up?" came Wade's friendly voice from Frank's headset.

"Elsu dropped a bollock and we need to undo it," said Frank swiftly, his fingers already poised over several interfaces.

"He messed up one key press?" asked Wade, puzzled.

"Apparently, fucking up is now so natural to him he quite literally does it in his sleep!" growled Frank, straining to keep his voice quiet. "So, Wade," he continued hopefully, "how do we go back a person?"

"Go back?" repeated Wade sounding confused. "You can't go back, that's not how it... wait, why do you want... you can't mean...?" he blustered with dawning comprehension.

"What do you mean we can't go back?" demanded Frank in a panic. "What kind of idiot doesn't include a back button?"

"You can't add a back button when there's no history, Frank!" yelled Wade indignantly. "There'd be nothing to go back to!"

"Well why the hell didn't you include a search history!" replied Frank, incredulously.

"The screen you're looking at…" said Wade curtly.

"What about it?" asked Frank impatiently.

"Does it look like fucking Google?" raged Wade. "No! It's actually a complex bit of code that contains a powerful bit of black magic that no one, I repeat literally no one else on the whole planet knows how to write. I mean for crying out loud, do you think this shit runs on Windows 95?"

"Fine! Fine, you made your point!" said Frank in a subdued tone. "But, can't we do anything?"

"No," said Wade sadly. "But if it helps the program will continue to run in a perpetual loop," he added with an attempt at optimism.

Frank gave his temples a firm rub and withdrew and lit a cigarette. "And how is that helpful?" he asked through a thick cloud of smoke.

"Once the algorithm has exhausted itself it will start again," replied Wade simply. "Sooner or later the person you found will show up again."

"They'll probably be dead by then," groaned Frank who collapsed against the desk, defeated. "That little freak has been ahead of us in everything," he added as his head fell on the console with a mundane thud. "He's probably eviscerating them right now!"

Gyasi rubbed Frank's back soothingly and picked up his headset which had become partially dislodged. He could hear Wade yelling indistinctly through the ear piece so he fitted it on his own head and, wincing a little at the volume, told Wade to calm down.

"CALM DOWN?" bellowed Wade in disbelief. "LOOK AT THE MAP!"

Gyasi glanced upwards toward the large, oily world map and his jaw fell open. He reached out a hand without looking, found Hoowo3oow and gave his clothes a little shake.

"What?" growled Hoowo3oow, turning to look at Gyasi. Hoowo3oow followed his gaze and saw exactly 'what'.

Four giant bursts of light were shining like suns across the planet. They were bright and extremely big, so big they could only be made by someone like…

"It's him!" said Hoowo3oow with a start.

Frank lurched up from his torpor and joined the others in staring at the map. "What the fff…?"

"And it looks like he's brought friends!"

"Diversion?" asked Frank who rallied at once and began work on isolating the locations.

"Probably," said Hoowo3oow. "But the timing is very suspicious!"

"Agreed," said Frank who was placing a conference call to Barry and Richard.

A few seconds later they were both staring with bemused expressions at a room full of very anxious people.

"Details later, right now I need a full sensor sweep of the institute and Conclave. Check everything! Once the scans are running, I need everyone battle ready."

Frank disconnected the call before either could react and immediately made another call to Amos.

This time Frank was able to appear instantly in the surface of Amos' cup of tea. His timing couldn't have been worse, as it coincided with Amos taking a particularly large gulp. When the surface finally stopped rippling, Frank caught Amos' attention.

"Amos, impressed as I am that you still have all your own teeth, it's urgent I speak with Ignis, is he there?"

Mildly startled by having his tea talk to him, Amos slopped a little of it down his jacket.

"Frank? Good gracious, you gave me a bit of a start," said Amos wiping himself down with his handkerchief. "What were you saying? You need to speak with Ignis?"

Ignis, who had been stood next to Amos, pricked up his ears.

"Yes, Ignis! Is he there? We have an emergency," said Frank desperately.

Amos, turned to lower the cup but Ignis had already scaled a fence and was stood shoulder to shoulder with Amos, peering into his cup.

"S'up Frank? What's going on?" asked Ignis in a casual but curious tone.

"Four massive energy signatures have just touched down mate and they are the kind of reading one of you guys would give off on a really bad day! It's got to be him!" said Frank with real panic in his voice.

"Four?" asked Ignis sounding puzzled. "There are more of them?"

"No, I don't think so," said Frank in rush. "All four of these just happened to appear right when we discovered a static visual in the search. I'm certain that one is our assassin on his way to murder whoever was behind the static and the others are distraction."

"Why distract?" asked Ignis sceptically. "Why not stealth in like he has previously? The previous attacks were always glamoured, is he trying to get caught?"

"Because I don't think he had time," said Frank knowledgeably. "I have a feeling the institute has been bugged, the building is being scanned as we speak. Listen," he continued as Ignis made to speak. "I am certain that they only know there's another because they know we found one. Somehow we are being watched."

"But…" said Ignis but Frank cut him off again.

"Preparing a glamour takes time but he has to act now to get there before we do. He must know if he just shows up, the four of you will descend upon him and he can't handle all of you. He still needs to search the area to find the right person and that can't happen while you guys are kicking him around, so you drop three more energy bombs in other locations."

"Split us up!" said Ignis grimly. "Make three of us chase phantoms, while avoiding just one," he was understanding Frank's viewpoint now and he didn't look pleased.

"Exactly!" said Frank. "And unfortunately, it's worked. I need you back here now and ready for redeployment."

"What about the nephilim?" asked Ignis with concern. "We can't just…"

"Amos," interrupted Frank. "Can you stay here and make contact with the busker. If it's him, call in and we'll whip you both back here in a flash.

If it's not, then continue with your enquiries, and report back when you're finished."

"Not a problem, Frank!" said Amos into his cup before turning to Ignis and looking uncharacteristically bloodthirsty.

"If you are fortunate enough to be placed at his location…" he began, his voice quiet and shaking with suppressed rage, "…be sure to rip his head from his body and bring it home with you. We would all like to pay our, 'respects'!" he finished without any trace of humour. Ignis looked at him with a mixture of shock and amusement for a moment and then nodded, grinning malevolently. Amos and Ignis bumped fists, and seconds later, Ignis had vanished from the square and out of sight to find a hidden place for Nephthys to bring him home.

"Best of luck, Frank," said Amos staunchly. "Let me know if anything changes. Speak soon." And with that Amos tossed the rest of his tea out of the cup and threw it in the bin. "Going to be one of those days!" he sighed.

Ten minutes later Ignis appeared in the elemortal lounge with a whoosh of purple flame. He wafted a plume of violet smoke out of his face and spotted Hoowo3oow and Aarde who sat at a table reviewing aerial maps of their imminent destinations and were sifting through reams of paper that detailed census information on everyone within a one-mile radius of the contact points of the massive energy readings. Both had looked up at Ignis when he appeared but only Hoowo3oow acknowledged his presence. Aarde instead looked grumpy and sullen and returned to his work without a word.

"Where are you being sent?" asked Ignis to Hoowo3oow and acting like Aarde wasn't there.

Hoowo3oow gave a surly, sideways glance at Aarde and rolled his eyes.

"Lambaré, Paraguay," he said gathering up a wad of paper and slamming it in the middle of the table.

"Only 170,000 possible subjects. Shouldn't take more than a week to investigate them all," he added sarcastically.

Aarde raised his eyes as though he expected Ignis to asked him next. When he didn't, he flicked a page from his own pile into the middle of the table. The map showed an overhead view of Abu Dhabi. Ignis snorted with a half-suppressed laugh and met Aarde's eyes with his.

"One point four million, give or take?" asked Ignis to Aarde who, after a moment of hesitation, grinned appreciatively.

"And all next door to each other. Very convenient!" snarled Hoowo3oow.

"Convenient?" chuckled Aarde with disbelief. "Do you have any idea how steep security will be?"

"Yeah!" agreed Ignis supportively. "And he doesn't exactly blend in does he. I mean they're all classy and posh!"

Aarde shook his head smiling. "Still a dick!"

"Still a pussy!" replied Ignis with a sly tenuous grin.

Aarde pursed his lips looking deeply offended, but a moment later he cracked a large smile.

"Sorry," he began bashfully. "For y'know… being a…"

"Twat?" supplied Ignis with a smirk. "Apology accepted. But may I offer you some advice?"

Aarde raised his eyebrows, gestured for him to continue and waited for what he assumed would be a childish insult. But to his surprise, Ignis actually looked quite sombre.

"Most people," began Ignis in a resigned tone, "when confronted with the end of the world would just say 'fuck it!' and tell a person how they feel! Exactly how many 'end of the worlds' do you need, man?"

Of all the things Aarde had been expecting Ignis to say, this was clearly the last on that list. He felt torn between annoyance and something like gratitude. Unable to think of a response and not wishing to cause further argument, he deflected the statement by scooping up a brown envelope and thrusting it at Ignis who took it politely and tore open the edge.

Hoowo3oow craned his head around to try and see what was written on the pages Ignis had emptied onto the table. Ignis quickly rifled through the pile of paper and withdrew an aerial photograph of somewhere that looked mountainous on one side.

"Switzerland?" asked Hoowo3oow interestedly.

"Hmm, yeah!" said Ignis distractedly.

"What locale?" asked Aarde who was also trying to peer round at the map.

"It's called Meyrin… Meyrin?" said Ignis thoughtfully. "Why do I know that?"

"Small population," said Hoowo3oow sourly. "Just over 21,000 I see," he added glancing at the land statistic sheet. "You can help me when you're finished!"

"Uugh!" growled Aarde, frustratedly. "For a man who can literally move on the wind you do a lot of complaining."

"At least I'm here to complain!" grumbled Hoowo3oow. "I see four operation dossiers… but only three people."

"That's not fair!" said Aarde plaintively. "Grieving is a process!"

"It's a process she is doing her best to avoid!" muttered Hoowo3oow, scooping up his file and planting himself down on the sofa.

Aarde looked at Ignis and silently asked. "What's his problem?"

But Ignis agreed with Hoowo3oow, it had been long enough. It was time for some healing and in Ignis' opinion nothing healed the soul like kicking the crap out of something bigger than him. Wordlessly he plucked the remaining envelope off the table and strode towards Shui's door.

"No! No!" whispered Aarde as he gesticulated frantically for Ignis to move away.

Ignis gave Aarde a remorseless look. There was a mischievous smile stretched across his face and with obvious delight at the panic on Aarde's face he kicked Shui's door with the toe of his shoe, three times.

"Ffhuck offff!" bellowed Shui in a slurry, angry manner.

"Rude!" chuckled Ignis and he booted the door more firmly this time. "C'mon dude let me in, or I'll huff and I'll puff then I'll kick your door in!"

Aarde looked scandalised, but Ignis wasn't done. He started drumming on Shui's door with his knuckles in a fast and purposefully off beat rhythm whilst singing in nonsensical sounds and noises that didn't follow the beat at all. A sudden series of thuds from inside Shui's room travelled closer to the door until, CRASH! The door was smashed open and Shui fell through it and collapsed face first onto the floor. Ignis who had dodged out of the way when he heard the footsteps, prodded her with his toe. She groaned mournfully, and with much wobbling and hesitation, pushed herself up to her knees. Ignis screwed up his nose as a powerful aroma invaded his nostrils. It smelled flammable.

"Holy shit, are you drunk?" asked Ignis as he backed away, in case he caused a spark.

"Wha' of it?" replied Shui aggressively.

Aarde was beside himself with shock as he crept closer to inspect Shui's condition. "What the hell, Shui," he said in terrified whisper. "We are being deployed in a couple of minutes."

Shui's vision swam as she looked around, spotted the envelope in Ignis' hand and, concentrating very hard, tried to take it without success. Ignis moved forward and placed it in her hand.

As she tore it open and held up the pages to the light, Ignis caught another strong smell of alcohol. "Seriously…" he said wafting his hand in front of his face, "…have you been bathing in vodka or something?"

"Yessh!" said Shui jubilantly before toppling over backwards. "Sho it's a good job I'm going to Russia!" and she tossed the pages into the middle of the room.

Aarde rushed to the kitchen area and frantically rummaged for a jar of coffee. "Quick," he shouted to Shui behind him. "You need to sober up before…"

"Guys, are we ready to go?" interrupted Frank who had flickered into view on the holographic display. As he gazed around the room his eyes fell upon Shui, lying on her back and rocking from side to side in a futile effort to get up again. "What is she doing?" he asked sternly.

"She is… er…" stammered Aarde but Hoowo3oow cut him off.

"She's acclimatising to the Russian lifestyle," he said unsympathetically.

"Acclimatising? Hoowo3oow, is she drunk?" demanded Frank incredulously.

"As a sailor!" Hoowo3oow growled back just as Shui released a loud reverberating burp, laughed immoderately and then began crying abruptly.

Frank was so angry he was struck dumb. Unable to summon words and form sentences, he simply screwed up his face and waggled his fists in the air with unsuppressed impotent rage.

"Shh'cool. I got thish!" said Shui launching from the floor and onto her feet but then stumbling forward and colliding with Ignis who caught her before she fell again.

"Get off!" she spat, shrugging Ignis off. She turned to face Ignis and fixed him with an unfocused blurry glare. She wobbled in place for a moment, then pointed at the empty space one foot to Ignis' left, accusingly.

"What'd you shay? Hmmm?" she asked with a hiccup.

Ignis' mind drew a blank. "Come again?" he said.

"Jush before..." began Shui, she paused to burp, "you... you said... ugh... something!". She snapped her fingers trying to conjure the memory. "With th'..." she snapped her fingers again, "...the prince dude!"

Ignis still looked completely lost. "I don't know, mate," said Ignis apologetically. "Bunch of stuff probably!"

He glanced between Aarde and Hoowo3oow to see if either of them appeared to be following this conversation better than he was, but both could only shrug their confusion.

"Don't know shay ya don't!" said Shui unhelpfully. "Before freesh! You know... you do, you know!"

Shui stumbled away from Ignis toward the window simulator at the back of the room and slumped against it.

"I don't like secrets," she mumbled before falling silent and drooling on the glass.

A second later she mumbled something about, "That woman," before slumping to the floor.

Aarde was about to check on her when purple flames exploded between them and Nephthys appeared looking sweaty and harassed.

"Someone order an Uber?" said Nephthys moodily.

Frank found his voice at last.

"Never thought I'd be so glad to see you," he said gratefully. "You guys are going to have to get going!" he added to Ignis, Aarde and Hoowo3oow.

"I want updates every ten minutes, no exceptions," he said seriously. "Bear in mind that we are working to the assumption that the others are a distraction. However, there is nothing to say there aren't three more like him... like you, waiting to jump you the second you land!"

Aarde and Ignis shared an uneasy look, it was after all a valid concern.

"What are you gonna do with rub-a-dub?" asked Ignis pointing at Shui with his thumb.

Frank gave a sad sigh and massaged his temples again. "She's just going to have to go with Gyasi and Elsu," he said weakly.

Aarde looked incredulous. "You can't be serious," he said disapprovingly. "She's hammered."

"She may be hammered but she can still cause some damage," said Frank defiantly.

Aarde made a sound that was somewhere between a laugh and a sneer.

"That's precisely my concern!" he said in a quiet, but impatient tone. "She could start an international incident in her condition."

Shui stumbled back over to where Ignis and Aarde were stood and vomited all over the floor.

"Let's do this!" she said wiping her mouth with her sleeve.

Nephthys gave a squeal of laughter as she observed the inebriated Shui slip a little in the pool of sick she had made.

"I think I like her better like this!" she said with wide-eyed delight. "Can I go with her too?"

Frank eyed Nephthys suspiciously. The circumstance of Nephthys volunteering to do anything like work was unheard of.

"You want to go on a mission?" Frank asked sceptically.

"I do if it's with the party animal over here," said Nephyhys who seemed genuinely excited. "I haven't had a girl's night out in… well ages."

"This isn't going to be about having a laugh Nephthys," said Frank who was obviously having misgivings about this. "It's search and rescue, people might die!"

"Darling, you and I have obvious differences in what we call a laugh!" said Nephthys with a grin.

Some of the colour drained from Frank's face at this. "People *might* die!" he repeated imploringly. "Might! It's not an objective."

"There'll be something I can kill though, right?" enquired Nephthys dubiously.

"Probably," said Frank feebly.

Aarde marched forward and stood between Nephthys and Frank's hologram. "You aren't seriously considering this?" he said aggressively. "She's in no condition to go, probably not even with Gyasi and Elsu and certainly not with her," he added, nodding his head at Nephthys.

"That's enough out of you," said Nephthys, pulling Aarde next to her and crouching to his height. "Do bring me back a flask of Karak Chai won't you!" and before Aarde could protest, she snapped her fingers and Aarde disappeared in a whoosh of purple fire.

"Wait a minute," barked Hoowo3oow, rising to his feet and showing every sign of arguing. "You can't just…" he began but he never got to finish the sentence.

Spotting Hoowo3oow approaching, Nephthys had snapped her fingers a second time and Hoowo3oow had been dragged to Paraguay amidst a swirl of violet flame. She rounded on Ignis who was under no illusion about what was coming. Accepting his fate with a wan smile, he shrugged in acquiescence and a second later he too was gone.

Nephthys then sauntered over to Shui and scooped her arm with her own and held her steady.

"Apparently, we have two handsome chaperones coming with us," she said merrily. Shui gave another loud belch.

"Let's go and break the good news," finished Nephthys with a cackle.

There was a final flash of bright purple fire and the pair was gone leaving Frank's hologram alone in the room.

He looked around bemusedly a moment before saying to no one in particular. "What the hell just happened?"

Chapter Five
The Creator

Snow had been falling thick and fast in Meyrin, Switzerland for a little over two days and the air was icy and bit the skin if any was left exposed. It was late and most of the Swiss population had hunkered down for the night, warm in their living rooms and blissfully ignorant to the cold. For those who still braved the blizzard, the night offered no comfort. It was very difficult to walk in the mounting snow, let alone drive, but Martha Bailey was determined to make it to her destination. She was a scientist at the LHC (Large Hadron Collider) and had a workspace in building 40, which she was desperately trying to reach.

During a very unsettled night's sleep she had experienced an epiphany, a real eureka moment and had spent the day in her apartment scribbling on a whiteboard to check her maths. Certain she was onto something very significant, Martha had wrapped herself up in as many layers as she could comfortably manage and set out in her car toward the office in the hopes of running a simulation before submitting her proposal. Martha gazed dreamily at a plastic model of a lithium atom that dangled from the car's rear-view mirror, and as she drove along the slippery roads that led to building 40, her mind raced. Martha was certain she had discovered a new particle and as her modesty gave way to hubris the words 'Nobel Prize' frequented her thoughts. No matter how hard she tried to contain her excitement the idea of being recognised in the scientific community for such an achievement was intoxicating.

For the briefest of moments, she indulged in a flight of fantasy, but just as her mind wandered a small figure appeared in the darkness, obscured by the snow and in the middle of the road. Panicked, Martha slammed on the brakes and swerved to avoid hitting whoever it was. The wheels of her VW Golf locked and the vehicle slid off the road and partly down an embankment, missing a tree by the narrowest of margins. Martha sat clutching the steering wheel for a few minutes, her eyes were wide and she was breathing heavily.

As she came to her senses, she gingerly checked herself for any cuts or bruises. Content that she was unscathed, Martha breathed a huge sigh of relief before recalling that she had nearly hit a person and began rummaging for a torch and mauling the door handle. As the car door opened a huge gust of wind blew a few pounds of snow into the vehicle but Martha was unconcerned with the cold right now. She pulled herself free of the seatbelt and scrambled up the embankment and onto the road.

Using the light from her torch she followed the grooves cut into the snow by her car wheels to where she had veered off in the first place. She expected to see a person, at the very least tracks that would show where they had fled to, but there was nothing that indicated a person had been there at all. The only oddity in the area was a one-metre-wide hole in the snow that, from what Martha could deduce, probably contained what she had tried to avoid hitting. What made it so odd was that the hole appeared to have been formed by the snow melting, an unlikely occurrence given the circumstances of the weather.

"Did I actually hit something?" wondered Martha under her breath. "Something really hot whatever it was!" she added as she crouched down and examined the gap in the snow that had begun to refreeze.

Her words fell out of her mouth like a string of icy clouds before being swept away by the wind and disappearing into the darkness. Martha stood up and gave a last look around for any sign of what it might have been, then feeling at least satisfied that no life, including her own, had been lost and no injury sustained, she made her way back to her car and set about thinking how to extract it from the embankment.

After a lot of revving and rocking of the car, Martha had managed to free her vehicle and turn it around in the adjacent field. Uncertain if she would be able get up the steep slope in such deep snow yet unsure what else to do, she was now driving along the edge of the embankment hoping that it might become shallower further up the road. It was difficult to steer as the VW Golf's wheels kept falling into the furrows that ran the length of the field and as she fought with the wheel to maintain control, the car suddenly shot up the slope as she broke free of the grooves and over-steered.

The car leaped several feet into the air and landed with loud groans and creaks of the chassis. Martha wrestled with the steering wheel in an effort to keep the car firmly on the road. She half expected the car to just slide across to the embankment on the other side, but to her amazement, the tyres dug into firmer ground and the car swerved away from the verge. For three whole minutes Martha just drove. It wasn't until she spotted Clinque des Vergers medical centre loom out of the blizzard that her senses caught up with her and she started to cry. Once she had turned onto Route de Meyrin and the bright lights on the Globe of Science and Innovation came into view, her sobbing turned to laughter and she wiped her face free of tears and took a calming, steadying breath.

As she approached building 40, she contemplated the notion of dying at the birth of a groundbreaking moment. The thought chilled her, but not because she was afraid of dying. No, it chilled her because she would have died in obscurity. Died before she had accomplished her goals and before she had been recognised for her contribution to science. Of course if she was right in her theory, someone else would discover it eventually. But they'd get all the credit. She pulled her car into the snow blanketed car park, giving it a best guess as to where the bay lines were and glanced around. Visibility was low through the howling storm but Martha felt surprised to see no other cars.

"Scared of a little snow, guys?" she muttered jokily under her breath as she fastened her jacket a little tighter and gathered up her things.

The car door opened against three feet of snow that had piled up against the tree-strewn reservation and Martha had to struggle to squeeze herself out. Snow driven by a fierce icy wind pelted her face, making it difficult to see the entrance until she was almost completely upon it and she burst through the doors, panting heavily and bearing a striking resemblance to a snowman.

"Are you OK?" asked the security guard stationed at the reception area.

His voice was light and accented with a Swiss tongue.

Martha shook her head and enough snow to make a snowball fell from her hair. "Leandro?" she said wiping water from her eyes and spotting someone walking toward to her.

"Ah, Miss Bailey," said Leandro recognising her immediately.

"Martha, please," said Martha embarrassedly. "It's a bit Baltic out there," she continued, shaking off her coat and brushing off yet more snow. "I'd drag your shift out if I were you, it's getting very thick."

Leandro gave Martha's clothes a cursory wave with a security wand and then turned his attention to the relentless weather that was rattling the heavy double doors of the entrance. "You may be right," he said a little dejectedly.

"Is anyone else here?" asked Martha with an attempt to sound like this was a throwaway question.

Leandro checked the sign in sheet. "Thirty-two people," he said helpfully. "Thirty-three now you are here," he added with a boyish, shy laugh.

A committed introvert, Martha instantly felt awkward and forced a laugh which came out louder than she had intended. Martha averted her eyes upwards and spotted the mural of the CMS detector. She intended to ask if he liked this particular mural, but the question got muddled in her head and she instead asked. "Are you a fan of murals?"

Leandro was still smiling politely but he looked confused. "Not... not really," he said apologetically.

Martha smiled weakly and then pointed off to the side to indicate her leaving. "I'll be off then!" she said awkwardly. "See you later?" she added, the pitch in her voice rising.

Leandro pointed outside and said, "I expect I'll still be here."

It was hard to tell if he was happy or sad about this. His tone was indiscernible.

"Of course... um... sorry," said Martha contritely and she left before things became any more uncomfortable.

"Real smooth, Martha!" she whispered as she rounded a corner and made her way up a flight of steps. "A brain like mine and I still can't talk to boys," she added ruefully as she climbed the next flight.

"Probably wasn't even flirting with me," she finished sadly as she reached her floor and kicked open the door to her workspace.

She dropped her things on her desk and groaned. "What if he tells everyone what a weirdo I am."

She unpacked her belongings with unnecessary force, slamming each item down on the counter one by one until she heard a crack, and realised she'd broken the screen on her phone. Martha succumbed to a silent fit of anger during which she mouthed a stream of curse words and eventually told off her phone for being weak. She soon deflated, and gazed remorsefully at her phone while contemplating how ridiculous she was being. Deciding that she was simply overexcited by the prospect of her impending discovery, she gracefully decluttered her desk and turned on her computer terminal. She stared at it for a few seconds, waiting for the black to reveal the computer desktop, but when nothing happened, she banged impatiently on the side of the monitor. Still nothing. She checked the power switch, then the cables and even the plug sockets. Everything was on but the screen was still resolutely black. She tried the next terminal along.

"Brian won't mind if I borrow his station," she thought to herself, but to her frustration and disappointment, Brian's screen stayed black too.

When she tried all of the other terminals in the room only to receive the same results, Martha's temper erupted and she stormed back to her desk, snatched up the landline phone receiver and pushed the button for IT Services so hard, she broke her nail on the plastic cover.

Quietly seething and chewing angrily on her nail, Martha waited for the dial tone to start but it never came. The phone also appeared to be faulty. She slammed the receiver down on the hook and grabbed her ID. She was just about to march down to IT herself when all of the monitors in the room blinked on to a single white dot glowing against the black in the middle of each screen. Perplexed, Martha paused in her tracks.

"Maybe this is scheduled maintenance," she thought to herself reasonably. "I really need to calm myself down," she continued aloud, sitting herself back down on her chair and giving her scalp a vigorous scratch with both hands.

She scraped her phone off the desk and craned forward to examine the crack. Sighing deeply, she unlocked it and swiped a few times until she found a game she liked about atoms. Feeling she should just have a minute to ease her nerves, she began to play while leaning sleepily on the desk. As her score rose her notice of her surroundings dimmed and she failed to notice the white dots moving in unison on each screen, drawing in bright white pixel thick lines, a spider web emblazoned with a litany of sygils and iconography that represented a diverse range of theologies.

When the drawing was complete a series of beeps echoed around the room as each computer indicated its end, and Martha, at last, looked up from her game. It took her a moment to take in what she was seeing and her first thoughts were those of hackers. "Someone is trying to hack into CERN," she gasped, standing so abruptly she knocked over her chair.

Closing her game, she opened the call 'app' on her mobile phone and called the security station downstairs. The call wouldn't connect. The storm raging outside had stolen her signal. She ran to the door and swung it open with the full intention of hanging over the balcony and just yelling down to the foyer. However, when she attempted to raise the alarm, no reassuring voice answered back.

Martha filled her lungs to straining and bellowed as loudly as she could. "HELP!" but still no one answered. Not even a curious fellow scientist.

"See you later my arse!" she spat in disbelief as she turned around and ran back to her terminal to disconnect the network cable. Martha's data was not stored on CERN servers, but rather external hard drives that she carried about with her.

"Not getting my files!" grunted Martha, yanking out the cable from the back and unplugging her drives. Martha stood her chair back up and dropped heavily into it and examined the spider web pattern on her monitor. A couple of seconds later she sighed despairingly — she recognised some of the icons.

"Ugh! Religious nuts!" grumbled Martha. "Sabotaging bastards!" she added, pulling out her phone, loading the camera app and photographing the monitor screen.

Martha gave the enter key a few vigorous taps with her finger. As expected, nothing happened.

"It's so nice you guys have finally found a common interest," said Martha sarcastically, noting how many religions were included in the image.

Acquiescing to the fact that this night had turned into a complete shambles and her experiment would have to wait, she pushed a few items into a lockable drawer, packed away her things and made her way back down the stairwell to the foyer.

Still marvelling at the complete lack of people when Leandro had said there were another thirty-two people in the building, Martha made her way through the reception, noting Leandro's absence, and looked out through the main doors to examine the weather. It was still snowing hard and appeared to have settled to a height of nearly four feet. As her eyes strained to see through the increasingly violent storm, she spotted the partly buried bike rack in the distance and, her heart raced, what looked like a large man walking away in the direction of restaurant one.

Martha barged the glass door open and yelled after him but even she could not hear herself over the howling wind. Before long the figure had vanished into the blizzard and Martha felt herself racked with indecision. The idea of chasing a stranger through this storm was not appealing, but on the other hand the sudden and unexplained emptiness of building 40 had unnerved her. Steeling herself for something drastic, she pulled the collar of her jumper up over her mouth and nose, dragged back on her still damp coat and set out into the furious and tempestuous night.

As the doors to building 40 swung closed behind her, and Martha was engulfed by an icy blast, a body fell from some twenty-seven metres above and smashed into the floor with devastating force. The mangled body of Leandro lay broken and splayed on the cold tiled floor. A large pool of blood was forming around his head and a wide gap in his hair revealed a crack in his skull. Brain damaged and dying, Leandro's eyes fell upon Martha beyond the door and he followed her progress as she battled against the elements. His last thoughts were of calling out to her. To shout for her to run, to get help or even just hide. But his body would not respond to his thoughts and the only sound he could make was a quiet, slurred wail of pain.

Someone walked over to where Leandro lay and stood beside his head. The person was small like a child and shrouded in a black cloak which hid their face in shadow. Their solid white eyes, which were still visible beneath the hood, half closed as they dropped their gaze to stare at Leandro who was still whimpering helplessly. The figure raised their right foot and placed it gently against Leandro's head. Leandro closed his eyes and a tear trickled over the bridge of his nose and mixed into a stream of blood still pouring from his wounds. A second later the hooded figure rammed their foot through Leandro's head and into the floor, cracking the ground and utterly obliterating Leandro's skull.

Wading through the waist-high snow, was proving to be extremely difficult and exhausting for Martha. Her jeans were drenched with ice cold water and her legs and feet were freezing. By the time she reached the shelter that was the entrance to restaurant one she had lost sight of the person she was following and was seriously considering just heading back to building 40 and getting some sleep under her desk.

Just as she was making up her mind to leave, the mysterious man appeared silhouetted against the swirling grey and white world only this time he was not alone, he was with someone else. They were stood across from her in the car park for building 32 and from what she could discern through her snowflake-strewn eyes, they were huddled close to each other as if trying to be heard in conversation over the deafening wind. Martha gave another pointless yell to garner their attention but her voice was swept away by a particularly strong gust so she summoned all her determination and broke away from the door and back into the drifts. She had only walked a few feet when the strangers suddenly bolted away from her again. This time they ran in the direction of the CERN Main Workshop and Martha wondered briefly whether that was their building and if they too were having hacker problems like her.

By widening her stride, Martha reached the Main Workshop in good time and thought she would have closed the gap between her and the strangers but as she came around the corner of the building and saw where they were, she felt nothing but frustration and annoyance to see they were already over by the Synchocyclotron and by the looks of it, heading in the direction of point one.

"FUUUUCK!" bellowed Martha into the storm and fueled by pure irritation, continued to give chase.

This cat and mousing took Martha all the way to the ATLAS building where at last the strangers could be caught up to as both had gone inside. This only increased Martha's sense of panic and fear. Had this hack affected the detectors, had it even affected the accelerator? A surge of adrenaline coursed through her veins and she ploughed through the snow like a woman possessed.

"This is gonna fuck up my experiments!" cried Martha, desperately clawing at the snow until she finally reached the service entrance and threw herself inside.

It was a battle to close the door on the ever-fierce wind that had followed her in. When the metal door eventually clanged shut, Martha sank to the floor on her hands and knees and tried to catch her breath. The surge of adrenaline had been exhausted and her knees felt wobbly when she got to her feet. She shook the snow from her hair and brushed herself down once more, becoming very much aware of how cold and wet her clothes were with each pat. But it was warm inside here. Really warm, almost sauna hot even. So Martha removed her coat, folded it over her arm and wafted her jumper to let the warm air circulate to her skin.

It was very pleasant after the bitter cold outside and Martha sighed with momentary relief. A chill was still able to run up her spine, when she noticed the floor of the corridor was peppered all the way along it with splashes of blood. It was a substantial amount of blood too, someone must have been seriously hurt to lose that much. Carefully tiptoeing to avoid standing in any of the puddles, Martha made her way further inside, following the trail of scarlet spatter. It was very dark as the emergency lighting was all that was on and Martha was starting to feel scared now. Maybe it was just the copious amount blood she had been following that had set her teeth on edge, but a creeping, sinister something was tickling the back of her brain that she couldn't put a finger on. Something that she felt ought to scare her more than CERN being hacked.

A sound of metal clinking against metal sounding from a stairwell that led to the underground levels caught Martha's attention. She crept quietly to the top step and strained her ears just in time to catch the echo of fleeting footsteps that appeared to be making their way deeper into the bowels of the building where the detector was located. Alarmingly, the trail of blood followed the same direction and Martha's sense of anticipation grew dramatically. What could be so important down there that a person could ignore bleeding to death. Nonetheless, Martha's curiosity had overtaken caution now. Indeed, this strange new turn of events had even caused her to forget the hack that had driven her out into the snow in the first place. Silent and slow, Martha made her way deeper into the lower levels of ATLAS, tracking the splashes of blood like bread crumbs. Martha had to stop for a moment and wipe the sweat from her brow. Why was it so hot?

"I must be twenty metres below ground," gasped Martha, the air in her lungs overly warm and uncomfortable.

Martha was indeed twenty metres deep under ATLAS and had another eighty metres below her. This place was riddled with high-tech and expensive equipment and it was normally kept so intentionally cold that Martha usually wore a coat when coming down here. Martha considered for a moment that perhaps a fire had started, but surely one of the emergency systems would have triggered. Another sound of hurried footsteps interrupted her thoughts. They were closer than before so Martha quickly took off after them, determined to get to the bottom of all this. As she reached the floor where the footsteps had originated, her curiosity and her courage evaporated on the spot. She had slipped in a very large pool of blood, one so large it had completely covered the floor. As Martha's eyes scanned the dimly lit space, they fell upon a body propped up in a reclining position against the wall, intermittently illuminated by a flashing green emergency light. She was able to discern that the body was dressed in a white security uniform and that it was drenched with dark black and scarlet stains. A modicum of sick lurched into her mouth and she spat it into the corner behind her. Without thinking, Martha took a few tentative steps closer to the body, and as she drew nearer, the blinking light showed her the bloodied and bruised face of...

"Leandro!" exclaimed Martha in horror.

She dashed over to him, splashing through the blood without care and crouched beside him. He looked dead already. Martha wrapped her fingers around his wrist and made to check his pulse. Nothing. She raised his arm to get a better feel but Leandro's arm cracked and crunched as the shattered bones in his arm ground against each other. Martha dropped his arm and recoiled in terror and disgust. It was then that her eyes sought his head and spotted the gaping hole between his hair. Trembling, she reached out and pressed her fingers against Leandro's head, raising it up. His face was completely misshapen and fragments of bone were sticking out of his cheek. It looked as though someone had crushed it and then attempted to put it back together again but very badly.

Martha released his head and fell backwards into the pool. Blood flooded around her and sprayed her face with droplets. When the splashing stopped Martha screamed... and screamed. Paralysed with shock and fear she stared wide-eyed at Leandro's corpse and screamed until she was hoarse. When she could no longer scream, she cried. Still sobbing uncontrollably Martha pushed herself back to her feet and looked down at the body. Her mind reeled with explanations. She was desperate for some sort of rationale, but clever as she was, Martha could not excuse this. With cold dread she realised this was not an accident. This had been done to him. This was murder. Even more unsettling was that the murderer had carried or dragged poor Leandro down here afterwards because off the blood trail. She wondered if Leandro had been one of the strangers in the storm and with a thrill of panic remembered there had been two. That means the other was still here and she had just alerted him to her presence by screaming.

She turned to leave but was struck immobile by another strange occurrence. The blood on the floor was rushing past her like a strong river current and back in the direction of Leandro's body. In fact, in felt so strong that she was having difficulty moving against it without stumbling. Martha turned slowly on the spot to prevent herself from falling and watched the current's progress. Somehow, the blood was running up the wall behind Leandro and was splitting off in many directions like roots of a tree. Her brain ached with confusion and abject terror. This was simply not possible. It wasn't.

"Maybe I'm hallucinating?" she asked herself desperately, examining her own hands for a psychotropic reaction.

When that didn't prove anything, she closed her eyes and pinched her skin. When Martha opened them again and saw what the branches of blood had left, she began to weep silently, her face drained of all colour and her body started to shake. Upon the wall, the blood had come to a stop, its paths complete. The route each branch had taken had reproduced the same spiral web of religious iconography and symbology Martha had observed on the computer screen in building 40. But there was no computer code that could do this.

"That's not possible," she whispered with a scared whine. "It's not, it's just not."

"If you don't like that," said a horribly familiar voice. "You definitely won't like this!"

To Martha's utter disbelief, Leandro was, with some difficulty, getting up. His bones popped and groaned with the effort of supporting his weight and he was not able to stand properly upright. His spine would not seem to allow it. Martha didn't try to rationalise this time. She turned and bolted toward the nearest door and slammed it shut behind her. As she stumbled forward and looked back to try to force sense into the situation, something banged heavily on the door. Martha jumped and stepped further away clutching at her chest. Her heart was hammering and she seemed unable to marshal her thoughts.

"This isn't real!" gasped Marsha through shallow breaths. "It's not, it can't be!"

The door crashed open violently with another loud bang and Leandro's disjointed body crept into view. His shattered jaw swung limply near his neck, forcing his mouth open wide, and when he smiled, the deformations in his face made it look like a sinister and manic leer.

"Can't?" cackled Leandro. "You still think this is in your head? I'll just have to try harder to convince you, won't I?"

Leandro started lurching in the doorway like he was being buffeted from behind by a crowd. From behind Leandro, arms, pale dead looking arms were reaching forward and pulling against the wall, heaving Leandro forward. Still grinning, Leandro braced against the door frame as more limbs jutted through and took purchase on the wall. His bones continued to crunch and crack as the horde of limbs swelled behind him, and as the strain mounted to breaking point, Leandro shrieked with delight.

"How about an orgy?" he crooned breathlessly before raising his voice and yelling. "AN ORGY OF EVIDENCE!"

Leandro gave a final insane laugh before his body broke apart under the pressure. His body parts scattered into the corridor landing in front of Martha as countless dead, rotting bodies cascaded through the door, landed in a pile and began scrambling to reach Martha.

Leandro's head looked up at her and still silently laughing, mouthed the word, 'Run!'

Martha did not need telling twice, she tore off down the corridor and began winding her way through the labyrinthine underbelly of ATLAS in a desperate attempt to shake off the wall of death flooding after her like a river, blocking out light and her only exit.

After several panic-stricken minutes of flight with the horde still swarming in all directions and gaining on her by the second, Martha considered her options. There were some rooms down here that were designed for safety in an emergency. Built out of concrete several feet thick and closed off with a heavy steel door that locked from the inside, these rooms were designed to take the brunt of fires, explosions and unforeseen circumstances. Martha figured her best chance was to get to one of these rooms and wait for help. She summoned her remaining strength and put it all into a final sprint, the rooms were close, she could make it. As she approached a connecting bridge that led to safety, she heard a voice echo from the other side which brought her to a full stop. It was a man's voice, British from the sounds of it, with a very broad accent and it sounded worried.

"Ignis?" said the voice with concern. "Ignis, are you there? Please respond!"

No reassuring voice answered the call though and the silence seemed to freeze Martha with indecision.

"Dammit Ignis, report!" came the voice again, his tone thick with fear and anger. But still no answer.

Martha came to the conclusion that Ignis must be another dead security guard and the last thing she wanted was a second confrontation with a reanimated corpse. Knowing full well that retreat meant death from a horde of zombies, Martha climbed over the bridge railing, and opening a maintenance service hatch, lowered herself inside and closed the panel. It was very cramped with all the thick wiring and pipes and very loud. But

Martha could still hear the calls to Ignis being bellowed from somewhere above. She could also hear the distant rumble of bodies clambering over each other as they raged ever closer. Indeed, she could feel the vibrations of their approach in the pipes. Trying her best to stifle her weeping, Martha reached up and like a child who believes there's a monster under the bed, she cupped her hands over her ears and squeezed her eyes tight shut.

In the Conclave, Frank was going spare. Ignis was not answering his attempts to make contact and no matter how hard he tried, he couldn't escape the idea that he had found the assassin and, it was almost impossible to believe, had lost the fight. Had lost his life.

"FUCK!" roared Frank, as his ninth attempt yielded no result. "Hoowo3oow, come in!" he continued, bashing the controls and zooming in on Paraguay.

Hoowo3oow answered at once but there was nothing displayed on Frank's mirror. It was just a blurry haze of mist blowing through a forest. Nonetheless, his voice was clear.

"What is it?" growled Hoowo3oow impatiently, "I'm a little busy right now!"

"What have you got?" asked Frank hopefully. "Is it him?"

"No!" said Hoowo3oow disappointedly. "It's a bunch of golems."

"Golems?" repeated Frank. "That's a relief! Hurry up and kill them then get back here, I need you to join Ignis."

The sound of bone hitting stone answered before Hooowo3oow spoke, and when he did, he was not happy. "That's a relief?" he snarled indignantly. "Are you joking?"

"Calm down lad, they're just golems. Should be a piece of cake for you!" said Frank reasonably.

"These are not normal golems!" yelled Hoowo3oow angrily and a stream of white-hot lava blazed across the mirror, dazzling Frank.

"They've been imbued with some sort of fire magic and I am struggling to be in any other form than inert gas. How about you bring Ignis here, this is right up his street." Another rush of fiery liquid rock lit up the control room and Frank averted his gaze.

"Ignis is down!" said Frank, who looked suddenly stunned for saying it aloud.

"What?" asked Hoowo3oow over the sound of punching and jets of fire.

"Ignis!" repeated Frank weakly. "He… he's not responding."

For almost a minute neither of them spoke. Only the sound of Hoowo3oow fighting crackled over the speakers. Eventually a cracking, crumbling noise of stone being smashed rang out into the room and Hoowo3oow appeared in the mirror, human and whole.

"I'll deal with these as quickly as I can!" he said reassuringly. "Keep some transport on standby and I'll join Ignis as soon as I…"

Hoowo3oow was cut short in his sentence by a blast of lava that hit him squarely in the chest which made him burst into gas. With a sinking feeling, Frank ended the connection and left him to it.

Communication with Aarde was not any better. He too was fighting golems also imbued with fire and while he was putting up a good fight in his normal form, he was still being overwhelmed. Watching the fight from car windows and mirrors on the crowded streets of Abu Dhabi, Frank could see scores of stone monsters, eight feet tall and brimming with lava rushing at Aarde, attacking one after the other in a relentless coordinated assault. He relayed the same message about Ignis and terminated his connection again. Aarde did not need the distraction.

With mounting dread, Frank finally called Shui. He expected to see her lying on the floor and covered in vomit, with Nephthys laughing hysterically. When the mirror lit up, he saw Shui borne upon a crashing icy wave that was smashing through a snow-filled Russian alleyway, washing several steaming golems with it. Even more surprisingly, Nephthys was in her Bathin form and was riding a slab of ice on the crest of the wave like a surfer. Bathin looked like he was having the time of his life as he held two halves of a golem in each hand and was waving them triumphantly in the air as he and Shui stormed between stone brick houses. A very unhappy Gyasi and Elsu could be seen in the distance, huddled together in a bath that bobbed about uncontrollably in Shui's wake. Try as he might, he could not make himself heard over the roaring wave and rolling ice and gave it up as a bad job.

"She seems to have that under control," he said to himself, quickly terminating the connection and lighting a cigarette.

The cigarette fell from his mouth into his lap, when Amos' voice sounded unexpectedly from a mirror beside him.

"You know those things will kill you," said Amos happily.

Patting his crotch irritably, he retrieved his cigarette and turned to address Amos who was smiling brightly and was standing next to a young, long-haired male whom Frank didn't recognise. The young man had a guitar strapped over his back and wore a polite but bewildered expression on his face. The pair appeared to be staring into a darkened shop window to disguise the conversation as every now and then Amos would randomly point at Frank without actually saying anything. He stared at them grumpily for a moment wondering why he was being shown this stranger when he suddenly remembered why Amos was not on operations. He choked on a lungful of smoke and his cigarette spluttered out of his mouth and onto the desk.

"Is that…" he began, wide-eyed and amazed. "Is that the…" Frank made a futile effort to hide his mouth from the boy and whispered, "…nephilim?"

"Yes, it is, and I've told him all about it so there is no need to be sensitive," said Amos helpfully. "If my knowledge of music is correct then he is quite keen to come and see the institute and meet the team!"

"What?" said Frank who seemed completely wrong-footed. "You told him everything? Like, everything?"

"Yes," said Amos simply. "He took it very well too. If you ask me, I think he always suspected something was amiss, poor lad. He's had a bad start, it's impressive that he turned out to be this well-mannered. Speaking of well-mannered lads, how is Ignis getting on? Has he whooped 'em yet?"

Frank's reply faltered, catching in his throat and as he looked into Amos' happy face, he visibly deflated.

"What is it?" said Amos, spotting something was wrong and becoming abruptly stern. "What's happened?"

Frank hovered on the edge of speech for a second but the words never came. Amos did not need him to speak, however. He could see the answer written all over Frank's distraught features.

"Is he confirmed KIA?" asked Amos. His voice was quiet and his tone soft but his eyes bored into Frank as if they were trying to see his brain.

Frank looked down at his hands, he could not bring himself to meet Amos' gaze.

"No," he said at last. "But communication went quiet about twenty minutes after he dropped."

"That could be anything," said Amos sceptically.

"I thought so too," said Frank still intently staring at his hands. "So I used a puddle at his location to have a quick look."

"And?" asked Amos impatiently.

"I couldn't see him. He must have been lying down," said Frank, his voice cracking a little. "Amos, the room, it was all quiet and… and… shit, it was caked in blood. It was on everything."

Amos' face became drawn and white as Frank pressed on.

"I told him to answer, I yelled it for a while."

There was a definite note of pleading in his voice, he needed Amos to understand.

"Eventually the silence was filled with white noise and the reflection changed to static. You know what that means, Amos. Ignis found one and I'm guessing so did the assassin."

Amos' eyebrows screwed together. "That doesn't mean he's dead," he said firmly. "Where is he?"

"LHC facility in Meyrin," began Frank. "But I can't get you there, Nephthys is with Shui and they are…" he thought back to the tsunami washing through a Russian village, "…in the thick of it!" he finished awkwardly.

Amos reached into an inner pocket and withdrew a small black box that was bound with seven delicate silver chains. Beneath the chain and on the box's surfaces were unusual drawings that crudely resembled eyes. Frank recognised the box at once and became very alarmed.

"What are you doing?" he asked in a worried whisper. "Put that away!"

Amos ignored him. Instead, he slid his finger beneath one of the chains and pulled. A snapping sound could just be heard over the speakers in Frank's control room.

"Amos, no!" ordered Frank. "You can't!"

He heard the sound of two more defiant snaps and flinched.

"Please Amos. You are in the middle of a crowded city," begged Frank desperately.

Snap. Snap. Snap.

Frank stared horror-struck at the determined grimace on Amos' face and with a deep feeling of dread, knew there was no stopping him.

"It was supposed to be used in an emergency," he said faintly.

"This is an emergency!" snarled Amos as he threw all caution to the wind and snapped the last chain apart.

The box lid popped open and a tremendously bright light lit up the street like a floodlight, turning night into day. Hundreds of shoppers and revellers in the city centre stopped in their tracks, dropped their bags and shielded their eyes. When the light calmed Amos could be seen clutching a large, glassy ball that was too big for the box and which was glowing from a white flame burning inside. The ball had garnered a lot of attention and a crowd was beginning to gather round Amos and the nephilim, the latter of whom was still watching with polite interest.

None of them seemed to be paying any interest to Frank reflected in the shop window who was leaning against the mirror and shaking his head in disbelief.

"You, stupid bastard!" he mouthed to Amos who was glaring back at him subordinately.

A roar. An angry terrible roar, boomed across the sky above Nottingham like an approaching storm. The roar grew in volume and ferocity, causing the populous to cower in fear and whispers of words like, 'terrorist' and 'missile' spread between them.

Suspicions of terrorism quickly evaporated, when the roar broke into words which raged from the heavens, "THAT'S MINE!"

A streak of white fire split the sky like a falling meteorite and before anyone could run or take cover, something crashed into the road behind Amos with such force it sent stone, concrete and steel tram railing flying in all directions. The debris destroyed lamp posts, tram shelters, several market stalls, one of two lion statues near the square and countless shop windows, one of which had been the one Frank had been using to communicate with Amos.

Amos stood resolute and unperturbed. Unlike many in the vicinity he and the nephilim were completely uninjured as Amos, who was feeling very motivated, had casually dodged and deflected any shards that had flown their way.

"That *hoshi no tama* is mine!" spat a raspy woman's voice behind him. "Give it to me! NOW!"

Amos turned to face the voice and saw a middle-aged woman stood in the centre of a crater a couple of feet deep. She looked like any other woman dressed in modern day clothing, but she radiated an intense energy that was felt by all as heat. Her eyes were fixed upon the ball in Amos' hand and her face was screwed up with fury.

"GIVE IT HERE!" she shrieked. Her vocalisation was rough and almost animalistic and she lunged at Amos without warning.

Amos stepped forward at the same time and punched the woman so hard in the face she came clean off her feet and slammed into the opposing kerb like a heavy rag doll. The people around them immediately began to protest, albeit cautiously, yelling about the mistreatment of women and condemning the abuse. Amos appeared quite unconcerned, as he strolled across the road to where the woman, dazed and shocked, was trying to get back to her feet. Noticing his approach, the woman drew back her fist and launched at Amos again but before she could stand he kicked her ungraciously in the head, driving it through the kerb this time, reducing the concrete slabs to dust. A large burly man suddenly burst out of a group of onlookers and seized Amos by the jacket with both hands, but Amos grabbed the man by his wrists, drew him closer and broke the man's nose with his forehead, instantly deterring any other would be 'have a go heroes'. He peered back into the hole his foot had made and saw the woman staring back at him. She looked murderous.

"If I had my ball, you would not find me so easy!" she growled.

"Behave for a few minutes and you might get it back," replied Amos sternly and he held out his hand for her to take.

Free from the ground the woman dusted herself off petulantly, all the while casting fleeting perplexed glances at Amos.

"How did you get that?" she asked after a pause. "I gave that to someone else a long time ago. Strong as you are I find it hard to believe you were able beat him and steal it."

"This," began Amos holding up the glowing fire filled ball, "is neither stolen nor lost. It is for all intents and purposes still in the possession of Ignis, I am simply keeping it safe at his request."

"You know Ignis?" said the woman, her anger easing.

"I do," said Amos, his voice urgent. "I am his friend and colleague and I need your help."

"My debt is to Ignis, not you," rebuffed the woman. "Now, give me the *hoshi no tama* and let me leave."

"Ignis saved your life and now I need to save his," said Amos desperately. "I know what you are and I know what you can do. Take me to him and your debt will be settled."

"Settled?" repeated the woman dubiously. "I get my ball back?"

"You can be complete again once more," confirmed Amos.

"And if I refuse?" asked the woman cautiously.

"Then Ignis dies and your debt will never be repaid," said Amos ruefully.

The woman eyed Amos as though determined to spot some sign of deceit, when she found none, she sighed deeply and asked. "What do you need me to do?"

"I know your species are capable of bending space and time," said Amos in a rush. "Ignis is somewhere in Meyrin, Switzerland. I'm certain you know where that is, I need to go there, now!"

The woman gave Amos a withering look, disappointed by his stupidity.

"I can't do that without my ball," she said with as much condescension as she could muster. "That sort of power is only available when I'm…"

Amos dropped the ball into the woman's gesticulating hand and she broke off looking thoroughly overwhelmed. "My… my ball."

The woman stared mesmerized at her treasure, rolling it over in her hands as if she had never encountered anything so wondrous before.

When it seemed like this would go on for some time, Amos cleared his throat and said very loudly. "Time is short!"

The woman glanced up and for a moment seemed surprised to see him there. "Thank you," she said at last, her voice quiet and strangely youthful.

She held the ball between her palms and squeezed it from both sides. The ball began to shrink as her hands closed together but the fire inside seemed to rage brighter under the pressure. Smaller and smaller it became until it was the size of a marble, but the fire that burned within had become so bright it was impossible to see anything other than pure white light, no matter where you looked. When darkness returned to the scene, it was a minute before anyone noticed, so intense had been the flare. When everyone's eyes had adjusted and their vision had returned to normal, they found a large fox with vibrant white fur, where the woman had been moments before. The fox was sat on its hind quarters yet was head height with Amos and swishing behind it were not one, but seven tails.

Camera flashes erupted all around them as smart phones were wrenched from pockets in a bid to photograph this auspicious and breathtaking creature.

"Stand beside me," said the fox calmly. Its voice was still female but it sounded more aged than before, like it was blended with wizened serenity.

Without thought for cameras and without fear for what awaited, Amos clasped the nephilim by the hand and dragged him along as he nestled himself against the fox's fur.

"The journey will be hard on you," said the fox warningly. "The stresses of warping space will make the energy that holds you together weak. It will take time to restore itself properly."

"That's fine, please let's just go," said Amos imploringly.

"Don't say I didn't warn you. What am I doing with this boy?" asked the fox benignly. "Is he coming too?"

"Sort of," said Amos awkwardly. "We'll be dropping him off on the way if that's OK?"

"Agreed," said the fox kindly. "I like him. He kind of smells like me."

Amos just had time to catch the look of concern on the nephilim's face before the fox's tails whipped through air, wrapped around them, and with a rushing, sucking noise, the three imploded on the spot, and were gone.

A twenty-sided die clattered across a large wooden table and onto a whimsical map bearing the title, 'Tiboria' in thick black marker. The die settled to show the number three and a chorus of groans and laughter broke over the table.

"What's your modifier?" asked Rich who was trying not to snigger.

"Which one is it?" replied Demi in a coy tone.

"Your strength modifier," said Rich, who was grinning broadly.

Demi scanned a character sheet for someone called 'Burn' and found the requested statistic. She sighed grumpily and tossed her sheet in disgust.

"Zero... Ugh! She's such a weakling."

Richard chuckled happily and considered his notes. He then picked up a die of his own and tossed it behind a curved board.

"Oh, my days!" he said jubilantly. "You jammy bugger!"

"Here we go!" said Stewart with a knowing smile. "Do you need some water first or..."

"Shut up!" said Rich, giving Stewart a playful push. "You love it, you know you do." He rolled up his sleeves. "Right then, Burn!"

Demi sat up straighter and leaned in to listen closely.

"Your attempt to sneak up on the troll and put him in a sleeper hold failed miserably. You clasp frantically at his neck and pull as hard you can, but the troll hardly seems to notice. He scratches at a tickle on his shoulder which dislodges your grip and you slip to the floor behind him. Dim as the troll is, he does not notice. Give me a stealth check."

Demi picked up the twenty-sided die again, gave it roll in her hand, blew on it and dashed it across the table. This time it settled on two. Stewart and Chloe who were sat either side of Demi laughed raucously while Alex, who was sat between Chloe and Richard, consulted her own character sheet for someone called Virgil before checking a hardback book with hurried swipes of each page.

"Let me just check," said Rich, rolling his own die again. His expression was wooden.

"You try to slip away unseen," began Richard in a whisper, "but as you turn to leave one of the planks beneath your feet creaks, cracks and then breaks. Your arm sinks between the boards and you collapse on the deck, banging your face upon the walk."

He gave Demi a tragic look.

"I'm afraid that this not only alerts the troll to your presence but it also causes you to lose two hit points!"

"Two?" yelled Demi indignantly. "Are you having a laugh?"

"One hit point is due to your arm being lodged in the board walk which has caused you a bleeding injury," said Rich blithely. "The troll lifts his massive club and takes aim at Burn's head…"

"I'm using a dart to knock his club out the way or to at least get his attention," interrupted Stewart lazily. He checked his own character sheet for a monk called Chug. "I've got twelve left."

"Yeah, but are you really going to be able to throw it hard enough to offset the swing of a club?" asked Rich scornfully.

"I'm a monk," said Stewart derisively. "I throw needles through glass, pretty sure I can nail a club with a dart."

"All right smart arse give me strength check!" demanded Rich smugly.

"I think you mean dexterity," said Stewart.

"You're trying to throw it hard enough to change its trajectory. That's strength."

Stewart threw the die irritably which landed on seven.

"You guys are not doing well with rolls tonight. The dart zooms through the air and finds its target with a soft thunk. An impressive shot for the distance but it has no effect on the club."

"I use the starfire amulet!" proclaimed Alex unexpectedly. "Blinding the troll causing him to miss."

"Interesting idea," said Richard approvingly. "Lemme check!" and he rolled behind his board.

"OK. So, Virgil, spying Burn in danger launches from the dock and down onto the boardwalk. He lands gracefully and withdraws the amulet from his pocket. Holding it high he summons the starfire to burst forth…"

"AHHHHH!" screamed everyone, Richard included as an actual burst of bright light erupted from the middle of the room beside the table and dazzled the group.

"You've outdone yourself with the effects mate," said Stewart, rubbing his eyes. "But tone it down a bit yeah?"

"Agreed!" chuntered Demi who was also massaging her eyelids and blinking to get the green blobs in her vision to fade.

"That wasn't me!" exclaimed Richard who had replaced his glasses and was actually looking for the source of the disturbance. "The strobe only does lightning fl…" He broke off looking dumbstruck.

Alex too was glaring open mouthed at something over Stewart's shoulder and although the light had diminished that 'something' was bathing her in a silvery glow. Their eyes adjusted, Demi and Stewart also turned to see what the others were staring at and they too, fell entranced at the sight. A very large, white furred fox that was glowing like a Christmas decoration stood before them with its head bowed as if sleeping. Swishing in front and behind were a number of tails that coiled through the air like serpents and were intertwined with two hard to see figures.

"Sorry to alarm you," said Amos a little weakly as he stumbled forward and clutched the back of Stewart's chair for support.

"Amos? What are you…? I mean how did…?" blustered Richard in confusion.

"Long story," replied Amos, lowering himself into the empty chair between Demi and Stewart and breathing deeply. "I'm afraid I don't have time to explain it all right now, I really need to be off."

Amos gave a small lurch like he might be sick, but he held it down and sat up straight.

"Could you take care of my friend here until I get back?" he asked, gesturing back toward the fox where a young, long-haired man wearing a long black leather jacket and a guitar strapped over his back stepped out from behind the tails.

Unlike Amos he seemed quite steady. Indeed, he was still wearing the same expression of polite interest he'd worn when the fox had first appeared. He came to stand directly behind Amos and smiled broadly. It was a smile that looked happy and genuine. It was also infectious.

"Can you play that thing?" asked Demi without preamble and pointing to his guitar.

The nephilim nodded enthusiastically.

"Yes!" said Demi jubilantly. "We can finally have a bard in our party."

"Steady on!" said Richard calmingly. "He's welcome to join of course but not everyone wants to play and you need to stop trying to force people. That's how you scared off the last three."

The nephilim examined the table interestedly and a moment later gestured, 'Why not?' with a nod.

"Quiet aren't you!" said Demi a little rudely.

"Oh, I'm sorry. I should have said," began Amos rising to his feet and giving his chair to the nephilim. "He can't speak!" he finished flatly.

Demi cringed and shrank into her chair. Stewart chuckled under his breath and whispered, "You idiot," at her and hid his eyes behind his hand.

The nephilim waved his hands placatively, his expression keen to show he was not offended.

"I'm sure you will get along just fine," said Amos agreeably. "Now, I really must go."

He looked down at the nephilim and gave a reassuring smile.

"Richard here and the others will take good care of you, until I come back. In the meantime please eat, rest, do whatever makes you comfortable. From here on after, you can consider this building your home like the rest us."

The nephilim blushed at such an offer and a happy tear swam down his cheek.

"While he may not speak, he cleverly converses through his choice of music," said Amos quickly to the group before turning to address Demi. "With your memory you ought to be quite effective at understanding what he is trying to say so try to help him out."

"Can't he just write it down?" asked Demi reasonably, yet still a little rudely.

"He has never been taught," said Amos delicately. "Something we will address at a later date."

Amos walked back to the fox and nestled back into the fur once more.

"Take care, all!" he bellowed before tilting his head up to the fox's ear. "If you would be so kind," he said stoutly. "Meyrin awaits!"

"This will be your second trip through folded space in a very short space of time," said the fox warningly, though she sounded indifferent. "Your body will be very unstable after."

"Yes, I know!" said Amos hurriedly. "Let's just go!"

"This must be your last time travelling in this way," said the fox benignly. "After this our business is concluded, yes?"

"Yes, let's go!" groaned Amos frustratedly.

"Very well."

The tails swished and wrapped around and with a great rushing sucking noise the pair imploded with a pop.

With the room plunged back into semi darkness, everyone seated themselves properly at the table again and Richard handed the nephilim a character sheet.

"Have you got a name?" he asked politely.

The nephilim shook his head disappointedly.

"Seriously?" said Demi with her usual lack of tact. "Well, that is something we are going to have to remedy."

The nephilim chuckled silently and nodded his approval of the idea. Then swinging his guitar to his front began to play *You've got a Friend in Me* by Randy Newman and everyone at the table sang along as play resumed and Richard introduced, The bard of Underbridge, into the narrative.

Poor old Amos emerged at his destination in total disarray. He fell heavily from the fox's tails and sank face down into several feet of snow. Even the fox's usual lustre was lost to the storm that still raged through Meyrin and her tails whipped furiously against the floor as the cruel winds gave them a churn.

"This is where I leave you," yelled the fox so Amos could hear her. She hesitated a moment then added, "If Ignis is still alive, tell him… tell him it was worth it!"

Amos spat into the snow and looking back yelled. "What was worth it?"

But the fox had already gone. Dejected, weak and shivering from the cold he attempted to stand himself up but the wind was pushing him hard and he found it difficult. He tried to get his bearings, he had after all been here before, but the blizzard had caused a whiteout and he had absolutely no idea where to go. He drew his tweed jacket tighter around his neck as he clambered through the waist-deep snow. He felt faint and numb and his shivering was becoming more intense. It felt to Amos like he was occasionally vibrating rather than shivering. He supposed that was something to do with what the fox had said. Either way he needed to get inside. He did not come all this way just to die of hypothermia.

He marched on toward the closest building he could see through the storm which wasn't very tall but was very wide. Not until he was almost right on top of it did Amos recognise the building as point one. He banged on the glass doors hoping to rouse a member of security or a cleaner, but no one came and the lights were all off. He decided he would check the side to see if there was a more easily repairable door he could break in through and was just coming around the corner of the building when he noticed a long groove in the snow. It had been recovered and made smooth by the relentless weather but Amos was certain it would have been made by a person carving a path a short time ago. From the way the snow was distributed at the edges, he was able to determine which direction the person had travelled in and for want of a better lead followed the trail. It didn't take long before Amos knew he'd made the right decision. He had followed the track all the way to the ATLAS building and had noticed immediately that there wasn't a single snow flake upon it.

"I'M COMING LAD!" roared Amos as he plunged forward. "HOLD ON!"

He soon reached the service entrance Martha had used earlier, and without pause, kicked the door open, breaking the lock. A wall of heat greeted him from inside and he felt it spread through him, warming his bones and he sighed gratefully. He wedged the door shut by bending part of the frame and took off his jacket. Now his body was warming, his clothes felt cold and nasty. But as he folded it over his arm for carrying, it simply dropped to the floor. Perplexed, Amos stared at it piled up at his feet. "How the hell did I miss?" he thought to himself.

He concluded that this too was probably more of what the fox had warned him about and scooped it up. It was then that he discovered the blood trail that had led Martha to Leandro earlier and hastened to follow it himself, eager to discover where it led to make sure it wasn't Ignis at the other end. It did not take Amos long to find the room full of blood and the web pattern stained on the wall. The sight of it filled him with anger. He turned to the only other open door and saw the scattered body parts of what appeared to be a security guard lying all over the floor. He knelt beside the torso and checked the name tag.

"Leandro Burri," he read aloud. "Poor kid."

A deep cackle of amused laughter sounded from further along the corridor and as Amos looked up, he saw a towering, monstrous figure strolling quite calmly in his direction, its red and black skin glistening in a sliver of green emergency lighting.

"He said to expect someone!" guffawed the creature incredulously. "He said they'd send backup, but…" the figure sniggered with delight, "…he never said it would be an old man."

Amos stood straight backed and slid a hand behind him. There was a steely glint in his eye and although he felt hot fury burn in his chest, he showed no outward sign of anger and when he spoke it was in a calm measured voice.

"Stand aside and no one need get hurt," said Amos graciously.

The creature roared hysterically, stomping its feet and slapping its knee.

"I'm almost sorry to have to kill you," boomed the monster as it drew right up to Amos and loomed over him.

Up close Amos could see discoloured mottled skin hanging off the creature like old wallpaper. In places it was green and yellow which ran into the red and black pigment like poorly performed tie-dye. The creature was massive, so tall it had to stoop to fit under the ceiling and was so wide its shoulders brushed against the wall either side.

"Ugly bastard, aren't you," said Amos almost conversationally. "Even by demon standards and that's saying something."

The creature did not seem bothered by the slight though. He laughed harder than before and wagged an admonitory finger at Amos.

"You've got balls mate, I'll give you that," said the demon appreciatively. "Reckon I'll wear them round my neck as a souvenir when I'm done with you."

Amos looked supremely unconcerned. "Your neck isn't big enough for these," he said with a grin.

The demon threw his head back in hysterics. "Not big enough!" he repeated gleefully. "Wait 'til I tell Asmodeus about this he will absolutely pi…"

The demon's sentence was cut short as a flash of steel split the air, spraying the walls with onyx blood. His amusement was replaced with a look of indignation as he looked down and saw a wide gash in his chest. His eyes then fell back upon Amos who was standing ready for a fight, a short partially concealed blade held tight in his hand behind him. A whine of steel pierced the tension.

"That's it, Amos!" said a voice in his head. "Game face mate. Cut this cunt a new one!"

"Language, Jack!" thought Amos admonitorily, but he smiled nonetheless.

"Bit rude!" said the demon in an almost sulky tone. "I thought we were enjoying some pre-match banter."

"I don't have time for pleasantries I'm afraid," said Amos dismissively. "I have a prior engagement and I'm already late."

"Oh, you're gonna be late all right!" growled the demon, balling up a fist and bashing it against his hand. "Late as in dead!"

Amos rolled his eyes morosely, but in that second the demon threw a punch so fast Amos did not have time to react. It connected with his cheek, smashing his glasses off his face and knocking Amos back through the door and into the pool of blood.

"Sucker punching bitch!" snarled Amos with a shake of his head.

"You wanna talk about sucker punching?" snorted the demon, holding up a torn blood-stained piece of clothing that underlined the gash Amos had made.

"Touché!" replied Amos fairly as he got sourly to his feet.

His grip on his blade slackened and it fell to the floor with a splash. Falling after it was a long chain that poured from Amos' sleeve and was attached to the blade's pommel. At the other end of the chain was a heavy iron ball which Amos caught and transferred to his other hand.

"Now we're talking!" said the demon confidently as he squeezed through the doorway and sized Amos up.

The need for discourse gone, the demon hurled himself through the air at Amos, his fist already drawn back. But when the punch landed it hit only wall. Amos had slipped under the attack and had moved behind him ensuring he was out of the demon's reach. When the demon turned to face him, Amos dropped the iron ball in mid-air and kicked it hard with the sole of his boot. The metal ball sailed through the air and collided with the demon's kneecap who let out a howl of pain, clutching at his leg. He recovered quickly and made to tackle Amos, but Amos dragged the ball by the chain back toward him, swung it behind and over himself and smashed it down hard into the back of the demon's head. The demon skidded through the blood face first and came to a stop where Amos had been standing but he was no longer there. Enraged, the demon flung himself to his feet and barged through the doorway smashing the frame and wall apart. Amos had not gone far.

He was waiting midway down the corridor, poised for action, the blade end of the chain being swung in a loop at his side. With an almighty roar the demon charged like bull, but when he came close enough to strike Amos had already slid back and was waving the blade in a figure eight movement, slashing the demon's face, chest and arms. Amos blocked a wild punch with his elbow but the force behind it was so strong he slammed into the wall. Seeing that Amos' was unable to retreat, the demon pressed his advantage and unleashed a torrent of punches that smashed relentlessly into Amos. With impressive speed and strength Amos braced against the blows until he spotted an opening in the attack. He parried a strike aimed for his face and snagged the demons arm with the chain. As the demon recoiled and tried to yank Amos closer, Amos thrust the blade tip through the demon's arm and kicked him hard in the stomach. The demon was too heavy for the attack, and the kick simply pushed Amos away. It was as intended, as Amos, able to move freely again, tossed the iron sphere into the air and with the grace and agility of a teenager span through the air and kicked the ball over the demon's shoulder.

"You missed!" said the demon as the ball whizzed past his ear, but when the chain pulled taut the weight of the ball tugged the blade still lodged in the demon's arm against his neck, the tip of which emerged abruptly out the other side. The demon sank to his knees, clutching at the wound in his neck and made a horrible gurgling noise as blood spurted from his mouth and down his chin. Amos stood facing him, panting and wincing from fresh bruises. He yanked on the chain aggressively and the blade freed itself with a meaty squelch. Amos approached the demon and held the blade up to its face.

The steel whined again as blood trickled down the blade's fuller, and dripped from the tip and in his head Amos heard an excited voice yelling, "Put it in his eye mate. Skull fuck him with it!"

Amos ignored it but still glared down at the demon with grim resolve.

"Would you like me to end it, or would you rather bleed out?" he asked quietly.

Unable to articulate words with a throat full of blood, the demon pointed to the blade with his eyes and, allowing his arms to drop to his side, raised his chin so Amos could get a clean shot.

Amos took aim and swung. The strike would have been the end for the demon, but as Amos' hand swiped through the air the blade slid from his grip as though the handle had literally passed through his flesh and landed beside the demon's dangling hand. Before he could consider the matter, the demon capitalised on his confusion and seized the weapon. Thoughts of a dignified death forgotten, the demon rounded on Amos and stabbed at his chest. Amos caught the demon's hand, holding the blade point at bay, but the demon's strength pushed him up off the floor and once again Amos found himself pinned with his back to the wall.

"Just an old man!" gurgled the demon as he pressed the blade harder against Amos who felt the tip start to sink into his chest.

Amos pushed back with all his strength but the demon was overwhelming him and he felt the blade sliding between his ribs.

"Bleeding out's not gonna be an option I'm afraid," sneered the demon giving the blade a twist. "This oughta be pretty quick."

Amos felt his death approaching and he knew there was nothing he could do to stop it. He thought of Ignis and wondered if he would meet his friend again in whatever passed for an afterlife for people like them. And with that amusing thought, he embraced his fate and stopped fighting.

With the pressure released the blade shot forward and sank an inch deep into the wall behind Amos. Yet Amos hadn't died. He had instead slid down the wall and was sat on the floor looking up at the demon who looked as equally surprised as Amos to see him down there.

Not wanting to waste this sudden reprieve, Amos kicked the demon in both knees, snapping them backward. As the demon fell his neck became tangled in the chain dangling from the weapon still stuck in the wall. Amos dived out of the way and grabbed the iron ball, then seizing a handful of chain, threw his weight forward and pulled. The demon clawed at the links bound tight around his neck but he could not get his fingers beneath them. Amos heaved with all his might and the demon's flesh began to split and tear. With a final effort that broke two of his fingers, Amos gave the chain a huge jerk. The demon's head popped off like a champagne cork and landed with a squelchy mundane thud on the ground near Amos' feet.

Amos collapsed on his back and sighed with relief. His body ached, his chest hurt and his head throbbed. Surely, he could just take a minute to catch his breath and wait for a second wind. The moment of tranquillity was ruined almost immediately, by a loud piercing scream that echoed through the corridors.

"For fuck's sake!" groaned Amos.

Several floors below him, Martha Bailey had been found. A hand had smashed through the maintenance hatch and grabbing a handful of hair, had dragged her and the hatch cover onto the platform. Scrambling to her feet she turned to see her aggressor, expecting to see a zombie or some mutilated monster. Instead, she found what looked like a child, dressed in a black hooded cloak. Whoever they were, at three and a half feet tall they didn't seem half as threatening and Martha visibly relaxed.

"DON'T YOU RELAX! DON'T YOU DARE FUCKING RELAX!" raged the child-like person in a surprisingly deep voice.

"It's exactly this…" he continued as he began to pace irately, "…always the same fucking assumption!"

"I'm sorry," said Martha perplexed. "I didn't mean to…"

"To what?" interjected the boy curtly. "To miraculously think you're safe just because the child is here? I just punched through a metal hatch and dragged your fat arse up here like a cuddly toy and yet somehow, I'm not threatening?" he finished incredulously.

Martha shuffled her feet nervously and pulled at the hem of her jumper.

"Please, I don't want to upset you," implored Martha. "I just want to go home."

"Well now!" said the boy with an alarming change in attitude. "That just happens to be something I think I can help you with!"

The abrupt change in the boy's demeanour was very disconcerting and Martha edged away from him slowly.

"You're... you're going to help me?" she asked hesitantly.

"Absolutely!" said the boy with exaggerated enthusiasm. "It happens to be exactly why I'm here."

"I don't understand," said Martha meekly.

A chill was creeping up her spine even though she was very warm. It also seemed to be getting darker. As though the emergency lighting was running out of power. Martha quickly scanned the area looking for escape routes. She knew the ATLAS building very well and if power to the lights cut out, Martha felt certain she could navigate her way to safety in the dark. The boy had been watching her with interest and the furtive quick thinking showing on Martha's face had not escaped his notice.

"You're not leaving, are you?" asked the boy with a mocking chuckle. "I thought you said you wanted to go home."

"I... I do." stammered Martha. "I... I need to go and get my keys," she invented quickly. "I left them in my coat which is upstairs."

As if by magic, the boy produced her coat from behind him and held it up for Martha to see. "This coat?"

Martha swallowed hard and her brain ached with confusion. "How did you get that?" she asked trying hard to keep her voice steady.

"Oh, I found this just lying around," said the boy casually. "Strange..." he added, giving the coat a shake. "It doesn't sound like your keys are there. Not to worry though, I'm pretty sure I have a spare."

The lights had dimmed quite substantially now and nothing could be seen of the boy now but a faint silhouette against the pale concrete floor. With his features now completely hidden in shadow, Martha noticed the boy's eyes which were totally white and glowing just enough to be stark against the black. Caught off guard by the unsettling sight Martha flinched and stumbled backwards toward to the stairwell.

"Um, I wouldn't go that way if were you," said the boy in a ponderous tone. "I haven't a clue how long it's been since they've eaten and I expect you smell quite delicious."

At his words a chorus of deep growls, drawn out rattling breaths and faint howling screams sang out of the growing gloom behind Martha and she froze.

"My, my. You have attracted a lot of attention," said the boy with mild amusement as he glanced around the room. It seemed he had no difficulty seeing in the dark at all.

"Wh… what are they? asked Martha who could no longer hide her fear and was weeping.

"Hard to say," said the boy wryly. "I mean it's not me who's making them so could be anything. I can tell you this though, they're not vegans."

Against her better judgement, Martha took a step closer to the boy and away from the greedy sounding noises that appeared to be getting closer. They were no longer just behind her either. The animalistic grunts and growls were coming from all around them.

"If you're not making them, why are you not afraid?" shrieked Martha, her voice much higher than usual.

"Me! Afraid?" giggled the boy scornfully. "Why on earth would I be frightened?"

The boy strolled over to Martha, took her by the hand and walked her onto the metal bridge that led to the CMS detector. Once in the middle he released her hand and turned to look up at her, his white eyes narrowed to slits.

"Do you want to see them?" he asked with whispered excitement. "Do you finally want to see, after all these years, what they look like?"

Martha blanched at the question and the thought made her insides clench. Her answer was unequivocally 'no', she did not want to see. But the rest of the question had been confusing.

"What do you mean after all these years?"

"You don't remember?" asked the boy, sounding a little disappointed. Several of the creatures lurking in the dark gnashed what sounded like large fangs and snarled angrily.

"Aww, bless, you've hurt their feelings… I honestly didn't think they had any, but there you go."

"Remember what?" whimpered Martha who was holding herself in her arms now.

The boy leaned relaxedly against the rails and rubbed his chin thoughtfully.

"You'd have been about seven years old. You and your parents were staying at that grubby farmhouse in the country and one night you got lost in the woods on the way home."

He started at Martha pensively for a moment, waiting for a glimmer of comprehension. As expected, a distant memory crept into the back of Martha's mind, a memory that was not fond. As dawning recollection spread across her face, the boy gave an unseen grin.

"There you go," he whispered coaxingly. "Do you remember them now?"

Martha didn't answer. Her eyes were wide like saucers, her expression rigid with fright. All she could do was shake her head in mute refusal to accept the nightmarish memory blossoming in her mind.

"You do!" said the boy with a satisfied sigh. "I can see you do. It was so dark and you were so alone. Your little mind racing as the forest creaked and groaned all around." The boy gave a derisive snort. "All those branches that looked like hands, and all those bushes that looked like monsters, your imagination went buck wild on you, didn't it?"

Martha found her voice at last. "I was just a child, my mind was playing tricks on me," she said defensively.

"Quite the trick to make you run all the way home," said the boy.

"What does it matter?" said Martha abruptly. "It wasn't real, it was just in my head!"

"Wasn't real!" repeated the boy. "Wasn't… past tense!"

Light had begun to return to the room, but it wasn't green any more, it was red and at the edge of her vision Martha could see movement in the distance.

"The problem is you made it real," continued the boy indifferent to the increasing illumination. "Your stupid, ignorant mind forced these… things, into existence."

"That's absurd!" cried Martha. "It's not scientifically pos…"

"ISN'T IT?" roared the boy and fire erupted beneath the bridge casting red and orange light in all directions.

Every inch of the room was crawling with monstrous creatures endowed with long spindly limbs, thick protuberant fangs and spiny lizard-like tails. Skin was stretched taught over where eyes would have been and a fleshless nose cavity sniffed hungrily at the air as they clambered over each other like spiders in their hunt for Martha.

"Fuck me!" coughed the boy with half a laugh. "I've had shits that were better looking."

Martha cowered as low as she could against the railing as though the thin bars would be sufficient to hide her and the boy looked down at her in disgust.

"You're all the same," he said contemptuously. "Reckless with your thoughts and quick to forget. No responsibility, no concern for your actions, you're selfish and pathetic."

The horde of creatures had begun to close in on them now. Salivating wildly and fighting amongst themselves to be first in line for feeding.

"I DIDN'T DO ANYTHING!" screamed Martha as one of the monsters placed a front paw on the bridge.

"DIDN'T DO ANYTHING?" raged the boy, incensed. He grabbed a handful of Martha's hair and thrust her face toward the approaching creature that was tasting her on the air. "DOES THAT LOOK LIKE NOTHING TO YOU?"

"Please," whispered Martha desperately. "Why are you doing this?"

The boy shook Martha's head viciously and gave an entirely mirthless laugh.

"This?" repeated the boy nastily. "I'm doing this because I just love fucking with you arrogant pricks. I'm doing this because I enjoy listening to you all screaming and crying and begging for it to stop. I'm doing this because I fucking hate all of you and it has to be said…" the boy placed his lips to Martha's ear and in an almost loving whisper continued, "…I hate your kind most of all!"

"My kind?" wailed Martha helplessly. "What kind? I don't have a kind!"

The boy threw her down in front of the creature and it licked her face leaving a sticky trail of black slime on her cheek.

"Not yet!" said the boy in a commanding tone and the creature withdrew a foot or so. "I will tell you what kind!" he continued with a touch of asperity and rounding on Martha. "You're a cancer. A disease. You infect the natural order and leave nothing but chaos behind you. You and yours are a two-hundred-thousand-year-long plague. You who would be Gods!"

"Gods?" blurted Martha through a thick sob. "What are you talking about? What do Gods have to do with anything?"

"Seriously, don't you have a PhD?" said the boy sardonically. "How are you this stupid? You…" he poked Martha in the forehead, "…are a God!"

Martha struggled to digest this bit of news and her confusion overcame her fear for a moment. "A what?"

"A God!" repeated the boy in a long-suffering voice. "Yes, I know. I'm disappointed too, but the fact remains!"

"Well, I'm obviously not," argued Martha rationally. "I'm a woman of science, I don't go in for religious nonsense."

"Dinner time!" sang the boy and the creature closest to Martha lunged forward and seized her leg in its teeth. It savagely gnawed and tugged at her leg and Martha screamed in agony as the teeth sliced through her calf muscle and cracked her shin bone.

"That's enough!" said the boy calmly and the monster released it jaws.

He then gave Martha a push with his foot and she rolled onto her back still wailing in pain. The boy glared down at her, his face directly above hers.

"You're not listening. This…" he gestured around the room at the encroaching creatures, "…is not nonsense. The hole in your leg is not nonsense. The fact that you are a God, not nonsense. Ridiculous maybe, but not nonsense."

"H… how? When?" cried Martha between wails.

"Well now, I'm glad you asked because that's actually quite interesting," said the boy indifferent to her suffering. "Interesting because of all the ones I've killed so far, you are the only one who actually deserves the title."

"K-killed?" repeated Martha weakly.

"Yes, killed," replied the boy coolly. "No great loss, bunch of posers entirely reliant on the faith of others. But you…" he wagged a finger at Martha, and chuckled with disbelief, "…you did it all on your own. Sod all this omnipotent and omniscient bollocks, you are a true representation of what a God is." The boy held his arms out in a grandiose gesture and the assembled creatures howled in praise. "You, the creator of a universe!"

Chapter Six
His Only Friend

Panting and sweaty, Amos fell against the wall and checked the wound in his chest. The bleeding appeared to have at least stopped but his vision kept swimming in and out of focus and he felt dizzy. He was still experiencing tremor-like vibrations throughout his body too. How long did the fox say they would last? He couldn't remember. A thick fog had encased his brain which made any kind of thinking exhausting.

A faint cacophony of noise drifting up from the bottom of the stairwell met his ears. It sounded busy like the noises from a hive, but he was sure it was not bees. He crept down the stairs, being careful to tread gently and cracked open the door at the bottom just as the din fell quiet and through the silence heard a shrill woman's voice crying her confusion.

"Please, I don't understand. I didn't do anything."

Amos slipped through the door and closed it softly behind him. He could see an orange glow up ahead and from the flickering quality of the light, concluded there must be a fire somewhere near. As he began to sidle down the corridor towards it. However, he heard another voice answer the first.

"Yes, you did," it said churlishly. "You made it… right here in fact, just the other side of those doors."

Amos knew that voice. It was one he was all too familiar with and he wanted to kill the person who owned that voice. He hastened his approach, his blade at the ready.

"The CMS reactor?" asked the woman between sobs. "It's just a tool, it gathers data."

"It's the birthplace of a universe!" corrected the voice Amos knew to be that of the assassin. "All set in motion, by your experiments. Yes, with the hubris of a child who has just found his father's gun you have been firing off shots without thought or concern for what might happen."

142

"My experiments…" began the woman tremulously, "…my experiments made a… a universe?"

"In essentials, yes," replied the assassin. "Though I don't believe you did it all on your own. It's more of a right time, right place sort of thing."

"I don't understand…" began the woman bewildered, but the assassin cut her off.

"How can you be this naive?" he shot at her. "Over a decade of collisions, of particles smashing against one another and always in the same place. How can you not have expected some sort of ramification?" asked the assassin in a spiteful condescending tone.

"Imagine if you will a tennis ball being repeatedly thrown at a brick wall. At the time it seems harmless, the wall is unscathed. But how long before that innocent little ball begins to wear away at the brick and cement, before cracks begin to appear and the wall begins to collapse. This is what you and your colleagues have done to the fabric of space, right here behind this door. That spot is riddled with subatomic fissures and you, you just happened to be the person who fired a particle through one. That innocuous speck of galactic dust tore through into the empty void between the multiverse and exploded. The resulting blast forced apart the void creating a brand-new universe in its wake."

Amos rolled the iron ball attached to his weapon around the corner and waited. Concentrating hard he said in his head, "How many?"

A whine of steel sang from the blade and in his mind heard the reply, "Loads mate. Hundreds by the look of it. You sure you want to do this?"

"Want is a strong word!" thought Amos. "But there is little choice in the matter. She's one of them and we need her alive!"

The blade sang again. "No offence Amos, but ain't no one coming out of this alive. You're good, but you ain't that good!"

"Thanks, Jack!" thought Amos grimly. "Your confidence in me is staggering."

"Just keeping it real, mate!" sang the weapon in his head. "So how're we doing this? Just gonna wing it?"

"Something like that!" thought Amos as he raised the iron ball by the chain and began to swing it to gain momentum.

"That doesn't make me a God!" screamed the woman painfully. "It's just an accident, a random event."

"Tell that to those who live there," sneered the assassin.

"To… what?" sobbed the woman in a baffled tone.

"There is a planet in this universe of yours," explained the assassin calmly. "A planet very much like this one. A planet where civilization and society has flourished much like it has here. The creatures that roam the world are humanoid in appearance, though quite different in features, and they, like the idiots here, put a lot of store, in religion." He paused for reflection but then with a snort of derision added. "However, unlike the uneducated fools of earth, they actually guessed correctly."

"Im… impossible!" wailed the woman. "Ten years is not long enough for anything to…"

"Ten years to you maybe. For them it has been several millennia and that has been more than enough time to develop an understanding of their material world. They postulated with surprising accuracy how their universe came into being, they even suspected it to be an accident."

The assassin gave a harsh laugh.

"They haven't got a clue what you look like, they don't even know if you're a man or a woman, but nevertheless, statues stand proud in every city, great monolithic androgynous figures that overlook the populace and all in homage to you."

Amos peered around the corner and took in the scene. Illuminated by a fire raging beneath a metal bridge were hundreds of squirming, misshapen bodies clinging to every surface of the room. They were eyeless and blind but their massive mouths bore monstrous fangs which drooled oily black slime down their pointed chins. On the bridge itself, Amos could see the assassin. He was pacing leisurely around a woman who was lying on the ground, clutching a bloody wound on her leg and crying miserably. As he looked on, the assassin seized the woman's top and lifted her roughly off the floor so they were face to face. He crept closer, still swinging the ball, he knew the assassin was about to strike.

"Full circle," growled the assassin in a low threatening tone. "It ends where it all began. Time to go home."

The assassin drew back his fist and muttered an incantation Amos had never heard before. A spider web bloomed before the assassin's knuckles, with the familiar series of symbols spiralling from the centre. The web glowed bright orange as the flames reflected off the threads. It hovered before his fist and Amos finally realised how the unhealing wounds were made.

Martha screamed in terror, she knew she was going to die and dreaded the end. But before the blow could land, the iron ball Amos had been swinging flew through the air, crashing into the side of the assassin's head and knocking him off balance. He dropped Martha as he stumbled sideways and fell to the floor. In a transport of rage, the assassin bashed his fists into the bridge floor and roared his irritation. He looked over to see who had disturbed him but the creatures lining the room had already swamped them. The sound of flesh tearing, blood splatting and bones breaking rent the air and the assassin raised himself up looking annoyed, but satisfied.

"Well, there goes the cavalry!" he chuckled dispassionately at Martha who was also watching the carnage. "Now, where were we?"

The assassin readied his strike again, but to his dismay, a yell of anger that was distinctly human burst from the swarm of bodies. One of the creatures tore in half and a fountain of scarlet decorated the riot with blood and bits of meat. In the middle of the throng and visible in the gap where the creature had been was Amos, maddened beyond recognition, shirtless and busy tearing open one of the monster's jaws with his bare hands.

The assassin did a double take. His body language betrayed alarm. It was clear he was unsettled by the appearance of this man and Martha had noticed.

"HELP!" yelled Martha as loud as she could, her last hope placed in this unexpected stranger.

"Shut it!" spat the assassin, backhanding her across the face and dislodging one of her teeth.

Panicking slightly, the assassin began to summon the web over his fist again, but he seemed to be struggling to get it going as he stammered through the incantation. Moments later the attempt was abandoned as Amos broke free and crashed against the assassin, wielding a dismembered creature's arm like a sword. The assassin blocked Amos' attack easily but he was not prepared for the amount of strength Amos had put behind it and he collapsed under the force and clanged loudly against the metal grid that was the bridge floor. Amos' face looked deranged, insane even and he didn't seem to notice the punches to his ribs the assassin was delivering as he pressed the severed arm against the assassin's throat, determined to choke him with it.

The assassin squeezed his feet up against Amos' chest and kicked out hard. Amos flew feet away and landed in front of the door to the CMS reactor where he found Jack, his blade and companion, on the ground beside him. Rallying at once, Amos sprang to his feet and charged at the assassin, his surprisingly large muscles bulging as he built up momentum in the chain. They met with a storm of punches and kicks that echoed through the chamber like a drum roll. The assassin ducked and weaved, avoiding Amos' strikes but it was with difficulty. The blade skimmed the edge of the assassin's hood as he parried a thrust, attempting to lock Amos' arm, but Amos swung the ball around his back which wrapped around them both and struck the assassin hard in the soft tissue on his back. He let out a yelp of pain and Amos wrenched his arm free but the chain had bound them together. Retreat was not an option.

Clash of elbow against elbow ensued as close quarters combat began. Vicious blows slipped through guards, breaking ribs, chipping teeth and blackening eyes. For several long minutes the pair fought on with speed and vigour and Martha took the opportunity to drag herself to safety.

After what seemed like an age, she reached the electronic lock that controlled the huge heavy door that led to the reactor. She tapped a code into the keypad and an alarm rang out as the circular slab of steel hissed open.

Distracted, the assassin glanced over and saw Martha crawling through the gap in the door and into the reactor work space. The moment of inattention cost him dearly as Amos' fist connected with his nose. Blood sprayed out from under the assassin's hood and he reeled from the impact. Like a bent spring let go, the assassin lurched forward and head-butted Amos in the forehead. The chain snapped as Amos recoiled and fell to the floor dazed and the assassin, abandoning the fight, dashed for the circular door as Martha's feet disappeared behind it and the door began to close.

Amos was not done, and grabbing the blade half of his weapon chased after him. He caught him at the door's threshold and they clattered inside as the door hissed shut with a soft clunk.

Martha continued screaming as the fight resumed in front of her, the combatants rolling over each other, the blade weaving between their hands. The assassin caught a wild swing, trapped Amos' arm and slammed his head against the concrete. The blade exposed, the assassin slipped out from under Amos' weight and snatched it. His eyes fixed on Martha. He had to end it now.

Amos pushed himself to his feet and threw himself in front of Martha, if he was going to die anyway it would be like this, as a shield between the monsters and the weak. For a fleeting instant, the assassin hesitated and something like sadness flickered across the white eyes beneath the hood. But his grip on the blade tightened, as did his resolve. The web bloomed before his fist, reflecting in Amos' worn and tired eyes and the assassin pounced. A flash of steel cut the space as the sharp edge passed over Amos' throat. But in that moment, a tremor flooded through Amos and he vibrated so violently he looked translucent and the blade, so true in its aim, passed through his neck as though it wasn't there. The assassin had not noticed however, and continued past Amos, his enchanted attack directed at Martha. Amos spun on the spot and tried to grab the assassin to stop him but he was just out of reach. His fingertips caught only at the hood of the cloak which fell back to reveal a shock of flame red hair. Amos watched in horror as the assassin, unaware of the reveal, struck Martha square in the chest. Blood ejected from numerous tiny cuts across Martha's torso and she slid to the floor gasping as a dark red pool formed beneath her.

The assassin turned to look at Amos and was mortified to see him still standing and wearing an expression of such hurt and betrayal he had tears swimming in his eyes. It was then that he realised his hood had fallen and Ignis stared back at Amos with a mixture of guilt and defiance.

For a while Amos just gazed at Ignis, a pained expression twisting his features. Oblivious to the sounds of Martha dying, he just stood there. His world had broken. It could not be. He could not believe it.

Ignis reached out to Amos, but Amos recoiled away from him looking disgusted.

Ignis searched for words to explain, to make Amos understand but before he could summon up any kind of excuse a light, vast and bright erupted beside them. In less than a second it had grown to immense proportions, filling the room and obscuring everything from sight. Amos and Ignis felt a tremendous pulse of energy course between them, punching their ribs and then with the sound of an explosion so loud it hurt their ears, the light collapsed in on itself and for a moment everything was black. When their eyes adjusted, they found Martha standing with her back to them and staring into the empty, endless abyss of space. They felt a cold rush of air push past them and into the void as if the room had gently decompressed.

Dominating the lower half of their view was a colossal galaxy which glowed a yellowish orange from the light of countless stars littering the arms that spiralled out from the centre. A whirlpool galaxy and one of thousands scattered in the distance.

"Is this it?" murmured Martha weakly. "Is this where they live?"

But there was no time to answer. Like water down a drain, the galaxy was being sucked away by something humongous and black. It drifted across space, warping their view of the galaxy and other celestial bodies behind it. An arm of the galaxy wrapped around the black monster as it tore away from the whole and hovered like a disc around the centre before it was devoured completely.

The black hole ripped through the galaxy without mercy, unfeeling and indifferent, until it was so large that all Amos, Ignis and Martha could see was the tumble of nebulas and stars as they spaghettified into the event horizon and were crushed. Martha staggered and fell to her knees. Her face was pale and grey. Despite this though her expression was one of contentment, as though she couldn't have wished to see anything more amazing and awe inspiring than this right here.

"It's so beautiful," she muttered quietly before she fell into the abyss and was gone.

"IGNIS, NO! YOU DAMN FOOL, WHAT HAVE YOU DONE?" roared Amos. His body was vibrating worse than ever and he felt like he was coming apart at the seams.

"Amos!" cried Ignis, panicked and he ran to his friend. He tried to hold him but his arms just passed through him. "What's happening?" he yelled staring at his hands uselessly.

"How could you?" murmured Amos weakly as the vibration increased. "You were my friend."

"I still am!" pleaded Ignis desperately as tears streamed down his cheeks. "I'll always be your friend."

"No!" whispered Amos contemptuously. "You are… a traitor."

Amos let out a long painful scream as the molecules in his body began to separate and float away like sand in a sea breeze. With Amos' bitter words still ringing in his ears, Ignis watched helplessly as Amos' body disintegrated before him and drifted away into the black of space and toward the black hole consuming creation.

Suddenly, as if it had never been there, the vastness of space shrank into nothing, imploding in on itself and returning the room to normal. No trace of Martha remained, not even a blood stain and Ignis remained on his knees and hung his head sadly. There was no sign of Amos either. A moment later he broke into tears and wept uncontrollably with his head in his hands. He punched the floor hard in anger. Punched it again and again till the crater in the concrete turned red and when punching was no longer enough, he raised his head to the heavens and gave a terrible, earth-shaking scream. Fire flooded out of him, burning his pain and fuelling his hate. He felt the last of his humanity incinerate inside his soul. Whatever love he had left for this world had just drifted into space with Amos.

When the fire cooled and his temper calmed, he tore the charred cloak from his shoulders, then raising his hands into the cool dark room, whistled in multiple tones.

"Ignis!" barked Frank with surprise. "You're alive! Fuck me, I thought we'd lost you. Did Amos find you? He went there too…" He paused a moment. He'd just noticed the solemn expression on Ignis' face. "What's wrong?" he asked hurriedly.

Ignis didn't answer immediately, he was breathing heavily and sagging under his own weight. He gave Frank a look of absolute incredulity and when he spoke his voice was thick with sadness. "Why did you send him here?"

"I didn't," said Frank defensively. "He sent himself. Used that orb thing you gave him and summoned the Kitsune."

"He what?" coughed Ignis with half a laugh. "He didn't!"

"Oh yes he did and right in the middle of Nottingham!" blustered Frank who was still visibly affronted by the lack of discretion Amos had shown. "Surrounded by hundreds of people too. I haven't even dared to check social media."

Frank peered around from inside Ignis' hands as though expecting Amos to be there.

"Where is he anyway?"

The happy thought of Amos summoning a magical fox in the middle of a crowded street vanished as quickly as it came. Swallowed by a flash of flame.

"He's dead!" said Ignis coldly. "He's fucking dead! That thing killed him!"

It took a few seconds for this information to penetrate Frank's skull. When it did, his face fell, aghast.

"He... he's dead? asked Frank feebly. "Amos? Dead?"

Ignis simply nodded his confirmation. He didn't want to have to say it again.

"I can't believe it," said Frank reeling. "Not Amos! Not now!"

A prolonged silence fell between them as the gravity of this loss sank in. Frank lit a cigarette and drew deep. He exhaled the smoke with a defeated sigh and wiping an errant tear from his cheek said. "I'm sorry, Ignis. I truly am."

Another drawn out silence followed his words until Frank asked quietly. "I don't suppose you found one of those mortal gods while you were there?"

Ignis gave a sober nod. "A scientist. But she's dead too," he said tonelessly.

"And the assassin?" continued Frank in a careful whisper.

"Gone! For now, anyway," replied Ignis. "Just get me back," he added irritably. "I don't want to be here any more."

"Nephthys should be back with Shui any minute, I'll send her your way as soon as she arrives."

Ignis gave a curt nod to show his understanding and broke his hands apart, letting them hang at his side. His fingers brushed something metal and Ignis looked down to see the remains of Amos' weapon lying next to him and covered in blood.

Ignis slid the blade half of Jack toward him and wrapped the broken chain around his hand. He gave the handle an almost affectionate squeeze before wiping the blade clean with his shirt.

"I'm sorry, Amos," he whispered.

Chapter Seven
Suicide Squad Assemble

An argument was raging in the elemortal lounge when Ignis and Nephthys eventually arrived back. Shui and Hoowo3oow were at loggerheads about something and as usual when Shui was involved it looked about to come to blows. Alerted to Ignis' presence, by the whooshing of purple flames, they broke apart awkwardly and sat at opposite ends of the room.

Frank had already relayed the catastrophic news about Amos and the scientist to the group and no one quite seemed to know what to do with themselves. Even Nephthys, to whom life and death were usually of equal amusement, had been brought to tears by the loss of Amos, something no one had realised could happen until now. Even more alarming was the sight of Shui comforting her. Apparently, they had bonded in Russia but no one knew how and Elsu and Gyasi refused to comment on the matter, as if the memory of their mission was too traumatic to revisit.

The first thing Ignis had noticed on his return was a framed photo of Amos resting on a tall legged stand in front of the weather window which showed a glorious sunset sky that was adorned with gold plated clouds. He walked over to the photo in a daze, paying no attention to the others in the room and picked it up.

He stared at it for minute before caressing the glass and returning it to the stand. In the absence of a body, it was customary to bury a personal item in the departed soul's place, but Amos was so minimalistic and carried anything of real value in his jacket, which was gone. The only thing that remained was Jack, the chained blade that was still wrapped in his hand. Ignis knew who Jack was and the fact that he knew had been their dirty little secret since Amos was a child, it had become a long running inside joke. Aside from not wanting to part with this last keepsake, Ignis didn't want anyone else to know who had been Amos' advisor during fights. He knew Amos wouldn't like it. So instead Ignis reached up, and using Jack, sliced off a hank of his own hair and tucked it behind a ribbon on the corner of the photo. When he turned back to face the room everyone hurriedly looked the other way as if ashamed to be intruding on his grief.

The lift to the lounge hissed and Ignis looked up to see Alex enter the room with Chloe and the nephilim. From the look on their faces, they too knew what had occurred this evening and it was obviously weighing heavy. The nephilim dragged his guitar apathetically behind him, shocked at a death so quickly into his stay and a look of uncertainty drawn upon his features. Chloe was carrying herself in such a dignified manner that she was almost unrecognisable and although tears fell steadily over her cheeks, her face remained completely composed. In stark contrast to them both, Alex had rushed over to Ignis the second she had seen him and dropping to her knees had dragged him into a tight, two-armed hug.

He was so disarmed by the gesture that he didn't resist and he sank into her embrace as though she were a blanket. The skin of her neck pressed against Ignis' cheek and the soft muted warmth of it made him feel somehow weaker. As Alex held him closer and he felt her heart beat against his chest, a great swell of emotion rose up inside him and throwing his arms around her neck, he began to cry in earnest. Alex cradled him to the floor and held him until he fell still. She stroked his hair and Ignis felt a pang of guilt for taking comfort from her touch. He did not deserve to be comforted, not for this.

The lift doors hissed open again and Chloe's mother, Cassandra, entered the room escorted by Richard and Wade. They quickly shuffled off to the kitchen and took a seat under the remonstratory glare of Shui who seemed determined to let Ignis have a moment to grieve properly.

For a time, no one knew how long, everyone sat in a mournful and respectful silence until Frank, opting to forgo the usual holographic presence, entered the room carrying an old book. The book was bound in dark red leather and inlaid with gold lettering on the front which read 'Amos Cromwell' and beneath it in smaller letters, 'Elemortal Steward'.

Shui recognised the book as one similar to the one she had taken from Wun Chuan's wake. It contained a record of their deeds and accomplishments during their time at the Conclave. This written hard copy would be on display for guests to read until the end of the ceremony at which point the elemortal the steward had served would add it to their ever-growing personal library of long-lost heroes.

Frank placed the book on the stand and opened it to the first page of records. The first line read:

1898 — Amos adopted by Conclave at age four.

"Wow!" cooed Frank in a low voice. "1898? You had a good run."

He turned and crouched down beside Ignis who was still huddled against Alex and patted him kindly on the shoulder.

"He was a great man!" said Frank staunchly, "Proud of the work you did."

Ignis' insides writhed uncomfortably and he turned away from Frank to hide his grimace.

"It's all right mate," said Frank consolingly. "He loved his life and he loved you, right until his final breath."

Amos' last words rang in Ignis' ears again. 'You are a traitor!' He had a sudden flashback of Amos' face and the disgust he saw upon it at the end. The hatred behind the words, the contempt in his voice. It was too much, he felt sick. He lurched forward and clutched at his chest, his heart was hammering. He was breathing fast and shallow and his skin had gone very white. Frank stood up in alarm, embarrassed at triggering such a response but Alex rubbed Ignis' back soothingly and he began to calm down.

"Shhh! It's OK!" she said softly. "Deep breaths, it's OK!"

Shui stared at Ignis with a mix of pity and surprise. As long as she had known him Ignis had never had a panic attack and he had been through things that would have caused one. But then Ignis had never had such a close relationship with a steward before. Her surprised turned to sympathy as she thought of Wun Chuan and how her loss had affected her. To an elemortal, losing a steward was like losing a child. It was why Ignis was usually so distant with his companions, death for them was always inevitable. But something about Amos had captivated him right from the start. That Amos reached such an old age, the oldest steward ever recorded in fact, and that he and Ignis had so much more time together, would probably make his loss all the worse. One thing Shui could be certain of was that lying on the floor in an emotional mess while everyone stood around and gormed at Ignis was not going to do him any favours.

"Alex, bring him over here," said Shui gesturing to the sofa. "Frank, do you want to get started."

His conscience pricking, Frank stood up and quickly activated a camera which displayed him on screens across the institute. He grabbed the book from the stand and turning to address those present, cleared his throat.

"It is with great sadness that we say farewell to our friend and colleague, Amos Cromwell," he began hoarsely. "A man who dedicated his whole life to protecting others and upholding the values of the Conclave. Never has there been a man more kind and fairer than Amos. Those that knew him benefitted from his wisdom and warm heart and his absence has diminished us all. The Conclave, indeed the world, owes him a debt but it is one that can never be repaid. We can only try to live up to his example so his legacy lives on."

Frank paused a moment while he sifted through the pages and cleared his throat a few more times.

"I will now read a few of his finer accomplishments and contributions made in service of the Conclave."

For the next hour the institute was alive with joy and laughter as the building was regaled with stories about Amos' adventures. Almost everyone had a tale to tell and they were getting wilder and wilder as the evening drew on. Even Nephthys made an effort to join in, although her stories, while full of affection, had a tendency to end up with her and Amos being found in a compromising position by local authorities. Shui shot Cassandra a filthy look about halfway through the ceremony when, as Wade was entertaining them all with a story about Amos getting drunk with a Strigoi he'd buried earlier, Cassandra's phone rang noisily. With embarrassed haste she had reached blindly into her bag and silenced the call but Shui could still hear the phone vibrate repeatedly inside the bag and privately wondered who needed to speak to her this much.

At the end of the ceremony, after toasts were made in Amos' honour and people began to mill about conversing amongst themselves, Shui impeded Cassandra as she moved to get a drink and pushed her into a corner next to the nephilim who was strumming gently on his two-necked guitar, playing 'Freebird' by Lynard Skynard.

"What was so damned important that you needed to be called twenty-four times during a funeral?" hissed Shui menacingly.

Cassandra looked taken aback at being accosted like this, but became much more perturbed when she tried to push Shui off her and discovered her unmovable.

"What do you think you're doing?" said Cassandra indignantly. "Are your parents here?" she added glancing around the room. "Let me go this instant!"

"Your phone!" said Shui impatiently. "Gimme!" and she held out her hand waiting.

"I will not!" muttered Cassandra as she squirmed against Shui's grip. "How are you so strong?" she demanded in bewilderment.

"Because reasons!" said Shui dismissively and quick as a flash, she reached inside Cassandra's bag with her free hand and withdrew the phone. She powered up the screen and saw twenty-four missed calls from...

"Gross!" said Shui, reading the name and then tossing the phone back to Cassandra in disgust. "You interrupted Amos' funeral for a booty call?"

Perplexed, Cassandra hastened to see the screen herself and her jaw fell open as she read the name.

"Oh my god!" she shrieked, loud enough to catch everyone's attention and to cause the nephilim to falter in his playing. "It's Bernard!"

Ignis snapped his head around, a look of surprise and anger flaring on his face. 'Impossible!' he thought disbelievingly.

Aarde sprang to his feet, as did Hoowo3oow and they both stared at Frank in amazement. Shui snatched the phone from Cassandra, only to have it snatched off her by Frank.

"Professor S..." began Frank quizically.

"It's him!" interrupted Cassandra loudly. She couldn't bear the thought of having the name read aloud.

"Quick, call him back!" said Frank passing the phone back to her and chewing on his fingernail.

Fumbling through the display, Cassandra shakily found Bernard's contact details and pressed 'call'. A few tense seconds dragged by as the dial tone whispered through the suddenly silent lounge.

"May I?" asked Frank, switching the phone to loud speaker without waiting for a reply.

After seven rings the line connected and a deep gruff voice answered in a relieved rush.

"Cassandra, thank God! I was really worried. Are you OK?" said Bernard Godfrey in one breath.

"Bernard, I'm fine," Cassandra reassured him. "But where have you been, I called you weeks ago and have tried every day since... I thought you were dead!"

"My dear, I'm so sorry," said Bernard sadly. "I had to travel in an emergency and was in such a rush to leave I left my phone behind. When I got back, saw how many calls I'd missed and heard that message from some guy called Mr Cromwell, I'm afraid I too thought the worst."

"What happened?" pressed Cassandra. "Where did you go?"

"France," said Bernard and he sounded disheartened. "My friend, Alfred..."

Frank and Wade exchanged a meaningful look.

"He... he passed away a few months ago," continued Bernard quietly. "I had no idea until his solicitor called and informed me, I'd been named as executor for his estate."

"I'm so sorry, Bernard," said Cassandra kindly. "Are you OK?"

He gave a deep regretful sigh. "I'd been meaning to visit him for a while," he began sorrowfully. "We hadn't spoke for a couple of months which was unusual and he hadn't been replying to..." he broke off and breathed tremulously. "He was murdered, Cass. Murdered! And the bastards burned down his house too."

"Oh, Bernard, you poor thing," wept Cassandra who had been moved to tears.

"I'll be all right!" said Bernard, his voice stronger. "It was just a bit of a shock. I just hope they catch who did it. Where are you anyway? I don't suppose you still need me to come and fetch you?" he asked jokily.

Frank waved in front of Cassandra's face to get attention and mouthed silently "Where is he?" before pointing repeatedly at the phone.

"Er, no!" replied Cassandra awkwardly. "I'll come to you. Are you at home?"

"I am my dear," said Bernard happily. "When should I expect you? I'll have some tea ready."

Frank silently asked for Bernard's address while handing Cassandra a pen and paper. When it was written, Frank thrust the address into Nephthys' hand who, to Cassandra's horror, vanished in a whirl of purple flame.

The phone in Cassandra's hand crackled loudly and Bernard could suddenly be heard yelling at what sounded like an intruder.

"Who the bloody hell are you?" he raged. "Get out of my house right now. Get out I say, you mad woman, before I…"

The phone gave another loud crackle, and a second later, violet flames erupted beside them which spat out Nephthys and Bernard into the lounge. Bernard was surprisingly tall and had long, thick chin-length white hair. Despite his age he was still very broad and straight backed and cut an impressive figure in his grey tailored suit.

"Call the police and have you arres…" continued Bernard, until he suddenly realised he wasn't in his living room any more. "What the devil?"

"What the devil?" said Nephthys with a scornful raise of her eyebrows. "What are you giving him credit for? I brought you here, not him!"

Bernard seemed to teeter on the edge of a response for a moment but then his eyes found everyone else and his mind seized. Cassandra ran forward and hugged Bernard, snapping him out of his stupor. She looked as alarmed as he did, people didn't routinely teleport though tunnels of purple fire in the archives, and her panic seemed to steady Bernard.

"Will someone please explain what's going on here!" he demanded in his deep gravelly voice. "Where am I? How did you bring me here?"

Frank stepped forward, his hands raised submissively. "Mr Godfrey," he said in a calm and quiet tone. "My name is Frank."

He held out his hand for Bernard to shake, but Bernard had already redirected his attention back to Cassandra.

"What's is all this?" he asked her firmly. "Who are these people?"

Before Cassandra could respond, the sound of hurried footsteps came from behind her and before Bernard knew what was happening, Ignis had grabbed a hold of his jacket and had lifted him angrily into the air.

"What the…?" yelled Bernard with fright.

He had not spotted Ignis approaching.

Ignis walked over to the stand that bore Amos' photo and slammed Bernard down in front of it. He then grabbed a handful of Bernard's white hair and pushed his face close to the photo of Amos. Bernard tried to resist, but he found Ignis to be too strong and was easily overwhelmed.

"These people," he began scathingly, "have just saved your life."

He then gestured to Amos' photo.

"This man was one of 'these people'," he continued bitterly, " and he died because you…" he poked Bernard painfully on the side of his head, "…forgot your phone."

Ignis let go of Bernard with another rough push of his head and stood to leer down at him.

"The least you can do is listen to why we bothered," he said in a menacing undertone. "Then we can decide if your life was a fair trade."

"Mr Godfrey…" interposed Frank with a nervous glance at Ignis, and Bernard turned to look at him. "I think you will want to hear what we have to say," he added, holding out his hand again to help Bernard to his feet.

Bernard took it this time and pulled himself up with a grunt. Straightening his jacket and shirt, he glared at Frank with indignation but when he spoke it was in a somewhat subdued and careful tone.

"And what would that be?" he asked with a cautious look at Ignis.

"Well for a start we know what happened to your friend, Alfred," said Frank matter-of-factly.

Whatever Bernard had been expecting to hear, it wasn't that.

The tale of what had happened to Alfred rocked Bernard to his core. But when he insisted on seeing the video as proof, he became quite sick and was forced to find a seat as his legs began to wobble. As if that wasn't enough to process, Frank ploughed on with an explanation of Bernard's own status as an accidental God, how the supernatural world actually exists, which Nephthys happily demonstrated by transforming back into her Bathin form, and how the assassin who had murdered his friend had been on a killing spree and was probably hunting him too. Unable to form coherent sentences to voice the million questions he had rattling around in his skull, Bernard had spluttered himself into a subdued silence. When Frank's brutally honest lecture culminated in Bernard being told he would need to travel beyond the mortal world to hunt giant spiders and stop a potential demon invasion, he stood up, asked where the toilet was, and after locking himself inside, was violently sick.

"He took that well!" said Shui sarcastically as she placed her ear to the bathroom door and heard him give another distressed wretch followed by the sound of liquid splashing. "Should make our jaunt into the other realms a real breeze."

Cassandra seemed to have found her voice again, and with a shriek of hysterics, rounded on Richard.

"You knew about all this?" she asked sounding hurt and scandalised.

Richard, who had been quietly minding his own business and eating a sandwich from the buffet, choked in alarm.

"Weeks I've been here. Weeks!" Cassandra continued, incensed. "And all these things I've been translating, antique spell books and scrolls on demons… you're telling me they're all real? What if I'd set something off by accident?"

Richard was quailing under the distraught look Cassandra was giving him so Frank dived forward and redirected her attention.

"Mrs Gibson, please calm down," he said imploringly. "It's not his fault. I told him not to say anything, if you want to blame anyone, blame me."

Cassandra stared intently at Frank, and her lips screwed together tightly as she fought to hold back the torrent of abuse she was dying to hurl at him. As Cassandra glared around the room at her colleagues, she felt stung by the realisation that no one else seemed surprised by any of this. All of them knew which must have meant that all of them had been lying.

"Did you know all about this too?" she snapped at Alex who looked nettled by her tone.

"I did," replied Alex coolly.

"But you're just a teacher!" raged Cassandra in disbelief.

"I was just a teacher!" corrected Alex disdainfully. "These days I am Chloe's dovetail. Suffice to say it has been an educational experience for both of us."

"Dovetail?" repeated Cassandra. "What the hell are you talking about? I thought this place was an educational institute. What have you been doing with my daughter?"

"I have been caring for her as no one else seemed to be bothered!" spat Alex who was now squaring up to Cassandra.

"And what's that supposed to mean?" snarled Cassandra in a posture of equal confrontation.

"It means I've taught your daughter for three years and I haven't seen you or her father once!" roared Alex with brutal honesty. "You haven't shown the slightest interest in her progress, I doubt you have even the remotest idea of how remarkable your child is. No, you are too consumed with your own shit to give a fuck about anyone but yourself."

Cassandra glowered indignantly and her face turned a blotchy red colour, but before she could retort Alex pressed on. "Have you even thanked her?"

Cassandra blanched as a confused grimace spread over her features. She had no response, but she had no idea what Alex meant either.

"I didn't think so," said Alex smugly. "Escaped your attention I expect, I mean she only saved your life, an easy thing to overlook, I'm sure."

"Saved my... what do you mean?" said Cassandra with a bewildered glance at Chloe who was standing next to Richard and stealing food off his plate.

"At the parade you stupid cow!" barked Shui who was feeling Alex's plight on this one. "That assassin was going to gut you like a fish and he would have done too, if Chloe hadn't used the same supernatural abilities you claim not to know about, to appear out of nowhere and block his knife."

Something stirred in a dark corner of Cassandra's brain. It niggled like an itch that couldn't be scratched and no matter how hard she concentrated, Cassandra could not summon the information hiding there, like it was hidden behind white noise and static.

"That is one seriously selective memory you have there!" sneered Shui. "Let's see what else you've repressed." Shui looked at her thoughtfully for

161

a moment and then said, "At the parade, that assassin spoke to you before he tried to kill you. He was all excited and distracted because he'd seen you there and he went out of his way to attack you."

Ignis looked at Shui with the slightest turn of his head and could feel concern creasing his face. Clenching hard on his back teeth he forced his expression to remain neutral and listened carefully.

"I want to know why he would risk losing his target for you," continued Shui in an accusatory tone. "I want to know what he said and I want to know now!"

"I… I don't know what you mean." argued Cassandra as she strained to remember. "What assassin? What parade?"

"Are you fucking kidding me?" said Shui disbelievingly. "The Remembrance Day parade!" she continued in a slow patronising tone.

"The parade?" repeated Cassandra quietly before her face dropped as something finally clunked into place. In a transport of panic as flashes of her attempted murder reeled through her mind, Cassandra wailed miserably and sank to her knees with her arms held over her head.

"He was… he was going to kill me!" she screamed so abruptly it gave Frank a turn. "Who was he? Why would he hurt me?"

She looked around beseechingly and saw Chloe.

"My baby!" she cried, getting up and running over to her. "Are you OK?" she said checking her for injuries.

"Mother! Calm down!" said Chloe in a kind but firm tone.

There was a commanding edge in the way she spoke, like it sounded fuller and carried more weight than usual. More interestingly still was that Cassandra did calm down. Her whole body had relaxed and she felt an impulse to sit on the floor. Chloe placed a half-eaten sandwich on Richard's plate and knelt down to look her mother in the eyes.

"There is nothing to be afraid of!" continued Chloe in the same soft but authoritative voice. "You are safe here and so am I!"

She patted her mother's hand soothingly and with a glance at Shui said firmly, "What did the boy in the hood say to you?"

Unseen by anyone, Ignis repositioned the blade called Jack in his hand and loosened the chain in preparation for a throw as his eyes burned into the back of Chloe's skull.

"He... he said he thought..." said Cassandra in a vacant and slightly monotonous voice, "...he thought it would take longer... to find me... and something about opening presents."

"Thanks, Mum. You can relax now," said Chloe in the strange soft but dominating voice, to which Cassandra obediently stared glassy eyed into the distance with a faint smile pulling at the corners of her mouth.

Frank gawped at Shui in bewilderment but she looked as bemused as he did and could only reply with surprised shrug of her shoulders.

Oblivious to the amazement being shown, Chloe got to her feet and continued eating her sandwich while stroking her mother's hair in a placating manner.

"He's a lunatic!" grumbled Hoowo3oow impatiently. "Only serial killers talk about opening people like presents, he just likes killing."

"Dude, you threatened to open Simon from HR 'like a present' last week," said Aarde fairly.

"Yes!" growled Hoowo3oow menacingly. "And I'm very good at killing!"

"He's got a point," said Frank peaceably before adding under his breath, "They can smell their own!" which made Shui chuckle and Ignis relax.

A few minutes later, Bernard re-emerged from the bathroom. He was still a little pale and his skin wet with water from the sink, but he had an air of determination about him and when he walked it was with purposeful steps.

"How are you feeling? Would you like a drink?" asked Frank cautiously.

"Some water if you don't mind," said Bernard, his voice hoarse.

Alex passed him a glass and he drained the contents in four deep, grateful gulps and sighing with relief, fixed Frank with an intrigued stare.

"When it comes to all things religious..." began Bernard ponderously, "I've made a career out of being the smartest man in the room. I thought I knew it all," he added sadly. "But what you've told me... and shown me..." he ran his hand through his hair and flattened his beard. "It makes my doctorate in theology seem childish and naive."

"Don't be so hard on yourself," said Frank sympathetically. "It's not every day you get promoted to deity."

Bernard grinned weakly.

"I'm not pretending to understand everything that's going on, there's a lot I still don't get," he said honestly. "But what I saw of Alfred's death is enough for me. If a journey to another world is the only way to get justice for my friend, then count me in."

"Wh… really?" asked Frank, his eyebrows raised in delight.

"I think I have one more expedition in me," said Bernard stoutly. "Besides, what scholar would pass on an offer like this?"

"Well in that case, I'd best introduce you to the rest of the team," said Frank happily, amazed for once at their good fortune.

Surprisingly, Ignis was first to make himself available for proper introduction and when they faced each other Ignis made a great effort to look suitably contrite.

"I'm sorry," said Ignis shamefacedly. "For before, I shouldn't have manhandled you like that!"

"You're stronger than you look," said Bernard respectfully. "I guess there's more to you than meets the eye as well?"

"Ignis is an elemortal," said Frank. "Just like Shui, Aarde and Hoowo3oow," he added as he gestured to them in turn.

"A what?" asked Bernard excitedly. "I've never heard the term before, is it Mesopotamian?"

"No," said Frank. "They aren't part of any religion or cultural folklore."

"Yeah!" laughed Shui dryly. "We're more like a homebrew kind of thing!"

"Homebrew? You mean you made them yourselves?" asked Bernard flabbergasted.

"Well not us personally," said Frank apologetically. "I mean they're seven thousand years old so it's a bit before my time, but yes, they were created by the Conclave."

"Seven thousand years?" gasped Bernard who was now examining Ignis more closely. "You look barely older than seven."

A shared look of consternation passed between the elemortals. Being seven years old for eternity was a long running gripe they all knew too well.

"Seven was considered the safest outer limit for our strength and abilities," said Ignis in an emotionless tone. "They didn't realise how powerful we could become until they'd already begun and unfortunately for us, they started when we were babies."

"Sadly so," said Frank sympathetically. "As I understand it, the founders feared the level of collateral damage their abilities would cause if they continued to increase their power. Part of that fear was exposure of their practices and fringe methods but most of all they feared annihilation."

"Armageddon!" said Shui, smiling at the quizzical look on Bernard's face. "They didn't want us to be powerful enough to destroy the planet."

Bernard glanced at Frank with his eyebrows raised as if to question the validity of Shui's statement.

"It's true," confirmed Frank. "If they were reattached and the exchange was made there's no telling how powerful they could become... I mean even a normal human could..."

"Frank? Are you there, Frank?" interrupted a voice over the internal speakers.

"Barry?" asked Frank as he opened communications and Barry's face appeared out of the lounge projector. "Is it urgent mate because we're kinda in the middle of something at the moment."

"Pretty urgent, yeah!" said Barry anxiously. "The sensor sweep has completed and it came back positive for contaminants."

"Shit!" muttered Frank before turning wide-eyed to Bernard and apologising for having to leave. "Can you guys show him around while I'm sorting this?" asked Frank casting his gaze around at Shui and the others. "I'll catch up with you later, so we can come up with a plan now that we have a full compliment."

All four nodded their assent and as Frank made his exit in a hurry, Shui took Bernard by the hand and led him toward the elevator as well.

"C'mon kid, I'll show you the dungeons!" said Shui giving him a roguish wink.

"Kid?" repeated Bernard with a chuckle.

"Compared to me mate, you're more like an embryo, but I figured 'kid' was more polite," said Shui.

Bernard laughed heartily. "You remind me of my granddaughter," he said happily.

"I'll let that slide because you're new…" replied Shui as they entered the lift. "And because Frank would never let me hear the end of it if I killed you now after all the trouble we've been to," she added with a crack of her knuckles.

As the lift doors closed, Bernard looked fleetingly like he didn't know if she was being serious or not and the last thing Aarde, Ignis and Hooowo3oow saw, was Bernard glancing at Shui who was grinning mischievously back.

Chapter Eight
Seven

"Don't be ridiculous?" whispered Ignis angrily. "To kill them now would be suicide."

He was on his knees in his room which was black walled, covered with a cage and illuminated by bolts of electricity that arced between Ignis' body and the walls. He had his hands raised in front of him to make a window as if communicating using the reflection song. But instead of the usual reflection of the person at the other end, there was a spider web that spiralled inwards which was littered with icons and symbols. It vibrated violently and out of its centre boomed what sounded like a multitude of voices merged into a one.

"YOU MUST!" it said with urgency. "WE HAD AN AGREEMENT!"

"Lower your voice," snapped Ignis with a glance at the door. "They will die I assure you of that. But it will be when I say so and not before."

"YOU FORGET YOUR PLACE!" roared the voice from the web.

"No, you forget yours!" corrected Ignis sharply. "And I said lower your voice. Look, it works out better this way. With the elemortals out of the way you can send Abyzou to tend to the woman. Meanwhile I can kill the old man and leave my colleagues stranded in the afterlife. There is no way they can stand up to the numbers we have at the breaches and with the God gates gone they'll have no way to move between worlds."

"You mean they'll be our problem?" said the voice more quietly than before.

"Are you trying to tell me you can't take them?" teased Ignis.

"OF COURSE WE CAN!" roared the voice with an abrupt return to its previous volume. "OUR POWER IS ABSOLUTE!"

"Absolute bullshit!" moaned Ignis under his breath.

"YOU DARE QUESTION... " began the voice but Ignis interrupted.

"Don't get too cocky!" said Ignis flatly. "We have killed Gods before!"

"Minor deities." scoffed the voice. "Weaklings born of poor imagination, they do not compare."

"Maybe not, but still, it would be a shame if one of you died before we accomplished our goal."

"Do not mock us!" growled the voice. "We know you want this as much as we do."

"I dare say I want it even more!" sneered Ignis. "I'm going to introduce the world to a new era… the golden age of fire. A glorious new beginning without all the mess caused by those who…"

A chime rang in the room followed shortly by the sound of the door being kicked.

"I have to go," said Ignis in a hurry, he knew who was doing the kicking.

"DO NOT FAIL US!" demanded the voice, but Ignis pulled his hands apart snapping the web and the room fell silent.

When he opened the door, he found Shui, as expected, leaning against the door frame, her expression one of amusement at being an obvious annoyance.

"Sorry dude, couldn't resist," she said smiling. But then observing him properly, asked, "Why are you all sweaty?"

"What do you want?" demanded Ignis impatiently.

"Meeting in ten minutes," replied Shui with restraint. She assumed he was still upset about Amos and decided to make allowances.

"Oh, right… thanks," muttered Ignis, wrong-footed by the lack of argument. "I'll be out in a minute."

As he closed the door, he saw Bernard sat at the large circular table in the lounge and he felt his temper rise. After all his hard work and planning it was an insult to have the only two people capable of ruining it all paraded right front of him. It would have been so easy to end their lives too, were it not for the others. Ignis was confident he could take on one elemortal, maybe two in the right environment, but all three? He'd never make it out of the building.

When Ignis opened his door a short time later, a shaft of bright light struck his eyes like a laser beam. Shielding himself, he entered the lounge and was greeted by a wall of smoke that was infused with such an eclectic mix of scents he felt overpowered as it burned inside his nasal passages.

Coughing a little as he wafted a path through the heavy low-slung cloud that filled the lounge, dodging the shafts of bright light that shot in every direction as he went, he found the table where his colleagues were waiting and sat down irritably, wishing he had water to douse his eyeballs. Peering through the dense grey smog, Ignis could just see Hoowo3oow and Aarde sat across from him. Bernard and the nephilim were sat either side of them at opposite edges of the table and finally to his left was Shui, who had every appearance of being relaxed as she reclined on her chair. However, her expression was one of deep concentration, so much so she didn't appear to have noticed Ignis had taken a seat.

"What the hell is all this crap?" asked Ignis moodily.

"Necessary precautions I'm afraid," said Frank, his holographic representation barely visible amongst the smoky atmosphere.

"Necessary for what?" he snapped as his left nostril caught a particularly strong whiff of burnt sage, cedar wood and peppermint. "Do you have a hag stalking you again?"

"That was one time!" whined Frank in a scandalised tone. "And if memory serves, it was your fault!"

Ignis shrugged looking amused. "You asked us to set you up on a date!"

"With a human!" shrieked Frank indignantly. "Not a cannibalistic grandma with no teeth."

"Really?" chuckled Shui unexpectedly. "I could have sworn that was your type."

Frank gave Shui what was assumed to be an admonitory stare, the smoke was getting so thick it was getting harder and harder to see.

He gave a great sigh of resignation and turned his attention back to Ignis. "In answer to your question, they are precautions against several unknown contaminants."

"Unknown?" repeated Shui questioningly.

"Afraid so. We were right to suspect that we had been bugged!" began Frank seriously. "Quite literally bugged in fact as four of the seven contaminants were spiders. I even found one inside my own bleedin' control room."

Through the haze came several sharp intakes of breath which disturbed the smoke and everyone except Hoowo3oow coughed.

"Not to worry, we got it. Not that the spider itself was dangerous, it was just a common house spider. But we know Anansi can and is using spider webs to traffic information to the upper realms. That will be how they knew about the scientist the second we did."

"Right, so if you have done fumigating the building, why are we still being suffocated with all this?" asked Aarde as he gestured distantly through the smoke.

"Well like I said, we had seven contaminants and only four of them were spiders. At the moment we are using warding charms, location spells and a mix of purification rituals to highlight and get rid of whatever the last three contaminants are."

"Do you believe there is a spy at the table?" growled Hoowo3oow in an almost bored voice.

"Not by now, no, there was a blip on our scans for near here about ten minutes ago, but it seems to have gone now," said Frank. "I'm certain that anything that had been down there would have been driven into another part of the building after this much cleansing."

"In that case…" began Hoowo3oow who whipped his hand in a circle in front of him so the smoke cleared from the table to make a wall of swirling grey fog behind them. It was like sitting in the eye of a hurricane, except it was indoors and littered with pillars of broken light.

Aarde took a grateful breath of fresh air and patted Hoowo3oow on the back to show thanks. "Oh, that's so much better."

"Agreed," said Shui who was likewise taking deep lungfuls. "Even my eyes are burning so yours must be melting."

Aarde gave her a lingering grin but Shui didn't hold his gaze, she had turned to look at Bernard who had been holding a handkerchief over his mouth and nose and was quite unaffected by the noxious effects.

"Why didn't I think of that?" she said musingly.

Ignis gave a soft laugh. "It's what Amos would have done."

His smile quickly faded, as his stomach gave another guilty lurch.

"If we can crack on…" began Frank with a touch of impatience, "…time as always is against us."

Everyone adjusted on their seats to give Frank their full attention and a noticeable shift in mood swept the table.

"The fates have at last thrown us a bone in what has so far been a game of catchup since this whole mess began," said Frank in an attempt at optimism. "To what I can only assume to be planetary alignment or some other bollocks, we have our team!" he finished with sarcastic amusement.

There was an exchange of looks across the table as everyone took a moment to size each other up. The nephilim looked quite pleased to be included in any sort of group, even if it was one heading out on a potentially lethal mission. Bernard appeared quite encouraged by the sight of the elemortals, though that faith was clearly causing him some internal conflict.

The elemortals looked anything but pleased and enthusiastic. When they looked at Bernard, they saw a glass chicken. Something that was going to run around in a panic until it was smashed. What they saw was problems. When they eyed the Nephilim, Ignis and Shui at least reserved judgement having met him before and were looking forward to seeing him do his thing. Aarde and Hoowo3oow seemed rather less impressed, but they did at least refrain from looking at him like he was fragile, scarred as he was.

"When the first breach triggered the global ordinance and divination system in October, we know it penetrated as deep as the third realm," began Frank matter-of-factly. "But that was two months ago and we know that the afterlife has been making a combined effort to use that damage to push deeper whilst widening the previous gaps in the barriers. When they finally break through and into the seventh realm there will be so much magical weight pressing down on the mortal realm that our barrier will fail completely and the world will be overrun by the worst horrors ever imagined by humankind."

"I'm sorry but what do you mean by realms?" interrupted Bernard sheepishly.

"Oh, er, well…" stammered Frank unsure where to begin.

"This universe is layered with what we call realms," began Hoowo3oow helpfully. "You are currently in the material or physical layer which sits, in the general scheme of things, on the outside of a stack of worlds all pressing against each other."

"Don't you mean inside?" asked Bernard who had recognised the theme from numerous theologies. "It sounds to me like you are talking about the seven planes of existence, a common theme in many religions."

"No," said Hoowo3oow flatly. "I mean outside. The realms do not span outward into the universe, past the edge and on into heaven. This is the not the universe's problem. All seven realms occupy the same space as Earth, you don't look up until you look down," he paused a moment with his lips pursed as though tasting something bitter. "What you have read regarding the planes of existence is rubbish. As are the naming conventions. When the Conclave discovered the realms, they knew exactly how they came to be and called them what they are, not the esoteric nonsense that you see in holistic healing guides. No, as I said, this is a contained and very localised system of reality and we are on the outside."

Bernard considered this for a moment before asking, "So it's more like a hard outer shell?"

"Precisely. An odd notion to grasp but believe me the view of the material world from a higher realm is quite the sight to see."

"You… you have been to one of these realms?" stuttered Bernard in surprise.

"Not with our bodies, but we have glimpsed the Ribatan realm, sometimes known as the astral plane or limbo, with our minds under the influence of certain herbs and extracts."

"Fascinating," said Bernard.

"But you'll get to see it with your own eyes mate," said Shui who then whispered under her breath to Ignis. "Just before a spider sucks those eyes out of his skull."

Ignis sniggered and Aarde sat back in his chair with his arms folded, an offended look on his face. Bernard had only heard the part about seeing it for himself and he didn't seem to know if he was excited or afraid.

"He's going to see more than that," said Frank warningly. "You will have to at the very least find a way into the Akashic realm and you can't do that without going through Alghatrasa."

"And we are expected to do that without going through the breaches?" asked Aarde with a touch of scepticism. "You remember we won't have the sword to start with, right?"

172

"Yeah, I was going to ask about that," said Shui, her eyebrows screwed together in puzzlement. "I get how we use this guy to get out of this realm and into limbo," she began with a lazy point at the nephilim.

"This guy..." interrupted Frank sternly. "...is, as Demi tells me, going by the name Flynn. So please address him as such."

"Fair enough," said Shui unabashed. "Where do we put Flynn in the other realms when we need the next lock?"

"Not a clue," said Frank disappointingly. "Death said that the gate in this world is Bernard's place of rebirth. But he won't have one of those in the other realms."

"Whoa, Frank. You're telling me we are stuck in there until we figure it out ourselves?" asked Aarde with a shock of realisation.

All faces turned to look expectantly at Frank who winced apologetically.

"Chill out baldy," said Ignis waving down Aarde's concerns disinterestedly. "You happen to be travelling with a genius."

"Well, I wouldn't go as far as to say genius," began Bernard with embarrassed modesty, "but..."

"I was talking about me!" scoffed Ignis.

Shui laughed very unkindly and punched Ignis on the arm. "You fuckin' wish! Good job I'm going or you'd all die!"

The conversation quickly degraded into an ego driven contest of intellect and eventually physical prowess when, ignoring Frank's attempts to restore order, Hoowo3oow and Shui got into an arm-wrestling match. It was starting to get very much out of hand when all of a sudden, Edmond the ghostly mail room clerk, pushed his head up through the table and was subsequently punched as Shui jerked Hoowo3oow's arm toward a victory but collided with Edmond instead.

"Every time!" wailed Edmond painfully. "Every damn time."

Rubbing his nose, he floated grumpily to a free space at the table's edge and looked reproachfully at Shui.

"One day," he began testily when no apology was offered, "I might be able to come to this room and leave without having my face bludgeoned."

"Don't be blaming me for that," retorted Shui dismissively. "You're the dumbass who stuck his head through the table. We do have a door you know."

"What did you want?" asked Aarde placatively.

Edmond rummaged in a bag he had slung over his shoulder and withdrew six clay objects that looked like sculpted faces.

"You asked me to bring these up, Frank," he said tossing them on the table with ill-disguised annoyance. "Who's this?" he added with an invasive glare at Bernard who recoiled with alarm at being interrogated so closely by a ghost.

"New recruit," said Frank who didn't feel like getting into the particulars right now.

Edmond gave a sort of half laugh and shook his head. "Get younger every year," he said before vanishing back through the floor.

Aarde slid the the face closest to him across the table and held it up for closer inspection. It was off-white in colour and very smooth like it had been sanded with great care. The face was that of a child, but it was not one Aarde recognised and it was difficult to tell if it was of a boy or girl. He looked over at the others and saw three more children, a teenager and the face of an aged man poking out at the bottom of the pile. Again, they were not faces Aarde knew, but he had an inkling now as to what they were for.

"Death masks?" he asked as he held one in front of his face and peeked through the eye holes.

"Indeed, they are," said Frank happily. "Everybody, take one. There's one each appropriate to your age."

A series of scraping sounds marked the masks being slid to each team member and pretty soon everyone had held one up to their face for size, except for Bernard. He was looking at his mask with some revulsion.

"Appropriate to my age?" he said despairingly. "There are creases on here deeper than the Grand Canyon. Exactly how old do you think I am?"

"Surprisingly enough," began Frank, "we have very few aged faces in our death mask collection. This will have to do, now please try it on."

Giving Frank a very derisive glare, Bernard raised the mask to his face and placed it gingerly against his skin.

"Get it on properly!" said Shui as she impatiently shoved the mask with her fingers so it sat flush on Bernard's face. "Lemme see…" she added turning his chin to look at her, "Perfect! You can barely see a difference."

Bernard shook his head and removed the mask, placing it upon the table with the face looking up.

"What do we even need these for?" he asked wearily.

"That's your disguise," said Ignis coldly. "Without it, the second your fleshy arse steps foot in the Ribatan realm you will shine like a beacon for everything to see. By wearing the face of someone who has died, you hide your life from view.

"That's right," agreed Frank. "And the last thing you want is attention so make sure that mask stays on your face until the world is the right way up again."

Bernard nodded his understanding and fell silent while he contemplated what he had got himself into.

"Anyway," said Frank with a loud clearing of his throat. "As I was trying to say earlier, chances are the breaches are much deeper than before and you will need to at least reach the Akashic Hall of Records to get Death's weapon. Then it's a simple matter of subduing the spider holding open each breach so Bernard can murder it!

"So I can what?" gasped Bernard, snapping about of his daze at once. "What am I murdering?"

"A… spider," said Frank tentatively.

"And why would a spider need subduing?" asked Bernard dubiously. "Spiders are tiny."

"These ones might be a little bigger than what you're used to," said Frank hesitantly.

"How big is big?" asked Bernard with a note of concern in his voice.

"If we are lucky, they'll be about the size of combine harvester," said Shui casually.

"A combin…" began Bernard before he slipped from his chair and disappeared under the table.

"Has he fainted?" asked Shui, peering under the table. "He has, he's fainted. Seriously Frank can't we leave him here once we get the gate open?"

175

Frank sighed disappointingly.

"Sorry, guys but you need him for more than just a gate, there are others if you can work out where they are. Besides he will be able to see things you can't like the spiders, not to mention he is the only one who can throw that sword about."

"I'm not carrying him when he passes out again… and he obviously will. That guess on the spider size was conservative, he'll slip into a bloody coma when he actually claps eyes on one," said Shui who folded her arms and legs very tightly in disgust and was determinedly not looking at Frank.

"Yeah, we're not carrying him either," said Aarde and Hoowo3oow together.

Ignis had jumped from his chair and had dragged Bernard out from under the table.

"Frank, get Chloe to come down here will you," said Ignis as he slumped Bernard on the sofa.

"Why?" asked Frank quizzically.

"You saw what she did to her mother before," said Ignis. "She's developing her abilities and whatever they are she chilled out Cassandra in seconds. Maybe she can make this moose knuckle get a grip on himself too."

"Worth a shot," said Frank, and he summoned Chloe over the intercom.

Chapter Nine
One of These Things is not Like the Others

A few minutes later, the elevator hissed open and a voice yelled, "A little help!"

It was Chloe who had just stepped out of the elevator and vanished into a wall of smog.

"Enough of this!" barked Hoowo3oow testily and holding his palm open in front of him sucked all the smoke from the room and pressed it into a turbulent ball of gas that swirled like the surface of Jupiter.

"What about the preventative measures?" asked Frank aghast.

"If anything was in here, I'm sure it has suffocated by now," said Hoowo3oow. When Frank continued to look distraught, he added with a sigh, "If a ghoul pops up, I'll throw this at them!" and he held up the ball of smoke for illustration.

Frank showed every sign of wanting to retort but he was distracted at once by a voice that made him do a double take.

"Frank, a pleasure as always!" said Chloe in a bright but direct tone that appeared to age her.

Her accent seemed different too. It was more enunciated and eloquent.

"For a moment there..." began Frank unnerved. "...I thought... sorry..." he added completely wrong footed.

And he wasn't the only one. The elemortals had been staring at Chloe with wide-eyed surprise too. There was no mistaking it. For the briefest of moments, she had sounded exactly like Amos.

"I assume there was something you needed me for?" asked Chloe encouragingly.

"Oh, er, yes... yes I did," said Frank pulling himself together. "It's your mother's friend, Bernard," began Frank, sadly. "He's not taking to the situation very well. His nerves are a little weak I think, well he is getting on in years."

Frank took a breath while he considered his next words but Chloe spared him the need to be delicate and asked for him.

"You want me to speak to him like I did to my mother and make him more… compliant?" said Chloe so calmly it was unsettling.

"Well… yes," said Frank, a little lamely.

"I'll certainly have a try," said Chloe and she gave Frank an affecting wink before strolling over to Bernard and dropping onto the sofa next to him. "I'm still not entirely sure what it is I'm doing, it's a work in progress for want of a better term. Strength of mind in the subject seems to be a factor," continued Chloe thoughtfully, "but as the saying goes, you can't make an omelette without breaking a few eggs, eh?" she finished with a chuckle.

"Er… OK!" stammered Frank nervously with a swift look at Shui.

There was a sound of chairs scraping as the other three elemortals fled their seats to get a better view, just in case. For Shui, Aarde and Hoowo3oow at least, it was hard to forget what she had done to Quentin.

"Will someone wake him?" asked Chloe.

Ignis who was still stood next to Bernard, leant in and slapped him with the back of his hand. Bernard didn't stir, but he did now have four finger marks blossoming across his cheek.

"She said wake him, not knock him out more," said Shui sarcastically and she made a small ball of water appear a foot above Bernard's head before dropping it, which splashed over his face.

"WHAAA!" bellowed Bernard as he woke with jerk and struggled wide-eyed to place his surroundings.

When his brain clicked back into place, a look of disappointment spread over his features.

"I was really hoping you lot were a bad dream."

He then sagged in on himself and rubbed his face vigorously with both hands.

"What on earth have you got me doing?" he added in a muffled, whiny voice.

"Mr Godfrey?" said Chloe kindly, placing a comforting hand on his shoulder. "Mr Godfrey, will you look at me?"

Bernard raised his head and slid his hands off his face. He appeared gaunt and pale, and as his eyes swivelled to glance at Chloe, a look of shame added itself to his already miserable features.

"What must you think of me?" he said in an embarrassed whisper. "I used to be an intrepid explorer you know. I was strong and fearless, like my friend, Alfred. He'd be disgusted if he could see me now."

"That's not true," said Chloe gently. "He'd be proud that you are trying to help and besides, bravery isn't about being fearless, you know that."

Bernard nodded half-heartedly but didn't speak. He just stared helplessly into Chloe's eyes, like a little boy being consoled by his mother.

"Pathetic!" whispered Ignis with ill-disguised disappointment, but Shui shot him a filthy look. "Sorry," he said to Chloe earnestly. "I meant him, not you."

"I know what you meant," said Chloe knowingly. "But I doubt that tone will help. Now, take a seat and give me some room, you're causing a distraction."

Ignis felt so disarmed by the way she spoke he couldn't think of anything to say. It was almost like having Amos in the room again. Chloe shook out her hands while she waited for Ignis to sit and then turned to fix Bernard with a penetrating stare.

A loud crackle of noise like that from a badly tuned radio thundered through Chloe's head, and some sort of force erupted between her and Bernard, and Chloe was thrown backward and tumbled across the floor.

"My word!" gasped Bernard, alarmed.

"Chloe?" yelled Shui and Frank together.

Before anyone moved to help, Chloe had rolled onto her stomach and was pushing herself up.

"Ugh…" grunted Chloe as she got to her feet. "That was unexpected."

Her nose was bleeding and there was a cut above her eye.

"You all right?" asked Shui with a tone that conveyed obvious surprise by how well Chloe was taking the blow.

Chloe withdrew a handkerchief from inside the fold in her top and wiped her nose clean. "Peachy!" she said stiffly.

"Any other ideas?" asked Ignis with an impatient glare at Frank.

"Hold your horses!" contested Chloe with a touch of annoyance and she marched back to Bernard before casting a reproachful glance at Ignis and adding, "Rome wasn't built in a day and all that."

"Can't argue with that!" said Ignis amusedly. "I was there and it took a long ass time."

"All right, Granddad, no one wants to hear your stories!" said Shui in a patronising voice.

"You sure you want to try again?" she added with a concerned look at Chloe. "You must have flown twelve feet and that's a nasty cut."

Blood was gently trickling down Chloe's cheek from the wound but she seemed quite unconcerned. On the contrary she was in good spirits, all things considered.

"There's no need to fuss, my dear," said Chloe in that unnerving Amos-like manner. "I'm surprisingly robust."

Shui giggled nervously and gave Chloe, who was rolling her shoulders, space to have another go at modifying Bernard's attitude.

Without warning Chloe unsheathed Yoshiro and in the same movement, brought the blade to a stop an inch from Bernard's face. Everyone flinched with surprise except for Bernard who appeared to be frozen in place from shock. Chloe held the blade level with Bernard's eyeline and, between the light bouncing off the cold metal surface and the reflected gaze of his own eyes, he seemed to be falling into some sort of hypnotic trance.

"Did it work?" whispered Chloe who shockingly had her eyes closed "Is he under?"

Shui leaned closer to observe the dreamy look on Bernard's face. His eyes were unfocused and from his half open mouth he was drooling.

"There's a face that's hard to unsee," she said with a soft titter. "Yeah, he's under."

"Thank you Shui, but I wasn't asking you," said Chloe gently.

Unheard by everyone but Chloe, Yoshiro replied, "Hai. He is receptive. The eyes of a God... Ha!"

"That was a good idea!" said Chloe softly as she reopened her own eyes and moved her head closer to Bernard's while keeping Yoshiro firmly at his eye height.

"His mind is quiet, you should try it now," said Yoshiro, his steel glinting.

"Listen…" began Chloe in the soft commanding tone she had used before and Bernard's whole body became suddenly stiff and attentive.

When she continued speaking her voice sounded blurred, like another voice overlapped hers.

"Once upon a happier time, you were worshipped as a god and they thought you brave and powerful. You may not have known it at the time, but you felt it and it gave you strength. Your mind may have forgotten but your body remembers."

Bernard seemed to swell at Chloe's words, like a sense of resolve was growing inside him and his face was no longer looking absent and dopey, on the contrary he appeared determined and confident.

"That power was real and it's still inside you," said Chloe firmly. "You just have to recognise it for what it was. Remember!"

At once Bernard's mind raced back to the days with Pacal Chan and a fresh understanding of those moments where Pacal had appeared awed rather than impressed lit up his brain. Comprehension of his mistake, indeed of Alfred's mistake, ricocheted around inside his head making him feel dizzy. It was obvious now that he thought about it, so obvious he couldn't believe he didn't realise it at the time. A familiar warmth rose up inside Bernard. A warmth he hadn't felt for years. Not since his time in Peru. Bernard bent his arm and flexed his bicep which strained against the fabric of his suit making it creak. He felt suddenly strong and energetic. He made a fist and then stretched out his fingers and felt the noticeable absence of arthritic pain.

"Stand!" commanded Chloe and Bernard stood so sharply it made Frank flinch.

A tense excitement hung in the air as they watched Bernard stretch out his shoulders and crack out the kinks in his spine. He appeared much larger than before, not just taller but more muscular too and Chloe gave a smile of relief.

"This is your destiny," said Chloe charismatically. "You are a soldier, an instrument of destruction. Be their eyes. See what they can't. See with the eyes of a God!" she finished in a dramatic whisper.

The few seconds of silence that followed seemed to stretch on forever as everyone waited with baited breath to see how Bernard would respond to such a grand statement. Anticipation quickly turned to alarm, however, as Bernard's eyes became pale and he was rendered blind.

"What the hell have you done?" wailed Bernard who made a sudden sharp turn and stumbled over the corner of the sofa. "I can't bloody see."

"Dammit!" said Shui as she moved in front of Bernard, and held him still for examination. "She's broken him."

Shui snapped her fingers briskly in front of Bernard's eyes.

"Yeah, those eyes look deader than Hoowo3oow's, maybe this is a joke about how the Gods don't actually see anything!" she added disappointedly.

Everyone turned to look at Chloe who was rubbing her chin as she pondered Bernard's predicament. She was just about to try and fix it when Bernard reeled in pain as a loud, high-pitched whistle overwhelmed his senses and he clutched wildly at his skull as he screamed through clenched teeth. His tightly shut eyes suddenly burst open wide as a brilliant light erupted behind them. For a moment it shone so bright it made everything in the room appear black by contrast and everyone else was forced to turn their heads away. Then, as abruptly as it had come, the light vanished and Bernard collapsed on the floor, smoke pouring from behind his closed eyelids.

"Well, if he wasn't broke before, that ought to do it!" said Shui dispassionately as she heaved Bernard up off the floor and slumped him onto the sofa. "Not having the best of days, is he?"

"Is he dead?" asked Frank who was flapping about, impotent to take action in his holographic form.

Shui checked for a pulse in Bernard's neck.

"He's still alive, Frank," she said at last.

Bernard stirred at the sound of Shui's words and he rolled in place, trying to sit up.

"Mr Godfrey?" whispered Shui gently. "Mr Godfrey, are you OK?

Bernard's eyes cracked open and a shaft of bright blue light illuminated his nose and cheeks.

"So that's still a thing," mused Shui as she squinted to get a better look. "He'll make a good torch if nothing else."

Bernard gave a couple of chesty coughs and a few puffs of bluish smoke escaped his lips.

"What happened?" he asked weakly.

"You levelled up!" snorted Ignis sarcastically.

Unable to suppress a giggle, Shui gave Ignis a withering look and turned back to Bernard.

"How do you feel, dude?" she asked cautiously.

Bernard coughed again and heaved himself forward before saying, "Like I swallowed a flare."

Shui was still examining Bernard's eyes with eager curiosity. "Can you… can you see?"

Bernard blinked a few times which dimmed and brightened the room like a strobe.

"It's a little bright in here, but the world is still there."

Frank sagged with relief and massaged his temples in attempt to smooth out the stress veins pulsating there.

"What on earth's happened to him?" he asked more to himself than anyone else.

"Well, it's like Ignis said…" replied Shui apathetically, "…he's had an upgrade. Achievement unlocked, 'Someone's eaten their carrots'!"

The elemortals all laughed at this but Frank was not amused.

"This is not funny!" spat Frank irritably. "He's the last one, if we cook his brain…"

"Relax!" interrupted Shui with a quelling wave of her hand. "You're all right, aren't you?" she added with a stout pat on Bernard's shoulder.

Bernard's face drifted lazily to look at Shui and he was on the verge of words but upon seeing her he looked aghast and as his eyes widened, the light emitting from the sockets glowed brighter, dazzling Shui. He stole a worried glance at the other elemortals and stammered, "Wh… what's happening?" he asked in an urgent shocked tone. "What's wrong with you?"

"We're fine!" said Shui a little offended. "What's wrong with you?"

Bernard leaned close and examined Shui with professional concern. Without thinking he reached out a finger to poke her in the shoulder.

"Oi!" snapped Shui as she batted his hand away. "You wanna lose that finger?"

But Bernard showed no signs of dismay. He was staring at Shui with bewildered amazement. "You're… you're made of water!"

"Of course I am you id… wait, what?" said Shui confused.

"Your body…" continued Bernard. "…it's like water poured into a human-shaped container."

"You can see it?" asked Shui horrified and she took a step back from him.

"I can," said Bernard in a low fascinated whisper. "Just like I can see that this boy… er… man, looks like he's on fire…" he added pointing at Ignis. "He's hardly there at all…" he continued pointing at Hoowo3oow, "…and he looks like he's been cut from a giant diamond," he finished pointing at Aarde.

Bernard rubbed at his eyes very hard and blinked several times as he glared at the elemortals with ill-disguised disbelief.

"I must be hallucinating," said Bernard rationally. "I took some weird things in the 70s, this is probably a flashback," he added calmly. "A few deep breaths and ride it out!"

Spotting the shadow of a tall man behind him, Bernard said. "Excuse me, sir," and side-stepped around Chloe before doddering back over to the table. He then leaned for a moment against the back of a chair and gave his head a little shake. Exhaling loudly, Bernard strode toward Ignis and reaching out, touched his shoulder with his whole hand.

"Fascinating," said Bernard interestedly, as he ran his fingers through invisible flames.

"The most convincing trip I've ever been on, much more tangible than that time I ate peyote." He then turned his attention to Flynn and added with jubilation, "My dear boy you have wings, giant beautiful wings… can… can I touch them?"

"What the hell did you do to him?" asked Ignis who was looking at Chloe with something like reverence.

Chloe shrugged and blew out of the side of her mouth.

"Buggered if I know," she said, perplexed. "See with the eyes of a God was supposed to be a metaphor."

Ignis burst out laughing. He couldn't help it. But Chloe laughed along with him and for a while they couldn't stop.

"So what do we do with him now?" asked Ignis once the laughter had subsided.

"We take him as he is," supplied Frank. "His new eyesight aside, he seems to have grown his balls back so he should hopefully stop freaking out every time he encounters something peculiar."

"Would you call this, not freaking out'?" asked Ignis, drawing inverted commas in the air with his fingers while Bernard began blowing into Hoowo3oow's back and chuckling amusedly.

"He's not scared at least," said Frank awkwardly. "So thank you Chloe for that."

"Not at all," said Chloe politely. "I'm just glad he can still move. I thought he was a goner for a moment there, I'm not going to lie!" she added while stifling a nervous laugh.

"Right then!" said Frank with an abrupt clap of his holographic hands. "Let's get your ramshackle arses geared up. I want you ready to leave in an hour!"

"An hour?" moaned Shui disapprovingly. "Is that it?"

"Yes, Shui!" retorted Frank contemptuously. "It's the end of the world, how much more time do you need?"

"All right!" sulked Shui moodily as she stomped over to the table, dragged Bernard's death mask off the surface and slapped it against Bernard's chest. "Don't forget this!" she grunted as she grabbed her own and made to leave.

"What in God's name is that?" roared Bernard who tore the mask away from his chest in disgust and held it away from him at arms' length.

"Now what?" growled Shui, impatiently.

"This thing you slapped on my chest..." roared Bernard furiously, pointing at the mask. "What the hell is it? And more to the point what is wrong with you, to make you think pressing something as freakish as this, onto living flesh, is OK?"

Shui was obviously confused and she wasn't the only one.

"We discussed this earlier," said Shui with a heavy sigh. "These are what we need to wear to hide ourselves in the other realms. We put then on our faces, like this!"

Shui demonstrated putting on her own mask but Bernard swelled indignantly.

"I am not putting this ruddy thing on my face. If I remember correctly, I had one like yours, I'll wear that and you can keep whatever sick hazing practice this is to yourself."

"What are you on about?" moaned Shui, exasperated.

"THIS!" yelled Bernard waving his own mask in Shui's face. "Is this yours? Is it some sort of pet you lot have been keeping? Whatever it is, it looks dangerous and probably isn't something you should be playing around with."

"Are you out of your fucking mind?" snarled Shui who was becoming visibly angered by the idiocy of the conversation.

"Me?" bellowed Bernard. "I'm not the one shoving monsters into people's chest."

"Mons… what…? I can't… I'm just gonna punch him… only way!" babbled Shui who seemed to have reached some final straw.

Aarde and Ignis lurched forward and restrained Shui just as she made to wind up a punch and Frank shot an accusatory stare at Chloe. An argument amongst them all was just breaking out when someone shouted from over by the elevator.

"Well bugger me, I haven't seen one of them in years!" chuckled Nephthys as she sauntered into the room and waved at Shui before turning her attention back to Bernard. "Ooh, it's only baby too," she crooned as she approached the mask still being held at arms' length. "Where did you get it? Actually, why did you get it?"

Bernard was too busy averting his eyes to attempt a reply.

"Madam, er, apologies but, you're… um… well, naked!" spluttered Bernard embarrassed.

"Is that so?" asked Nephthys slyly. "Have you had a good look?" she continued with a twirl.

"My good woman, please show some decorum!" blustered Bernard, his face now a beetroot colour.

"You really can't see my clothes?" asked Nephthys with a mischievous grin. "Would that have something to do with why you can see this wondrous little creature you have in that very large hand of yours?"

Shui, gave Nephthys a disappointed look.

"Please don't encourage him, it'll only make it worse."

"The only thing that would make this worse is if he actually put that creature on his face," said Nephthys smoothly.

"You're going to need to elaborate," said Frank as he lit a cigarette and exhaled heavily.

"It's a mimic!" said Nephthys in a tone that suggested this was obvious.

"It's not! Is it really?" asked Aarde excitedly as he sidled over to stand near Nephthys and get a better view.

"Oh yes! And nasty little buggers they are even at this size," explained Nephthys indifferently.

Bernard turned the mask to face him and looked at it more closely, the professor in him taking charge.

"You mean to say this… mimic did you call it? It pretends to be things?" he asked in a calmer and interested manner.

"It is pretending, right now," chortled Nephthys who seemed to be enjoying the confusion the misunderstanding had caused. "They all see a mask, because that's the form it's projecting. It's the same reason you can't see my clothes. I am always naked, I just mentally project the fashion I desire and that's what others see… except you of course. I'm going to assume you can see it because of the flashy eyesight you seem to have acquired in my absence."

"The what with my eyesight?" asked Bernard.

"He hasn't seen it yet," whispered Chloe. "I don't think they were going to mention it."

"Oh, well, never mind that…" waved Nephthys distractedly. "Look here…" she added drawing his attention to a place near the nose on the mask. "…that tendril-like appendage just there just between the sixth and seventh pair of legs, it bores into the host and taps into the nearest artery. Once there it feeds itself through the circulatory system and into the brain stem where it can maintain autonomic control of the victim for several hours while it drinks the host dry and absorbs part of the genome for its morphological library."

"Fascinating!" said Bernard who was now prodding at some unseen part of the creature in his hand with a pencil. "And my eyes…" continued Bernard who had not forgotten the comment.

"Your eyes allow you to see the creature in its usual form," deflected Nephthys silkily. "What you don't see is the mask that this lot see." She jabbed a thumb over her shoulder at the elemortals. "But you could… if you try," she added in soft whisper.

"How?"

"Just stare at the mask and slowly allow your eyes to become unfocused."

There was a pause while Bernard did this. It took a moment as he was very aware of everyone staring but eventually, he muttered. "Now what?"

"Now look past the mask, far into the distance."

"Ridiculous!" groaned Bernard. "All that's going to do is… oh, I see!" added Bernard astonished. "It gets offset."

"Well done. All I need to do now is show you how to find some manners and my work here is done," said Nephthys brusquely.

"My apologies, dear lady. I spoke out of turn," said Bernard sombrely.

Nephthys smiled indulgently and patted Bernard gently on the cheek.

"You're forgiven, but only because you called me 'dear lady'."

"EXCUSE ME!" snapped Frank in a whirl of impatience. "BUT HOW THE HELL DID A MIMIC GET INSIDE THE CONCLAVE?"

"That is your problem!" said Shui coolly. "I've got about forty-five minutes left before us six leave for Peru!"

"Seven!" interjected Nephthys. "I'm coming too!"

"You're… what?" gasped Frank.

"I'm going with them. Amos… well he meant a lot to me…" Nephthys seemed trail off for a moment, but then she suddenly came back to herself and continued her case. "Anyway, I've become quite fond of this one," she added with a nudge to Shui. "Besides, if you can't recognise a mimic when you see one, you're going to need me."

"She's got a point!" agreed Shui who seemed quite keen on the idea of Nephthys coming along for the ride.

"Fine!" said Frank who couldn't think of an argument against it. "Just get rid of that thing. I'll send Edmond to look for the original mask the mimic copied. It'll be stashed around here somewhere… little shit!"

"Rodger dodger," said Shui and she gave a silly salute.

Frank rubbed his forehead despairingly before hitting a button on his desk which caused him to disappear without a word.

"Bit rude!" sniggered Shui as she turned to face Bernard and made to grab the mimic, but to her astonishment and disappointment, Bernard had already killed it. To Shui the mask sat crushed to powder inside his fist, to Bernard, the crushed remains of the mimic sat crunched beneath his fingers and where legs jutted out between his knuckles, blackish green slime, oozed to the floor.

"Sorry, but it was going to put its wiggly bit in my wrist so…" muttered Bernard, trailing off.

"I'm just glad I can't see the mess that you can," sighed Shui shrugging. "I'm not cleaning it either, you did it, you can scoop it up!" she added with a grin.

Everyone quickly departed to gather their belongings and prepare for the off before they got roped into helping and soon Bernard was left alone in the room with the remains of his first kill still dripping onto the floor and looking at a loss for what to do with it. He turned to look for any cupboards that might have cleaning products in them and promptly slipped over in the slime.

"Don't you have people for this?" he barked to the empty room.

"Yeah!" came Shui's muffled yell from behind her door. "You!"

Chapter Ten
A Grave Sight

"Settle down please," said Frank's hologram in a tired, worn-out voice which didn't quite carry over the loud joviality in the room.

The team had been talking animatedly since reassembling and were quite excited about the journey now they had packed. Of course packed didn't mean much for the elemortals. If it was not something they could secrete about their person, it wasn't going. Nephthys was likewise travelling light and when asked what she was doing for food, she said she had brought a travel snack and then leered at Bernard and licked her lips menacingly. Flynn was a little more encumbered. He had his twin-necked guitar slung across his back as normal but had elected to bring a satchel bag, the strap of which crossed with that of the guitar and was filled with food and a few picture books that Frank thought he might find useful.

Bernard was equipped like a real explorer. He had changed clothes into a tan-coloured shirt and matching knee-length shorts which were extremely tight fitting against his large frame and below all this were long green socks pulled up the length of his shins. On his feet were a pair of massive hiking boots which creaked with the slightest movement and strapped to his back was a large rucksack upon which various implements such as a cup and fork were clipped here and there while tied to the top was a thick sleeping mat. He was even wearing a wide-brimmed sun hat. There had been much sniggering and stifled fits of laughter when Bernard had first entered the room. Even Cassandra who had come to see him off had to pass off a snort as a sneeze.

"Mock all you like!" Bernard had scoffed. "But I've been there before. Mark my words, you'll wish you'd dressed like me before long."

It was when Ignis had replied by saying, "We already do. From the children's section!" that the joke had come out and the tide of hilarity the group had been suppressing broke free and the room collapsed with uncontrollable hysterics.

"Guys… guys!" repeated Frank loudly. "Can we focus, your flight leaves in twenty minutes."

"Flight?" asked Hoowo3oow, his brow furrowed.

"Yes flight. Bernard cannot identify the location of the village he found from aerial satellite imagery but he is certain he can get us there the same way he and Alfred went before."

"Right," said Aarde sceptically. "Just remind me again, how long has it been since you were last there?" he asked with an enquiring look at Bernard.

"Ooh, don't you worry Mr Owusu," said Bernard with an assuring grin. "The path we're taking isn't one you'll forget."

A look of bewilderment stole over Aarde's face and he mouthed the words 'Mr Owusu', silently back at Bernard, wrong-footed at being addressed as his surname and even more so, as Mr.

"Don't worry," began Bernard who had misunderstood Aarde's facial expression as one of concern. "I'll be there to help you out over the more treacherous terrain."

Aarde merely stared at Bernard incredulously who gave him a reassuring wink in return which almost reduced Shui to tears as she battled with her amusement.

"So how is this going to work?" asked Hoowo3oow gruffly.

"Nephthys can get us as far as the City of Rioja in northern Peru," said Frank pleased to be getting back on topic. "From there we will be transported by helicopter to Pavayacu at which point we will head into the reserve on foot. It's a few days' trek not counting sleep in between, but with a fast pace you should make it there in good time."

"Fast pace. In good time. A few days," said Shui, holding a finger for each point. "One of these things does not belong in that sentence!"

"Allowances must be made," said Frank scowling.

Shui frowned at Bernard and Nephthys whispered something in her ear which made her smile mischievously and made Frank uncomfortable.

"Have you all got your masks?" asked Frank as he ran through a few last-minute checks on a clipboard.

Everyone held up their masks in the air and Frank made a tick on his notes.

"Bernard, are all the masks, masks?" he continued with his pen poised.

Bernard, who had learned how to turn his eyes normal while cleaning mimic guts, fired up his eyes and cast a look over the faces held above each person and nodded his approval.

"Fantastic. Nephthys, if you would stand over in the space near the weather window over there," continued Frank, signalling to the area in which the elemortal sometimes trained. "And everyone else, if you could all gather in a circle around her... no, Bernard, you don't need to hold hands... Flynn your guitar is snagged on the sofa... Shui, just pick a spot and stand still... Aarde will you grab the mobile emitter from the counter..." Frank paused to light a cigarette and take a deep drag. "Nephthys, have at it!"

Nephthys stood straight backed and said. "Now click your heels together three times and say, *no hay lugar como el hogar*!"

"There's no place like home," translated Bernard helpfully for Flynn who had been looking confused. "They speak Spanish in Peru... for the most part anyway," added Bernard as an afterthought

"But we forgot to wish Ignis had a brain!" said Shui teasingly.

Ignis opened his mouth to respond but WHOOSH! The team were dragged beneath the floor by the force of a colossal implosion of purple fire that erupted around the circle and crashed over them like a giant wave. A second later they were gone.

It was customary for Nephyhys to make the reappearance of her passengers a discreet affair. Something that happened down an alleyway or behind some bushes, anything that was out of sight. So when the team arrived in Rioja and became instantly aware of being out in the open and in broad daylight no less, they panicked.

"Hey, what the hell?" roared Aarde, rounding on Nephthys. "We need to hide before someone sees us!"

"Really?" sneered Nephthys in a condescending tone. "Is it the bugs you are worried about, or maybe that worm near your foot? Perhaps you think the duck over there is going to run off to the tabloids and start quacking about the spooky happenings on Bob's road here?"

Aarde, looked at the duck. It didn't seem concerned that seven people had just appeared out of nowhere. Neither did the worm. Everyone took a moment to take in their surroundings properly and could see why Nephthys was behaving so nonchalantly. They were stood on a dirt track dotted with clumps of grass growing in long tufts, and while there were buildings around them, they were old, battered, covered in graffiti and more importantly empty.

"Oh!" said Aarde. "Sorry, Neph. I didn't mean to snap!" he added shamefacedly. "I just thought..."

"No, no!" said Nephthys coolly. "I assure you I'm quite used to it by now." And she strode off toward the gates to the airport, her head held high with indignation.

"You're such a dick sometimes," muttered Shui as she barged passed Aarde to catch up with Nephthys.

Aarde looked after her, a look of hurt on his face. Bernard stood beside him and placed his massive hand on Aarde's shoulder.

"If you haven't figured women out after seven thousand years," he began with a sigh, "the rest of us have got no chance." And he gave Aarde a kind smile, which Aarde returned.

Juan Simons Vela airport was not a large facility. A mere fifteen steps took a person in one side and out the other. But this, it turned out, made finding their pilot a doddle, made all the easier because he seemed to be the only person there. Wearing dusty jeans and a vest jacket, the pilot was found smoking a cigarette against the wall next to the helipad.

His helicopter was waiting a few feet away and at first glance appeared to be an impressive machine. A black Airbus with white trim that gleamed in the midday sun. Once the pilot had showed everyone to their seats and the team were buckled in, they began to suspect Frank had opted for a budget flight. There seemed to be a lot of rattling even though the engine was off and some of the fixtures wobbled in an unnerving way. There was also an alarming amount of visible rust which was so severe in places it perforated the hull. The upholstery was patched and frayed too, as were the seatbelts and Ignis chuckled incredulously when he tightened his straps and part of one tore.

"All the things we've survived and we're gonna die in this thing!" said Ignis who was caught between highly amused and astonishment at this absolute deathtrap.

It was a wobbly take-off. The helicopter pitched and turned, then touched down again as the propellers momentarily slowed down. Thankfully the pilot was able to correct this issue with a few well-placed thumps on the ceiling which seemed to return full power to the blades and they were finally away. Soon enough they were flying over a mountain range drenched with jungle and Bernard became very excited. He was bouncing on his seat like a little boy on his way to Disneyland.

"Not far now!" he bellowed happily. "I can't believe I'm here again."

He looked rejuvenated. It was as if a man many years younger was sitting before them. No that wasn't right. It wasn't like he was years younger. He was becoming younger. His skin was smoother and some of the colour had returned to his hair. The liver spots on his hands had gone and his physique strained the fabric of his already tight outfight even more.

"Dude, are you seeing this?" asked Shui nudging Ignis.

Ignis didn't need the nudge in the ribs, he had noticed. In fact, everyone except the pilot and Bernard were all acutely aware of this bizarre occurrence. By the time the helicopter had landed and they had all disembarked, Bernard didn't look a day over twenty-five. Dark haired and handsome he caught Nephthys' attention immediately and she eyed him hungrily.

"You should have come here years ago mate!" said Shui who couldn't contain her obvious amazement.

"You're not gonna be a kid by the time we get to the village, are you?" asked Ignis who was laughing but being quite serious.

"Oh, I do hope not!" said Nephthys in a silky voice. "I quite like this new and impro…"

"Bernard, how old were you when you came here last," interrupted Hoowo3oow impatiently.

"I'd have been twenty-six," said Bernard, who was happily pacing around, taking in the scenery and inhaling the hot jungle air as if it smelled like fresh cookies.

"He looks about twenty-six to me," said Aarde appraisingly.

"Agreed," said Hoowo3oow in his usual growl. "It's likely this is as young as he will get. We should keep an eye on him though, just in case."

"Oh, I'll keep more than an eye on him!" tittered Nephthys which made Shui snort with laughter at the look on Bernard's face.

After the helicopter had begun its journey back to Rioja and was safely out of sight, Frank appeared out of the mobile emitter that was strapped to Aarde's wrist.

"Glad to see you've made it here safe and sound," he said cheerfully as he took in the dense jungle environment that encompassed the landing zone.

"Don't you mean relieved?" said Shui irritably. "How much did you rent that shit heap for, eh?"

"Ah!" said Frank sheepishly. "Well, you see there weren't that many options for an off the books flight and believe it or not he was the best out of what was available."

"Would have thought it difficult for the underground to go downhill," said Ignis sarcastically. "Just doesn't seem logistically possible."

"Trust Frank to find the very dregs of the pit," teased Shui.

"Oh, c'mon. That wasn't the dregs," said Frank defensively. "He got you here, didn't he?"

Frank quailed at the look everyone was giving him. "Look we're here now, let's put it behind us and…"

"I'll put you behind us!" said Shui, snatching the emitter off of Aarde's wrist and strapping it to Bernard's instead. "He can babysit you, instead."

"As Bernard is the only one who knows where we're going that's probably for the best," said Frank who didn't think he was being penalised the way Shui had intended.

"Lead the way then!" said Frank with a gesture for Bernard to get going.

Bernard heaved his rucksack onto his back and clipped it over his chest.

"Try to keep up!" he chuckled roguishly and he set off with a brisk walk toward the edge of the clearing and toward the thicket and deep jungle.

While Bernard knew the elemortals were strong, he had assumed that their small stature would have been a hindrance in such dense terrain. Returned to a younger body he had intended to put in a show of stamina and speed and win some respect from his companions. All hopes of this quickly vanished however, when the elemortals treated the jungle landscape like a playground as they bounced between trees, swung on vines and even sparred with each other as they travelled. They considered this a great place for training.

Four hours in, Bernard huffed and puffed his way through the winding plants that weaved across the ground and shot envious looks at the four warriors, laughing like the children they outwardly were as they leapt through the treetops with ease.

Flynn strolled along at his leisure, following the path Bernard was trampling and was plucking lazily at his guitar with a gentle smile on his face. He too was watching the elemortals play up in the canopy and he played 'Forever Young' by Youth Group to express his enjoyment. Even Bernard couldn't suppress a grin. He knew what Flynn was getting at with the song, but considering he'd just shed decades off his age, he was feeling forever young himself.

Nephthys rode as Bathin about a hundred metres behind them all to keep a look out for anyone or anything that might be following or hunting them. When they made camp Nephthys complained loudly about being the only one doing any work. She was quickly mollified by Shui, when she produced the head of a Pishtaco and dropped it into Nephthys' lap.

Bernard, horrified at the sight of a severed head being unceremoniously tossed about, pushed the bowl of beans he had been cooking away from him. Flynn, peered over his guitar at the grizzily sight with an expression of mild surprise. The head was for all intents and purposes that of a human, with obvious gruesome differences. The most obvious of which was the foot long protrusion with a sucker like tip that sat where the tongue ought to have been.

"And when exactly did you get this?" asked Nepthys incredulously, as she held it up for scrutiny. "I was hunting this entire time and saw nothing but a few snakes and furry critters."

"It was right when you hid behind that tree to pinch one o…" began Ignis but Frank cut across him.

"As delightful a story that is, may I ask why you brought it with you to camp?" he asked looking disgusted. "Surely there was a rock you could have hidden it under?"

"I brought it for you," said Shui brightly and giving Nephthys a look of genuine care. "Been a while since you ate and I figured you'd like a snack."

Nephthys looked genuinely touched by the sentiment. It was one thing to bring someone food, but quite another to overlook the very gratuitous manner in which a rich meal like this would be consumed. When people overlook something that repulses them, friendship is normally behind it.

"You... you really got this for me?" asked Nephthys in a surprisingly soft and quiet voice.

"Course I did!" said Shui with a wide smile. "It's by way of appreciation. We don't say it enough but you do a lot for us... for the Conclave like..."

There was an embarrassed pause that hung in the air and tugged at the corners of mouths till everyone was grinning like idiots.

"It's true," said Aarde. "We don't show our feelings often enough. I think we have become a bit too hard-nosed and too used to nothing but sarcasm over the years. When time bleeds into one infinite year it's easy to forget the niceties and we have been remiss in our gratitude."

There was a general muttering of "Here, here!" and "Well said!" from around the group and Nephthys pawed the air bashfully.

The wonderfully serene moment of camaraderie shared around a crackling campfire was shattered by the sudden and voracious tearing noises made by Nephthys eating the head with indecent enthusiasm.

Noticing Bernard turning a little green, Flynn nudged him in the ribs and played the beginning of *Dueling Banjos* from the movie *Deliverance*.

"I can see why you like him," said Hoowo3oow looking from Shui and Ignis to Flynn and back again and offering a rare and somewhat uncharacteristic compliment.

Night fell and the jungle turned black, but the firelight shone bright even though the wood was almost gone. The elemortals, Nephthys, Frank, Bernard and Flynn chatted, joked and laughed long into the night, sharing stories and showing off.

It was only when the embers were dying and everyone got comfortable and ready to sleep, that it occurred to Frank just how long it had been since the elemortals had laughed like this. He had feared the loss of Amos and Wun Chuan had broken something in the team. Things had been a little frayed in their relationships for some time anyway, he knew that, but still. When was the last time they did this? Frank made a note to organise regular evenings of no missions and no orders for them and he switched off the hologram and slumped against his desk. That happy thought made sleep come with ease. He did not know, could not know, that the four elemortals would never share a night like that ever again.

It was with fresh determination that the team awoke and began their trek with an almost militant attitude. Aarde and Hoowo3oow took point surveying the land from on high while taking direction from Bernard below. Meanwhile Shui and Ignis darted around in the undergrowth unseen and subdued potential threats to Bernard and Flynn's life, like anacondas, jaguars and giant centipedes.

Nephthys, feeling more like a team player than ever, had resumed travelling as Bathin and had offered to carry Bernard's luggage and more shockingly had given Flynn a ride. This allowed Bernard who felt more energetic the further they travelled to traverse the forest at a much faster pace and Flynn, throwing himself fully into his role as bard, played *Run to the Hills* by Iron Maiden to spur them all on.

They continued like this for another day and a half, relentless, unwavering, obsessed. Nothing distracted them from their march. Nothing except a smell. An unmistakable smell. It was the familiar aroma of destruction and death. After a further half an hour of following the awful aroma of wet charcoal, burned wood and charred flesh, the team finally came upon the outskirts of the village Bernard had discovered all those years ago, but it was not the village he remembered. What he saw now was the remains of a massacre. Every hut and structure and home had been razed to the ground, many with people still inside. Blackened and crisped bodies were scattered around the scorched clearing, frozen in time, posed forever in their final moments. Some had been fleeing, some had been pleading, all had been cowering. The worst of these were of children being held and sheltered in what must have been the arms of parents, though they were all burned so badly it was impossible to tell if it was the mother or father. Even Nephthys winced at the sight and she moved closer to Shui, though she didn't know why.

A feeling of emptiness washed over Bernard as he stumbled around, struggling to take in the horror of what he was seeing.

Near where Pacal Chan's hut had been, several bodies had been lined up on their knees, ready for execution. They too had been burned fiercely, but it seemed to have been done in a measured way to ensure the fat and skin would melt just enough to hold the skeleton in place without destroying it. Statues of a crime the killer wanted to share.

For what might have been a minute, maybe a hour, could have been a day, the team just stood in silence, their vigour and motivation crushed beneath the sight of such monstrosities.

Only Ignis was undisturbed by what he was seeing. Indeed, he was proud at the effect he had caused. The demoralisation he had inflicted upon them at this critical juncture. However, he did very well to hide his feelings as he moped around with his eyebrows furrowed in an angry frown and kicked debris about in a fine imitation of frustration.

Bernard crouched next to the remains of a body who had something clutched in their hands. As he pulled it free, he realised it was a brass cigarette lighter. As he turned it over in his fingers, he saw the letters 'A.B.' engraved on one side. Alfred's lighter. He gripped it tightly in his hand and held it to his forehead.

"I miss you, old friend," he whispered quietly. "He's going to pay for what he's done. For what he did to you," continued Bernard bitterly.

"I'm sorry, Bernard," said Frank solemnly. "I really am."

"Thank you," said Bernard without looking at him.

"Take all the time you need." offered Frank kindly. "We'll be waiting over here when you're ready."

For a while Bernard searched the grounds alone as he picked at the piles of wreckage. He didn't move any of the bodies even though he wanted to. They, like many cultures, practised sky burials and were already where there needed to be. Every now and again, Bernard wailed with anguish and shed more tears. This usually happened when he found the remains of children who had been huddling together for some imagined sense of security.

When he eventually rejoined the group, his eyes were glowing bright blue, and with his face drawn gaunt, he looked wild, incensed, manic.

"Let's do this!" he said with calm aggression though his voice boomed. "Let's get that door open."

"Are you OK?" asked Frank, alarmed at the change.

"Of course he is!" growled Hoowo3oow approvingly as a sudden gust of wind swept through them.

"Yeah!" said Shui stepping forward and summoning water from the ground to briefly rise up and around her in a vortex, showering them all and grinning broadly. "He's got his game face on."

Aarde flexed his muscles which made him look temporarily like hard, polished marble. "A wise move considering what we're about to do."

Ignis glanced at them a moment and then burst into flames. "Well, if we're showing off."

Nephthys became Bathin and reared his horse which sneered flames and stomped the floor to the sound of thunder.

"I really like hanging out with you guys!" he said in a deep rumbling voice.

Everyone turned to look at Flynn, expecting to hear some sort of riff or maybe a ten second shred on his guitar, but he was not there. They looked around and spotted him in the centre of the village. He was kneeling on the floor next to some sort of totem onto which the body of a toddler had been nailed before it was burned.

"Flynn?" shouted Frank, but Flynn ignored him.

"You OK, dude?" shouted Shui, a look of concern creasing her eyes as she began walking toward him.

"Flynn," began Shui in a quieter voice when she was close enough to be heard properly, "are you all right? Can I he…" but Shui broke off mid-sentence, distracted by a sound.

It was hard to tell where it was coming from, but it was unmistakably the sound of a church bell chiming. The chimes were slow and rhythmic and considering they were in the middle of the Peruvian rainforest, quite impossible.

"Do you hear that?" called Shui to the others.

Everyone pricked up their ears and became aware of the sound at once which seemed to increase in volume as if in response to the extra attention.

"Where the hell is that coming from?" yelled Ignis, striding over to Shui and looking all around him as if expecting to see a church amongst the trees.

"No idea!" replied Shui who was craning in every direction herself.

As Ignis drew close, he glanced at Flynn who was still on his knees. He was visibly shaking and Ignis noticed tears falling thick and fast down his cheeks and splashing on the ground. Ignis inwardly mused that his tears hitting the ground were in perfect sync with the bells when a bizarre thought occurred to him.

"It's him," whispered Ignis with dawning comprehension.

"What's that?" asked Shui distractedly.

"Flynn!" cried Ignis enthusiastically. "His tears," he continued pointing at the ground in front of Flynn. "His tears are chiming when they hit the ground."

Shui gave Ignis a look that showed she thought him mad but she checked Flynn anyway. Sure enough, and to Shui's utter astonishment, the tears did indeed seemed to be chiming upon impact. She reached a hand forward to let one droplet land on her hand. Not only did the sound line up perfectly, she could also feel the vibration of the sound ringing through her palm.

"That's just weird," she said perplexedly.

Everyone else had gathered around now to see what was happening for themselves and were eager to offer comforting words to Flynn. A disturbed hush fell over them when a chorus of voices like a choir echoed a soft melody through the trees. An unseasonably cold and stiff breeze rifled through the village and where the long grass and plants swayed in the wind came soft beautiful music such as that played by a string section in an orchestra.

"What is going on?" demanded Frank who felt uneasy by this sudden and unexpected musical apparition.

"This must be it!" growled Hoowo3oow with interest and casting his eyes to the sky to observe the gathering storm clouds above them. "It's how Death said it would happen. This must be how he summons the gate."

Although his tears were still falling at regular intervals, Flynn had calmed at the sound of mystical strings and he slowly rose to his feet, his twin-necked guitar dangling from his neck. The instrument glistened with beads of rain that had started to fall from above and when he finally stood tall, his long hair fell lank over his face which bore no expression at all. In the space of a second the heavens had opened and the spots of rain turned to heavy and fast bullets of water in an instant. A flash of lightning split the sky as it arched overhead and a tremendous crack of thunder burst from the clouds like a snare drum as Flynn gripped the neck of his guitar.

Chapter Eleven
Knock, Knock

Another percussive crash of thunder rolled overhead and Flynn lurched forward, bringing his pick down across the strings. From the start he played hard, heavy and fast. Whatever song was inside him, it had evidently been forged with metal.

The team backed away to give Flynn room as he chugged at the bottom neck and led on the top with angry melodies and dizzying flourishes. Flashes of lightning flashed behind dark clouds and thunder pounded the air, drumming for the music in Flynn's soul. By the second bar the ground had cracked and split right across the village in several places and a fierce storm had kicked up with Flynn in the eye.

The strong winds began to gather together the rubble and ruins of thatch, bamboo, wood and person that had once been the village and swirled them around the clearing in a giant loop like a tornado. Everyone in the team stood firm and shielded themselves from the debris and dust hurtling around them. Everyone except Hoowo3oow who stood unfazed but impressed.

As Flynn continued to play, the ground where the cracks had appeared began to rise in blocks. Cut shapes that would have pleased a master mason erupted from the earth as though they had always been there, sleeping until summoned to rise from their dirt tombs.

Shui, Aarde and Bernard had to leap down from a beautifully crafted archway that burst up from beneath them and, despite its weight, rose into the air and was scooped by the ever fiercer storm raging around them.

As the music built in pace more blocks, pillars, columns and slabs shot out of the ground and joined the maelstrom of architecture sailing at speed above them in a giant column.

The ground beneath Flynn's feet rose in a clean vertical column, platformed beneath him like a pedestal and decorated with vines that wound tightly around the base. As his playing became more vigorous so did the sky. Forked lighting struck the ground with every snare beat forcing the team to take cover beneath an improvised shelter made by Aarde. More stonework ripped itself from the earth, cluttering the sky and darkening the land. But a new light had appeared. It was a soft, golden light that radiated a warmth you could feel in your soul and it was coming from Flynn. His whole body was glowing with a sunset aura that crackled against his guitar, sending it into overdrive. From atop his stage many feet up, his song broke into a crescendo and the pedestal exploded from the force of huge bright wings that erupted from Flynn's back and shone with such intensity it turned the jungle white.

The rhythm stopped, giving volume to the storm, but a series of high notes sang out louder than ever and cut through the wind as Flynn, his body suspended in the air by his stretching wings, allowed his fingers to ricochet back and forth on the top neck.

Throwing the guitar forward he played a cascading flurry of notes that told the listener, 'things were about get real'. As he did the scar across Flynn's throat healed and as he revved himself up with more chugging on the lower neck, Flynn let out a tremendous, ear piercing, monstrous scream that chilled the spines of all who heard it. His lungs seemed to be everlasting as his cry to the storm tore through their heads with painful resonance.

The fearful sound stopped and Flynn gave a huge flap of his gigantic wings. He shot to the ground at speed, landing on his knees and power sliding with his guitar raised as a bolt of lightning struck his chest. The second he had hit the floor, Flynn had broken into a blazing, adrenaline filled guitar solo powered by the energy of the storm. As he played, the collection of objects that had been floating above them fired from the sky like javelins, impaling the ground and stacking at odd angles that balanced on each other in impossible ways.

As the land was repopulated all six of Flynn's fingers darted about the frets at incredible speeds, writing a masterpiece as they moved for this tiny audience gathered at a concert for the gods.

As though his first solo had been a challenge to himself, Flynn switched necks and ripped out an answer, hammering the strings with exquisite proficiency and creativity. This embellishment was reflected in the world as more refined groupings of architecture formed, though with no less aggressive force than their larger predecessors as detail rained down like cannon fire.

With another flap of his massive wings Flynn raised himself to his feet and resumed his verse on both necks with enthusiasm bordering on insanity. What had once been a hidden village in a small pocket of jungle was now a wide expanse of smashed earth and randomly scattered stonework. Plants and vines climbed the structures and bound everything in place as Flynn's song began to slow and play out with a sombre tempo. As the last few notes rang out into the evening, the storm collapsed with a final drum roll and the sky cleared. When the last chord was played, the chaos ended. Flynn's wings vanished, his scar reappeared and his glow faded to nothing.

For one whole dumbstruck minute, the storm battered team gawped at Flynn who was bent forward and panting with exhaustion, his guitar hanging limply from his neck. Fragments of wood and stone were still raining gently across the clearing, clattering and clinking as they fell and an orange fog of dust and dirt covered everything, the team included.

"Well, that escalated quickly!" said Shui whose hair was windswept so badly it stood on end in clumps.

"That, was your tune?" laughed Ignis excitedly. "That was metal as fuck!"

"Seconded!" said Aarde approvingly.

"That was certainly intense!" said Frank with a nervous shake in his voice.

"I loved it," said Nephthys cheerfully. "Reminded me of my six hundred and seventy-fifth birthday."

"Not to criticise," began Hoowo3oow in a tone that suggested nothing but criticism, "but is it supposed to look like that?" he added pointing to the random assortment of block shapes and structures that littered the area.

Several heads swivelled on necks to take a good look at what Flynn had created.

"Hoowo3oow's got a point," said Aarde, surveying the new arrangement of things with an expression of equal bewilderment. "This makes no sense."

The 'new arrangement' was quite something to behold. Columns of stone and wood of varying heights and widths, rose into the air before jutting off at random angles for no obvious good reason. Long flat slabs stuck out here and there like diving boards and beneath a handful of these more stonework hung beneath them like stalagtites. It was almost like looking at the pieces of a three-dimensional jigsaw puzzle laid out on the ground before assembly. It was certainly interesting, but there was no getting around the fact that it was basically useless. It didn't even resemble a gate of any description, just a gallery of oversized abstract art.

"Hmm!" intoned Frank. "Maybe there's something else we need to do."

"Like what?" scoffed Shui. "An encore? No offence mate," she began with an apologetic look at Flynn, "but all of that came from an emotional breakdown triggered by seeing that kid nailed to a post. Are you trying to tell me that to use these other gates he's gonna need to experience more psychological trauma? Because I for one forgot to bring extra children to sacrifice when he needs amping up."

Flynn looked apologetic and forlorn and Shui filled with guilt.

"I wasn't having a go at you, mate," she sighed, regretting her tone. "I appreciate this is all very new and yet you still showed out just then. That was an epic performance, believe me this isn't on you."

"So I suppose this is somehow on me," sighed Frank, acquiescing to the inevitable.

"Oh, don't be such a martyr, this isn't on you either," continued Shui curtly. "But we can't pretend this isn't more complicated than we expected."

"Could it be because the village was destroyed?" asked Bernard, his voice cracking as he spoke.

Frank hesitated before answering. "I suppose as we know so little, we can't rule it out as a possibility."

"Then it's my fault," said Bernard bitterly. "They're all dead because I interfered. Because my own pride was more important than their isolation."

"Don't talk nonsense," said Frank consolingly. "None of this is because of you."

"Actually, it is," said Nephthys callously but fairly. "If you had never met these people they would not have been brutally murdered as your disciples. But that's no reason for this gate thing to be broken. Religion is full of sacrifice and it never broke anything before."

Bernard fixed Nephthys with a stare that conveyed defeat and misery. "Maybe this time the thing that's broken is my heart."

Nephthys seemed to realise she had been insensitive and reached out convulsively to comfort Bernard, to apologise, but he had already turned and was walking away with his head hung low.

"Don't worry about it. That you know you said something wrong is what matters," said Shui with a cheeky grin.

Frank waited until Bernard was out of earshot before speaking again and when he did, he addressed his question more to Nephthys than anyone else.

"Do you think that could be true?" he whispered as discreetly as he could. "A broken heart means a broken gate?"

"You know I honestly don't know," began Nephthys, nonplussed. "I don't think any of them have ever actually cared about anything enough to get a broken heart before."

"Well, that's a bleak sentiment!" said Frank disappointingly.

"Hey, just saying it how I see it," replied Nephthys dismissively.

"Fine!" said Frank frustratedly. "How about just emotions in general then?"

"They're very good at jealousy and anger!" said Nephthys brightly as if they were traits to be admired.

"Not what I meant," sighed Frank.

"I know what you meant and I have no idea," said Nephthys flatly. "The fact that he is a god is weird enough without all this nonsense," she pointed at the statues, "being thrown in."

"Remind me again why I agreed to let you come along?" asked Frank coolly.

"Because I am the David Attenborough of the supernatural. That and obviously a bit of eye candy... you're welcome."

Shui chuckled, so did Ignis.

"Amos would have loved all this," he muttered softly to Shui.

"Wun Chuan wouldn't," said Shui honestly. "She would have been moaning this whole time."

"Amos would have said something helpful like we just needed to approach this from a different angle," said Hoowo3oow reminiscently.

Hoowo3oow's words nudged something in Ignis' brain. A sort of formless idea, a thought that hadn't yet developed sound or image but was growing at a dizzying pace. With the suddenness of a thunderbolt, an epiphany struck his mind and he lurched upright, wide-eyed with excitement and armed with a plan.

"Fan out!" he commanded as he began jogging backwards away from the structures. When no one responded and instead watched him as though they thought him an idiot, he repeated the order with much more volume. "Spread out as far as you can, all the way around… all of this!" he said adding the last part with a gesture to the cobbled together mess that ought to have been a gate.

"What are we looking for?" bellowed Hoowo3oow as he headed away to the opposite side.

"You'll know it when you see it!" replied Ignis who had gone far enough back and was now strafing around the edge of the clearing.

"What must we look like?" laughed Shui as she also jogged sideways in a wide arc around the colums and slabs.

"Like pillocks I would imagine!" said Nephthys in an amused tone as she followed suit.

A loud 'kerrang' from Flynn's guitar echoed in between the stone pieces instantly grabbing everyone's attention. Copying Ignis' example, he had been running sideways in a big circle too but had stopped because he seemed to 'know he'd seen it'.

The team made their way around the blocks and pillars to where Flynn was waiting. As they walked their eyes turned inward watching for anything unusual and a thrill of anticipation crackled like electricity in the air. What they saw as they drew close to Flynn was almost impossible to believe. The many disparate objects, columns, platforms and blocks seemed to line up in such a way that they appeared, when stood in the right place, to look like part of something bigger. Much bigger.

Indeed, by the time they could all see exactly what Flynn could, they were beholding a titanic two-pronged pyramid that glowed in the evening sun. A bright golden flare of light was reaching skyward from between the prongs, illuminating their goal — the gate at the top.

On the side facing them and chasing the full height of the pyramid was a flight of wide stairs that was broken at intervals by wide platforms which were decorated with the statuesque bodies of villagers and gilded with vines.

"Dude, that is a lot of steps!" said Shui with a withering sigh.

"You're not kidding," added Bernard with a gulp.

"Kinda makes you appreciate being a hologram," said Frank who let his eyes run the height of what appeared to be thousands of steps.

As if to check he wasn't hallucinating Aarde ran a short distance up the steps, jumped up and down to test the sturdiness and then back down again. He then ran back around the side and watched the pyramid break apart and back into random blocks again.

"The logistics of this are insane," he said scratching his head.

Hoowo3oow strolled slowly over to Aarde and observing the same effect understood Aarde's concerns.

"What happens to anyone on this structure when it is viewed from any angle that disrupts the illusion?" he asked rhetorically.

"We should do an experiment!" exclaimed Shui brightly and she grabbed two handfuls of Ignis' clothing, swung him around very fast and threw him up the steps.

Ignis flew through the air at speed, yelling as he careened headlong into what he perceived to be hard slabs of stone. But he did not crash into the stairs. Instead, he continued to fall and past through walls and pillars like they were not there and for most of his fall his vision was obscured by the dark depths of solid rock. Aarde and Hoowo3oow had watched him be thrown into the air, over a couple of blocks and slabs and then into basically nothing until the ground.

They both let out a cry of warning, when they saw what was scattered on the floor beneath him.

Ignis realised what the warning was for at the last second when he emerged from the pyramid interior and saw the ground riddled with shards of wood and jagged rocks. Ignis tried to excite his molecules to make things hot and incinerate the hazard, but for some reason it wouldn't work. Yelling a stream of obscenities, Ignis twisted in the air and braced against two sharp edges of stone with his hands and thrust his leg against a piece wood that was sticking up behind him. The wood snapped as he pressed it, and he fell several more inches before he could stop himself properly. Those extra inches cost him as a spear of rock pierced his leg and he received multiple lacerations to his torso.

Shui and the others had run over to Aarde and Hoowo3oow, to see where Ignis had disappeared to. When Shui saw the predicament she had placed Ignis in, she covered her mouth in mortified astonishment and charged forward, smashing through the minefield of spikes until she reached Ignis and could gently lift him free.

"My hero," said Ignis with spiteful sarcasm.

"Ya welcome," chuckled Shui, still carrying him back to safety.

"You're a dick!" growled Ignis.

"Did you die though?" sniggered Shui, promptly dropping Ignis to the floor now they were clear of lethal debris.

"Why didn't you blast the area clear?" asked Hoowo3oow, his voice thick with concern.

"I couldn't," said Ignis, raising his hand and creating a little test fireball in his hand. "Oh, now it's working."

Shui stepped within the area allotted to the pyramid pieces and tried to summon a ball of water. Nothing happened. As she stepped back beyond the boundary, a sphere of gloopy liquid grew before her.

"That's not good," she said, throwing the ball of water behind her and splashing Bernard by accident.

"Everyone back this way!" ordered Frank, who was pointing at the spot where the pyramid could be seen. "Bernard, if you wouldn't mind," he added with a meaningful look at him in a painful reminder of his limitations to lead as a hologram.

When they were all gathered in full view of this ludicrous testament to Bernard's godly status once more, Frank turned to address them.

"The odds of being disturbed right now by another human is very slim. However, given the inherent danger presented by alternate perspectives we should try to prevent anything from being able to view this thing while we're on it just in case," said Frank with a take charge attitude. "For all we know a monkey could be enough to disrupt the whole thing. Aarde can you erect some sort of barrier around the perimeter to stop anything coming close. Hoowo3oow perhaps you could add some heavy wind to kick up some dust."

The elemortals did as commanded, and with a rumbling of earth and rush of wind, formidable barriers appeared around them and the pyramid.

"Right then. Let's go!" said Frank confidently.

The second Hoowo3oow and Aarde set foot on the first step, the barriers collapsed and vanished.

"Seriously?" gasped Aarde looking back as his walls of rock disintegrated.

Hoowo3oow showed equal dismay at his storm blowing itself out and he tried to summon wind again without success.

"Nephthys?" began Frank with a nervous glance at the tower of steps. "What do you make of all of this?"

"Hmmm," said Nephthys pondering the situation and placing a foot on the bottom. "Well now, that is interesting."

"What is?" asked Shui who was watching her closely.

"I can't transform," said Nephthys with mild surprise. "In fact, I can't do any magic. This place must be nullifying our abilities."

"Amazingly enough, we figured that much out for ourselves," said Ignis scornfully. "What we wanted to know was why?"

"I'm getting to it," retorted Nephthys hotly. "I have been to places where my powers have been muted before," she continued with forced calm. "This usually happens when the place is central to a belief structure, but a structure you are not part of. It's just differences in cultural folklore and religion."

"So… that means…" began Frank hesitantly. "What? What does that mean?"

"It means that we are in a place that's all about Bernard here," continued Nephthys knowledgeably. "The villagers who worshipped him, believed in him and things like the pishtaco, but they didn't know who you were and they evidently didn't know who I was either or our powers would work."

"That actually makes sense," said Frank who was growing increasingly concerned. "What now?"

"We are just going to have to be quick about it," said Ignis and without warning he broke into a sprint and dashed up the stairs, seven steps at a time.

Grinning at each other, the other elemortals immediately gave chase and soon they were racing each other up the side of the pyramid, concerns of falling to their doom forgotten. Flynn and Bernard jogged along some distance behind them but still managed to maintain a good pace. Nephthys, although in her human-like form, ran up the stairs on her hands and feet like a panther scaling a tree and joined in the race to much cheering and whoops from Shui.

Their concerns over the pyramid being disturbed turned out to be unfounded as they all reached the top without incident. To the surprise of the elemortals Nephthys had won the improvised race. She had taken the lead when Ignis and Shui got into a fight halfway up while arguing about cheating. Bernard had arrived some twenty minutes after the race had ended but with Flynn at his side. They had been talking and laughing as they scaled the steps, occasionally looking out over the treetops at the sun still setting in the distance, while Flynn serenaded their climb.

"Glad you could make it," said Shui with wink.

"Glad you brought me," said Bernard with a grateful smile.

"Well, there it is," said Frank directing Bernard and Flynn's gaze somewhere off to the side.

What they saw was a set of large wooden doors, gilded with gold and framed with a stone arch. But the door wasn't in anything like a wall. It was just there on top with nothing but air on either side. It was illuminated by an inexplicable shaft of gold and bright light that did not seem to have a source, it was just there.

Bernard stepped toward the door and into the light and felt his body fill with a peaceful warmth that tingled across his skin. He walked around the door to see the other side. It was exactly the same as the front.

"Is it wrong that this is the least weird thing I have seen all day?" he asked to no one in particular as he reappeared around the other side again.

"It's good you're getting desensitised to this sort of thing, dear," said Nephthys encouragingly. "It will make the rest of this voyage much easier to cope with." And she patted him gently on the cheek before staring into the sunset and drawing a deep satisfied breath.

"Take a good look!" she continued with soft tug on Bernard's arm and directing his attention to the sky overlooking the almost alien landscape of the jungle. "It may be the last time you see it!"

"Nephthys, can we not?" interjected Frank, appalled by her blasé tone.

"Just keeping it real," she said fairly. "It's meant to inspire."

"Inspire what?" asked Frank with the same disgruntled edge in his voice. "All consuming dread?"

"No, Nephthys is right!" said Bernard firmly as his gaze fell upon the horizon, his face ablaze with orange and gold sunlight. "This could be a one-way trip. I have no illusions about that. But Nephthys has reminded me why I'm doing it. This world is a wonderful thing, full of infinite mystery and endless beauty. We humans have done enough damage and I look set to be the cause of the greatest act of destruction the planet has ever seen. If my life needs to be traded to stop that from happening, so be it."

Everyone shared a moment of silence as they all stared out into the endless sunset and appreciated the view. After all, it wasn't every day you got to stand on top of a metaphysical wonder and watch the sun never setting over a glistening rainforest.

"Just don't die on us too quickly," said Shui breaking the silence and getting to her feet. She strolled over to face Bernard and gave him a playful punch in the ribs. "I'm starting to like you," she added with a smile.

"Well, I guess this is where we part company for now," said Frank a little awkwardly. "No way you're getting a signal in there. I doubt the reflect song will work either so it's radio silence for a while. I'll have Richard get R&D to join up with the coven and see if they come up with a pan dimensional telephone or something."

"Way to science, Frank," chuckled Ignis. "Catch you on the flip side."

Everyone bade farewell to Frank, and stood in a row before the enormous double doors that led to the Ribatan realm and beyond. They felt no dread at their mission, only a deep resolve and excited anticipation. Come what may this was going to be a hell of a journey.

Shui nudged Bernard forward out of line and toward the door. It seemed only right that he opened it. It was his gate after all. Bernard understood the gesture, and after a pause, reached forward and grabbed a huge door handle ring made of gold. The seam between the two heavy doors split down the centre with a thin sliver of brilliant blue light and a loud mechanical clunk sound echoed from within the wood indicating the door was now unlocked.

There was a collective intake of breath as Bernard pulled at the ring and the heavy door slowly creaked ajar. The thin sliver of light expanded as Bernard heaved the door open, engulfing the team and momentarily blinding them. As such no one saw the fist as big as Bernard's head emerge from the gap and smash into Bernard's face.

Chapter Twelve
The Beginning

The punch lifted Bernard clean off his feet and sent him toppling down the steps. The elemortals backed away and out of the light to regain their sight pulling Flynn with them and hiding him behind them. Nephthys shot down the stairs to assist Bernard who had come to a stop seventeen steps below. All had their eyes trained on the door and were poised, ready to attack whoever was foolish enough to come through.

The doors burst wide open with tremendous force and slammed into the stone frame. In the centre of the doorway stood a huge figure with hulking muscles and wild, long straggly hair. A pair of ragged feathered wings jutted out at awkward angles from his back which twitched rather than flapped. Wrapped around the fist that had struck Bernard was a viper that reared and hissed angrily at the elemortals, and from between the figure's legs, appeared the monstrous face of a giant beast which raised its neck and carried the figure to its flanks. The beast stretched out massive, dragon-like wings which unfolded out of the door, and as it stood on its hind legs, it let out a blood curdling screech which made the ground tremble.

"KNEEL IN TERROR AND AVERT THINE EYES FROM THE GLORY OF ASTAROTH," boomed the demon from atop his giant beast. "GREAT DUKE OF HELL AND…"

"Inanna, darling," interrupted Nephthys with polite greeting. "What the devil are you doing here?"

Astaroth looked down to see who had spoken and upon seeing her dropped formalities at once. "Nephy? My goodness, how are you?" he said in a deep voice that exacerbated a certain campness in his words.

"Better than my friend here I dare say. Did you have to hit him so hard?" replied Nephthys playfully.

"Your friend?" asked Astaroth his thickset eyebrows gathered in puzzlement. "You're not helping these humans, are you?"

Nephthys teased her hair away from her face before saying, "Well, yes!" as though it ought to have been obvious.

In a single movement, Astaroth removed his outer skin revealing a stunningly pretty woman in dark blue flowing robes and rushed out of the door and over to Nephthys in a panic. Her face was stricken as though she thought Nephthys had lost her mind.

"Nephy, you can't be serious. Come and stand with me and it'll be all right."

"Oh, my dear Inanna," said Nephthys sadly. "I'm afraid it's not going to be all right at all."

With a casual grace that bordered on insulting, Nephthys examined her nails as she continued. "Step aside, Inanna. You don't have to die."

"Me?" shrieked Inanna with hysterical laughter. "I'm not the one who's going to die. I have an army."

Sure enough, silhouetted against the brilliant bright light of the doorway appeared a crowd of dark figures that grunted and growled in anticipation of a fight.

"And we enter proper this time, Nephthys. No borrowed bodies."

"Then you know your death will be final, right?" asked Nephthys with a wry grin. "No do-overs in the afterlife."

"That will not be a problem," sneered Inanna. "I see you have made your choice... and so have I!" she added, turning her back on Nephthys.

"Fair enough," said Nephthys indifferently and without warning she produced a knife and grabbing hold of a handful of Inanna's long black hair hacked off Inanna's head in one clean sweep. She held the head up to the doorway, an action that was greeted with angry jeers and roars from the throng ready to burst through.

"That was cold," chuckled Shui as she came to stand beside Nephthys and took up a fighting stance.

"Yeah," agreed Aarde who did the same. "I'm glad you're on our side."

The rest of the team took up position alongside them, ready for a fight as clawed hands scrambled at the doorframe and floor, eager for flesh. Bernard wiped the blood from his nose and spat a globule onto the floor.

"Don't they know it's sacrilegious to strike a god?" he asked with a playful nudge on Flynn's shoulder.

"Hark at this one," chuckled Ignis. "He gets one pyramid and it goes to his head. Hey, Flynn. Play us some murder music, if you will."

Flynn obliged by playing a rapid dance on the top neck with two fingers, creating a thrill of anticipation before he allowed 'the beat to drop'.

"Would you like to kick things off?" asked Nephthys with a wink at Shui.

"Always!" grinned Shui.

Nephthys hurled the head into the air and Shui leapt toward it. Her foot connected with Inanna's head with a sickening crunch and it shot into the doorway like a bullet as Flynn lunged into a power stance and began to thrash the guitar with frantic riffs. Something screamed and blood exploded from within the light. There was a second of confused silence, but then yells of rage unpaused the world and the army charged. Demons poured from out of the doorway in droves and elbowed and barged into each other in an effort to reach their opponents first. By the time the first demon had reached the line, more than a hundred stood between them and the gate. The first demon had his face driven into the stone floor by Shui as the team scattered to divide the numbers. Bernard and Flynn remained close to Nephthys and Bernard assisted her by duelling with anyone who tried to flank her while Flynn raged on with ever more furious strumming.

Though stripped of their powers, the elemortals still had their strength and their speed and were armed with techniques that had been honed with experience and training over thousands of years. The platform upon which they fought was not very big and the elemortals darted about as they dispatched demon after demon, switching places with their teammates and tag teaming unsuspecting aggressors who never saw it coming. Unable or perhaps unwilling to fight as a team, the demons never stood a chance and soon the air was thick with bodies as they were kicked, punched and thrown from the top.

Nephthys was fairing equally well and was leaving a trail of limbs in her wake as her knife slashed through the air again and again. Seemingly out of nowhere ten massive monsters launched themselves up out of the crowd and dived at Nephthys. With incredible reflexes, she spun herself round and sliced their throats the second they landed. All except for one, who had escaped her blade and had taken the opportunity to duck beneath her arm and tackle Bernard down the steps. Flynn, worked a warning siren into his playing to alert the elemortals to the situation and Ignis was the first to respond.

The sound of bones breaking could be heard from the cluster of demons he was fighting as he incapacitated them at speed and threw one over his shoulder, face first onto the steps. Ignis then drove his foot between the demon's shoulder blades and pushed off hard with his back foot. The demon's face clattered and shook violently against every step as Ignis rode his body down the pyramid steps like a surfboard, chasing after the cascading form of Bernard and his opponent tumbling ahead of him. When level with the pair, Ignis waited for his moment then slammed his foot into the head of the demon holding Bernard when his body was against the steps, killing the demon instantly and catapulting Bernard into the air. Ignis swerved the body he was riding diagonally across the steps leaving a streak of red behind him and caught Bernard before he hit the steps again. Unable to slow the descent, Ignis slalomed the corpse beneath him the remaining distance as bodies rained down around them as they were punted from the top by the other elemortals with rhythmic precision to Flynn's solo echoing overhead.

The second Ignis put Bernard back on his feet, Bernard began scrambling back up the steps as fast as he could manage. Ignis, however, did not. A demon at the base of the steps was stirring. He had somehow survived his encounter with one of the elemortals and his subsequent fall to the ground. In another time and place he might have been considered lucky or fortunate. But not right now.

Ignis grabbed him by the scruff of his neck, which was easy in this case as this demon had a ginger mane that was matted thick with dirt. It protested as Ignis yanked it upright so Ignis placed a silencing hand over its mouth.

Bernard looked back to see what the noise had been and as he did, Ignis began to needlessly wrestle with the demon who, with a broken back, could no more have walked away let alone fight.

"Run Bernard, get to the others!" urged Ignis, forcing the demon's head back with the hand over its mouth, pretending to stop it from biting him.

Bernard, confident in Ignis' ability to kill one demon, resumed his charge up the stairs and Ignis watching him leave, held the demon's face next to his own and forced its gaze up the pyramid.

"That's a hell of a view, eh?" said Ignis with a leer. "But if you think that's nice, you should see how it looks from over there!"

The second he finished speaking, Ignis swung the demon behind him and hurled him across the edge of the clearing and straight at a tree. The demon hit the trunk with mundane thud and collapsed on the roots in an upright sitting position. His eyes were closed but Ignis could see he was still alive and took the opportunity to race up part of the pyramid and gain some ground on Bernard. It had to look convincing, just in case.

As the demon against the tree came to his senses his eyes creaked open and for a moment, meaningless blurry shapes and colours swam in front of him. But then his head cleared and his vision sharpened and the true state of the pyramid was revealed.

In an instant of pure horror and confusion, the elemortals, Flynn, Nephthys and Bernard suddenly found themselves falling through the pyramid with a horde of demons tumbling after them. Ignis who had been keeping a weather eye on the demon he had thrown had spotted the moment when the illusion had been interrupted and had leapt clear of the lethal debris below and fell to the ground with a sense of impending victory swelling within him.

Not for nothing had the elemortals survived for thousands of years. Their quick thinking and ability to react with speed and precision whilst under pressure was something Ignis was all too familiar with and was something he should have given his counterparts more credit for.

Sensing their environment, the elemortals found solid foundations to swing, push and jump off. Several meaty thuds could be heard from behind brickwork, and like ghosts passing through walls, demons shot out in all directions colliding in mid-air with Bernard who narrowly escaped impaling Flynn who was still playing furious riffs, and Nephthys, who was still fighting two at a time, knocking them to safety.

Still operating blind, Shui, Aarde and Hoowo3oow ricocheted between pillars until they cleared the illusion and landed away from danger, albeit far away from their goal. From their new perspective they watched demons pouring from a doorway high out of reach and into an ever-growing pile on the ground beneath it.

"It's like when you fuck up on lemmings, isn't it?" said Ignis dispassionately who had rejoined the team and was watching the body count stack up with a smirk on his face.

"Guys, this is bad. You need to get moving," said Frank in a worried voice.

"Yeah, all right!" said Shui irritably. "We're on it."

"Well get on it faster," said Frank and he was starting to panic now. "They are starting to survive the drop. The longer that door stays open the more demons will be left in this realm when you've gone… and then the problem is you've gone!" added Frank with a hysterical yell.

"Say no more!" said Shui and she ripped a length of vine off a nearby stone column and lashed it around her waist as Flynn fired up the tempo and cranked up the volume. She did the same to the other elemortals and then ripping off one side of a tree's bark tied it behind them like a sled.

"Hop in, masks on and hold tight!" she commanded to Bernard, Nephthys and Flynn as she scooped up a rock and executed the demon against the tree with a well-aimed throw to his forehead.

Knowing there was no way of sabotaging this without getting caught, Ignis grudgingly took the strain of the vines and crouched down like a runner waiting for the starter pistol to fire. When everyone was on and had a good grip, Shui raised her eyes to the top of the reformed pyramid which now had bodies cascading down the steps instead and smiled. "Go!"

With acceleration that would shame a sports car, the four elemortals dashed forward and sped up the steps dragging an excited Nephthys, an alarmed Bernard and solo playing Flynn behind them. Shui suddenly snapped her neck around to look at Flynn — she recognised that tune.

"Have you been playing Dr Wily's theme from *MegaMan 2* this entire time?" she asked with wide-eyed amusement.

Flynn gave an enthusiastic nod of his head and flourished the theme signature on the top neck.

"There's something wrong with you!" laughed Shui and she increased her speed forcing the others to do the same.

Efforts were made to murder and maim as many demons as they could when they passed them on the way up, but they knew Frank had been right to be worried. A great number of demons and other entities had escaped Ribatan, and they knew these creatures, now unfettered by the separation of realities, would be able to prowl the earth with their full strength and powers at their disposal. They knew too that there was nothing they could do about it either. The only way to help now was to get through that door, lock it behind them and trust in the Conclave to eliminate what was left. There was no time for goodbyes. No time for one last look. No time to consider the danger ahead. There was only time to act.

The elemortals had reached the summit in a matter of minutes only to discover that the demons had attempted to gather themselves into a blockade. But with such fury and speed had the elemortals scaled the pyramid that they crashed into the wall of bodies with such force that many of them exploded into pink clouds as all four warriors tore a tunnel through their defence and slipped through the doorway dragging Nephthys squealing with delight and her arms raised, Bernard clinging to the bark as though it was the most precious thing in the world and Flynn bent back with his guitar raised and carrying a long piercing note until they vanished from sight and the door slammed shut behind them.

A second later Frank disconnected from the device Bernard had with him and he found himself back in his dimly lit control room alone. Without pause he immediately began dispatching auxiliary units and operational support across the globe to Peru in an effort to contain as many entities and demons as possible.

When the last unit left the Conclave Frank slumped against the back of his chair and lit a cigarette. He took a very long, deep drag and exhaled with relief. It had been an intense day. He looked up at the map and stared dismally at the bright blob of light in South America and watched it slowly spread out as though it were infectious.

"Hurry home guys!" he whispered under his breath.

Firing up another cigarette he fell back into his chair again and swivelled it back and forth a bit. It was only then that he noticed the package wrapped in brown paper sat on his desktop. He picked it up and saw 'FAO Frank', written in black marker pen across a label addressed to the Qin Zhu

Institute of Science. Holding his cigarette in his mouth he dug a finger behind a fold in the wrapping and tore it open revealing the edge of a book. Confused as to why anyone would send him a book, he tore off the rest of the paper and turned it over to see the title. At once his eyes went wide as they roamed over the front cover and his jaw gaped open as he read the words emblazoned across the middle:

Magikal Thinking
The Conclave of Magikal Thought

by DQZS Robinson

Frank stared in disbelief for what seemed like a long time. His brain felt like it had jammed and he read the words in his head over and over again. That was of course until the cigarette fell from his mouth and onto his crotch which snapped him from his stupor.

"What the fuck is this?" growled Frank in an undertone. There was a note where the parcel had been on the desktop and Frank snatched it up. It read:

This is the book that guy wrote.
You know who I mean, the guy the assassin killed.

Wade.

"No way!" whispered Frank, sounding both excited and afraid.

With haste Frank opened the book and found the first page but his eyebrows furrowed together as he read the subtitle.

"Seamen? Really?" he said with a roll of his eyes.

He skipped ahead a few pages and found chapter one. With mounting dread Frank read the contents in fervour until he reached the words 'Bernard Godfrey' and instantly broke into a sweat. He soon felt like he was going to vomit. However, as he turned to chapter two and saw the words 'Coffee, Frank?' printed right there, on the page, in black and white, he felt quite faint.

Trying to keep it together he skimmed forward several pages and hurriedly read a few random lines aloud.

"AMOS!" bellowed Frank a little more sharply than he had intended. Amos came into view on a mirror that showed the inside of the circular room. He looked very dishevelled.

Frank threw the book at the desk in disgust or horror he didn't know which and backed away from it skidding his chair across the room. He stood up and paced about nervously, wringing his hands and running his fingers through his hair which was slick with sweat. Lighting up another cigarette he looked at the book and dragged his chair back to his desk. Pausing a second to smoke a few drags he grabbed the book with unnecessary roughness and split it open to view the middle and continued to read at random.

"Who was it this time?" enquired Amos who was beginning to feel more intrigued than lethargic now and had been keen to hear more news on the assassin's whereabouts.

"A…" began Frank, pausing to read something on a scrap of paper, "…DQZS Robinson."

Frank couldn't help but laugh a little as he read this. "Fuckin' hell! Can't say you didn't see it coming mate," he chuckled quietly before deciding to start from the beginning and flipping the pages back to the prologue.

As the hours slipped by Frank submerged into a world of secrets and lies, triumph and tragedy. It caused him frequent pause every time he read his name and learned about his own life from someone else's perspective. It caused him some distress to have to relive Wun Chuan's death which was reflected in the mound of cigarette stubs in the ashtray. But what hurt, what really cut to his core was learning how Amos had died and of course, of Ignis' betrayal and the plain truth that he had been the assassin all along.

Frank reeled from this information and his head swam as he was overcome with a panic attack. His heart raced, his body poured with sweat and stars popped in front of eyes. Ignis, a traitor. It couldn't be true. It just couldn't be. But everything else he had read had been accurate. It had happened, all been true. He screamed with impotent rage and bashed the book against his desk several times out of anger and confusion.

"WHY?" he roared as he slammed the book again and again. "YOU FUCKING BASTARD, HOW COULD YOU?"

His rage was relentless and in a fit of pure venom, he tore the book in two and cast the halves across the room before collapsing on the floor and breaking down in tears.

"We were a family," he whispered between sobs.

He continued to cry for nearly ten minutes before a terrible thought occurred to him, the urgency of which overcame his emotional turmoil. Shui, Aarde and Hoowo3oow. There was no way to let them know. To tell them their enemy had been with them this whole time. Suspicions of traps and ambushes crept through Frank's mind and he felt a swell of fear for the team.

Thinking better of his actions he grabbed the two halves of the book and held them together as close to where they should be as he could. Maybe there was something useful on the last page. As he read about himself reading this book and his subsequent fit of anger through which the book was damaged, his eyes impatiently dropped to the last few lines of text.

His eyebrows rose in surprise and he couldn't help a tiny snort of amusement as he said. "Well, I can't argue with that!"

He placed the book halves back on his desk and brought up Wade's contact details on his display. There were a few seconds of soft digital chiming before the call connected and Wade's voice crackled over the speakers and his face appeared on screen.

"S'up dude?" said Wade in a bored voice. "How did the mission go?"

"Bad!" said Frank snippishly. "And it's getting worse. That book you sent me, are there any more?"

"Well, no," said Wade in a puzzled tone. "I only ordered one. Seemed daft to get more…"

"Not more of this one, you pillock!" interrupted Frank angrily. "I thought it was a trilogy, where's part two and three?"

"I didn't order them because they weren't available yet," said Wade reasonably.

"I want those books, Wade," said Frank in a low menacing voice. "I want those books and I want them now."

There was an awkward pause while Wade stared back with an incredulous look on his face. What was he supposed to do? Pull one out of his…

"GET ME THOSE BOOKS WADE!" bellowed Frank as his last thread of patience snapped. "GET THEM FOR ME, NOW!"

End of Book One

In memory of Prince Philip, a true God among men.